I0561644

ISBN # 978-0-6151-6378-9

Five Years Part I

For Rai the
unfrozen cave
woman.

They said you died alone

Five Year

By

Patrick Fisher

They said you died alone

Prologue

It has to begin somewhere one would suppose. It started in Manhattan. Colleen Ferguson was twenty-nine. This had been a hard week for her. It started on the last page of the Daily News. Colleen never read the daily news but for some reason she had picked up a copy on her way home on Monday. She had been fired on Monday. There had been too many crying fits, too many long lunches and not enough work done in the last three months. Her life was falling apart and now she had the story in the Daily News. The headline read 'Reclusive doctor killed in botched robbery attempt.' The article started out with; Retired M.D. Colin Ferguson was found dead from apparent gunshot wounds in his Albany home last Thursday morning. Doctor Ferguson is survived by his estranged wife, Sharon McClain-Ferguson. The couple had no children. There were other details; Colleen didn't really care to read about, something about religious articles missing. That was her father and this was the first she had heard about this. Sharon was only her stepmother, fucking bitch, Colleen thought to herself. They were hardly ever on speaking terms; Sharon had been such a horrible mother. Still Colleen had to know.

"Why didn't you call me?" Colleen cried once Sharon picked up the phone.

"It really wasn't about you dear," Sharon answered cheerfully, "why do you always think everything is about you?"

"Fuck you he was my father," Colleen was shaking, in twenty-two years

They said you died alone

Five Years Part I

she had never stood up to Sharon before now.

"Was he?" Sharon began, "was he really? I mean the way you whored yourself around when you where in school I figured you were still looking for a father figure darling."

"WHAT?" Colleen was red with anger; she tried to crush the phone receiver in her hand. She felt her heart race as she thought of smashing Sharon with the phone.

"And that husband of yours," Sharon laughed, "he cheated on you and didn't he hit you as well?"

Colleen didn't answer she couldn't speak. She felt bile build up at the back of her throat. She wanted to scream out; instead she dropped the phone and ran to go throw up.

"Men and woman wasn't it dear?" Sharon asked the empty receiver. Colleen returned and hung up the phone. She wiped a bit of vomit from her lip and stared at the table by her front door. On the table was her freedom. Freedom from the prick, freedom from a loveless marriage that had been a four-year mistake. Colleen needed love, and she needed comfort. She grabbed her papers and her bicycle helmet and headed out. She needed a hot chocolate.

Her divorce was becoming final after a full year of lies and silent dinners. A failed marriage, she thought as she rushed to nowhere, at least that's out of the way. Her marriage had fallen apart when she discovered that she was sterile, well that and her husband fucking everything in town. Not only that but it was like she was a woman by default. Her doctor told her that it was rather remarkable; it appeared as though she

They said you died alone

Five Years Part I

never even had the parts necessary to
conceive. How did the doctor put it? She
thought to herself, ornamental and
entirely useless.

Colleen raced down Canal St.
toward Chinatown. She was pedaling her
ten-speed at an unruly tempo. The last
six years were racing through her mind.
What had it all been for? She wondered. A
degree in finance from Fordham and she
still had to talk her way into a job at
the Met. That's where she met Pete,
fucking cocksucker, she thought. It
brought a smile to her face even if it
was only a thought. She hardly noticed as
the landscape around her changed from
Soho to Chinatown. The streets were
suddenly busier, teeming with people.
Costumed children and exploding fireworks
and she didn't notice. She had to make it
to Mott Avenue. The Atomic Lotus Tea Room
was her destination. They served her
favorite hot chocolate (it was a
Carnation instant powder mixed with fresh
ginger root). It was a basement opium den
in the thirties and it sat across from
the Buddhist temple. It was Colleen's
sanctuary. Pete never liked the place, it
was always too smoky in there, and there
were always his allergies to consider.
And for that matter he thought they
agreed she would quit. Colleen always
wanted to say something like she thought
they agreed he would stop fucking other
woman but it was always a moot point when
she had a chance.

Chinese New Year was being
celebrated all around her as she burned
down Canal. She had forgotten this year.
She wasn't Chinese, but she did try to
observe something.

They said you died alone

Five Years Part I

The job at the Met, even if it was in the financial office, allowed her to be close to all the art she pored over as a girl. She always fantasized about the Soho loft and the gallery shows. The tragic love affairs she would have while she left her mark on the world. Well she had the loft now, though it was in Tribeca and not Soho. A blank canvas sat on an easel by her window. The canvas had been the symbol for her reclaiming her life, or at least how she envisioned it. The canvas would never see a drop of paint. All Colleen would ever do was stare at, she never felt ready to commit thoughts to art. Her high school sketchbook sat on top of her unopened paints and unused brushes. The canvas would always remain blank.

Colleen had reached her tearoom. She was covered in sweat and out of breath. She walked her bike down the same seven steps she's gone down for nearly a decade. It was dark in the tearoom, though it was always dark in there. Colleen's eyes slowly adjusted to her new surroundings, it was all so familiar to her, so comfortable. The yellowed portrait of Chairman Moa still hanging behind the counter and the same barista working the counter. Colleen could never be sure but it seemed as though he'd been smoking the same cigarette for the last ten years and had never really opened his eyes that whole time. He was from Mainland China and despite having been in America since seventy-three, he never really learned English. The only English he knew what whatever he learned from his David Bowie albums. He even wore his hair long, like Bowie from Hunky Dory. He saw Colleen enter and already had her hot

They said you died alone

chocolate in the steamer. Colleen smiled at him then she scanned the room. Some familiar faces, it made her feel safe. In the corner of the Atomic Tea room was a corner table that Colleen always sat at. It was the prime spot for people watching, which was a favorite pastime for her. It sat in the western corner of the basement.

At her usual table sat a man she'd never seen before. He looked nervous. He was smoking a cigarette like a man who had quit twenty years before. It was dark but it looked like he was dressed like her grandfather, or a mortician on holiday. He was wearing a non-descript gray suit with a dull colored tie. The David Bowie barista handed Colleen her hot chocolate, she smiled and dropped a five on the counter and moved toward the man at her table. He was fumbling with a large scrapbook that he had laid out in front of him. Next to the book sat an ashtray that was mostly full, a full cup of black coffee, three unopened packs of Dunhill reds. It wasn't the book he had been fumbling with; he was opening a pack of cigarettes.

"I used to be able to do this," he muttered.

"May I sit down," Colleen asked, "this is where I normally sit so I hope you don't mind."

"Not at all," he smiled, "I was beginning to wonder when you'd get here."

"Really??" she looked worried, "should I know you?"

"No," he lit a cigarette, "but I know you,
You might say I'm responsible for you."

They said you died alone

Five Years Part I

"What are you like my real father or something?" she said as she sat down across from him, "you know I always thought that I was adopted, I never felt like I fit anywhere, my family was always so strange to me and my life now is such a complete failure..."

"Perhaps you should listen to what I have to say before you get too excited."

"What you're dying, great I just meet my father and he's dying, my real father and he's..."

"Please stop that and listen," he said sternly.

"What can I call you?" she asked.

"George, call me George," he smiled in a very forced manner.

"George, I like that," Colleen smiled.

"I'm not dying and I'm not your father, not in any flesh and bone sense anyway."

Colleen remained silent. George pushed the book in front of her. She looked down and opened to the first page.

"Let me give you a history lesson," he took a long drag on his cigarette, "In spring of nineteen sixty-seven the N.S.A. took charge of a privately funded genetics program. The original goal was to modify a subject into the perfect soldier. At the N.S.A. we took this further. We used their research and most of their scientists to create a breed of assassins. We worked to augment strength, sharpen vision and heighten all the senses. This had limited success. By nineteen seventy we had around twenty-two such agents, most of who had become strung out, chemical monsters. They excelled at vicious,

They said you died alone

brutal killing and had become all but
uncontrollable."

"Pete sent you didn't he?" Colleen
accused her tone changing with the lunacy
of the old mans story, "well you can
tell that bastard to go to hell." She
took a long hard pull on her hot
chocolate.

"No please listen to me Colleen,"
George hissed.

"Pete is the only other person who
knew I thought I was adopted," Colleen
grabbed one the cigarette packs and tore
it open. George offered a light.

"Ms. Ferguson quit this foolishness,
you were adopted because you had no birth
parents."

"You're insane," Colleen said as
she got up to leave. George stamped his
cigarette out and looked her straight in
the eye.

"Your ex-husband has nothing to do
with either your adoption or my being
here."

"Then why are you here? why are you
telling me this?" she said as tears
welled in her eyes.

"Because in the simplest of term you
need to be activated," George lit
another cigarette.

"What are you talking about?" she
asked.

"You are a synthetic human being Ms.
Ferguson, you are not composed of any
organic materials," Colleen tried to
interrupt but couldn't make a sound,
"your lack of vital reproductive organs
was a fail safe design that was exclusive
to your generation."

"How did you know about that?"

They said you died alone

Five Years Part I

"I know everything Colleen," George began, "and now we've reached a point where you need to know as well."

Colleen sat silent for a moment playing with the tarnished wedding band that she still wore on her ring finger.

"What did you mean by my adoption?"

"Well you were right Colleen," George smiled, "you were adopted." George opened his scrapbook to a page showing a clipping from a Japanese newspaper. Colleen couldn't read the text and George kept tapping his finger on the picture next to the article. The picture showed a Japanese lady, flanked by police, being led out of a large door way. In the background was a large globe shape. It was really too blurry to make out what it was.

"Technically speaking that woman was your mother and I guess by proxy that would make me your father. The family you grew up in was carefully selected, they were part of our program."

"Your what?" Colleen exclaimed.

"No sense in beating around the bush," George laughed to which Colleen rolled her eyes, "You were the product of a now defunct N.S.A. program that's purpose was to cultivate a flawless assassin. Your generation was designed to manipulate basic features through simple chemical management as well as activate your other extraordinary abilities in a similar fashion."

"You said my generation, more followed me?"

"You were third generation, frankly the first success and there were two to follow before the project got suspended."

They said you died alone

Five Years Part I

"Do four and five have their parts?"
she patted her lower belly.

"Well yes, we did simplify the design
and we found other ways to limit breeding
without making the 'sleeper agent' stand
out."

"Unbelievable, well I guess that
would make me a barren Japanese woman,"
Colleen said as she got up.

"Half," George said.

"What?" Colleen snapped back.

"It would have made you half
Japanese, I was, technically an American
at the time, besides you officially don't
have a race."

"All right," Colleen turned her
back, "you've ruined my afternoon so now
I'm going home."

"Colleen wait," George began,
"outside on the street men are waiting,
men who saw me enter, then you enter and
who now are waiting for you to storm out
on to the street."

"What so they can kill me," Colleen
said

"Well actually yes," George finally
freed a cigarette from the pack he'd been
fighting with smirked rather
triumphantly. Colleen lowered her eyes to
the floor. It was a dirty red carpet,
probably hadn't been cleaned since the
sixties.

"What?" she said with tears welling
in her eyes, "I know to much now?"

"Well almost," George smiled, "if
you would listen to me we don't have a
lot of time.

"I can't do this," Colleen said.

"Colleen you must not go back
through the door," George protested.

"It's ok, you did a good job," she
smiled for a moment, "you really had me

They said you died alone

for a minute there but I have to go
now. "

"Colleen the world is going to end
in five years and seven months, " George
said dryly. She stopped as she reached
her bicycle.

"You really believe that don't
you, " she said with a raised eyebrow,
"and that's really sad, " she thought
for a moment as she put her helmet on,
"besides is there really something I
could do to stop it if it was coming to
an end? "

"No, " George said.

"Then if there are people waiting to
kill me outside then it really wouldn't
matter would it? "

"No, I don't suppose it would, " he
answered. Colleen turned and started to
walk her bike back up the steps. It was
still light outside but kids were already
starting fireworks. The little explosions
were getting louder as she got up the
steps. The setting sun blinded her long
enough for her not to see the sedan
parked across the street. It blinded her
to the single shot fired from the
passenger. The shot was masked only by
the din of the fireworks. The bullet
screamed across the street and through
her forehead imbedding itself in the wall
behind her. Colleen was dead as she fell
back down the stairs.

George looked up to see her lifeless
body stumble down the stairs. He put out
his cigarette, retrieved a notebook from
his suit pocket and crossed her name off
a list. Colleen was second to last on the
list under the group heading 'three'.
There were thirty other names that had
all been crossed out in the 'three'
group. Under the group heading of 'five'

They said you died alone

Five Years Part I

there were also several names crossed
out. However the name "Parker, John
Declan" was circled. George closed the
notebook and placed it back into its
pocket. He got up from the table,
collecting his scrapbook and cigarette
packs and left out the back of the Atomic
Lotus Tea Room. Colleen was dead on the
stairs her story was over.

They said you died alone

Five Years Part I

"Mexico City, Mexico. Maria Fernandez, 28, was killed Wednesday when the seven-month-old fetus that she was carrying dug its way out through her spine. Maria bled to death at the scene. Her very stunned husband and three remaining children survive Maria. At the behest of their Parish priest an exorcism will be performed on the three surviving children. The locals fear it is another of Satan's children coming to create Hell on Earth. When reached for comment Satan had this to say; "That's my boy!" The Dark Lord proudly proclaimed, "you're next America." The Prince of Lies and pain went on to claim in the exclusive interview from Hell....."

Excerpt from 'The Cyclops' Oct. 10-16 1978

They said you died alone

Part I
They said you died
alone.
Chapter 1

John Parker hated his job. This
was nothing new, especially if you were
in anyway familiar with John. He had
spent almost all of the last ten years
drifting aimlessly from one job to the
next. He had tried almost everything and
found that he enjoyed very little. For
the last year he held a position at the
"Book Silo". The Book Silo was a chain
of super bookstores that began in Nevada
in the late eighties. It made a foot hold
in Los Angeles before the chain crippled
itself with over expansion. John worked
at the largest store in the Los Angeles
county area. It was a three story super
store that sold books, magazines,
video's, music and only recently added a
coffee shop on the third floor[1]. John was
in charge of the Religion/Philosophy
section of the store, which was in the
back corner of the first floor. Like
anyone else John had slipped into a
routine. He works seven till four-thirty
five days a week. He has the same frozen
waffle, three cup of coffee breakfast
each work morning before running out to
catch the number seventy-seven bus that
he's always late for. He offers the same
tired excuse to any of the three bus
drivers he'll see any given week and then
it's off to work. Like clockwork John

---

[1] The Book Silo would disappear from the retail landscape in a few more
months when it would be bought out, the majority the majority of the
employees fired. It would later reopen as 'Cory's Casa of Books'. Cory
would be closed before the end of the year after failing to catch the
narrow porno comics/Advanced Dungeons and Dragons demographic.

Five Years Part I

will arrive with four and a half minutes
to spare in which time he'll try to smoke
half of a cigarette and try to get some
inane television theme song out of his
head before starting his shift. Typically
the theme song would have been from 'The
Rockford Files', which was usually what
his father was watching and the only
thing his father could hold a
conversation about. John's father retired
early and has done little since but watch
television and wake up at five-thirty
ever morning. "Not going to let you get
the drop on me you son of a whore," he
would say to John before John left for
work. Amazingly this behavior did not
surprise John in the least; in fact he
imagines that nearly everyone's father
was more or less insane.

John will arrive greeted by the same
people everyday, most of whom still call
him Mark or sometimes James because those
were the two previous heads of the
Religion/Philosophy department and no one
has really noticed that it's no longer
two people doing the job that John now
holds. They'll ask the same questions;
"How was your weekend?" or "Any plans
for your weekend?" John will almost
automatically respond with; "Fine." or
"Nothing much." at the end of each work
day he'll stop at the same coffee shop
and sit in the same waitresses section
and order the same cup of coffee and
whatever fruit pie may be on hand so long
as it's not apple. The waitress, who is
about John's age (which is twenty-seven),
likes waiting on John. He's kind of cute,
not creepy and always tips five dollars
on a four and a half dollar check. She
also likes him because he can be sweet
but he's not a very good flirt. Poor

They said you died alone

Five Years Part I

flirting has always been a problem for
John. He is neither good at flirting nor
at recognizing that he is being flirted
with. He is also a bit of a coward when
it comes to women.

John has been a regular customer at
the coffee shop almost as long as he's
been working at the Book Silo. The coffee
shop was once part of a national chain
called "Jim Friendly's". Jim Friendly[2],
who was born James Darren Vittelo to an
Italian family in Patterson New Jersey,
was a self made (campy) cowboy singer in
the nineteen seventies with a string
(four) top one hundred hits and an album
that went gold in nineteen seventy-four.
Jim parlayed this success into a number
of ill-fated ventures[3]. The only one of
his ventures that survived the seventies
was the coffee shop chain and only one
survived the eighties and nineties. The
last one of the "Jim Friendly's" is
where John Parker and the waitress, who's
name is Francesca Ann Morris, meet five
times a week and share fragments of a
conversation. John has come close on
three occasions to asking Francesca if
she would like to go out for dinner and
maybe a movie, but John has lost his
nerve each time. Francesca, in the
meanwhile, has been growing tired of
waiting for John to ask her that she will
soon resort to quasi-drastic measures.

---

[2] Jim Friendly was at best a parody of a cartoon cowboy. Though often compared to Spike Jones and other pioneers of musical parody, Jim considered himself to be a serious country-western artist and musician. His hits included: "My best girls is my cow", "Too old for the shootout" and "The Sharkskin Cowboy". His album "The Return of the Sharkskin Cowboy" sold well in part due to his large and influential extended family.

[3] Among Jim Friendly's failed ventures: the notorious Gas station/Topless bars where you could fill your tank see some tits and get a beer.

They said you died alone

Five Years Part I

Since he wasn't at the moment attending school, his parent's charge him rent for the above garage apartment he occupies. John's parents are quite far from needing the money, they are of the feeling that if John is not trying to better himself then he should contribute to the household in some way. Richard and Angela Parker, John's parents, are both in their own ways slightly detached from their own children and have made little effort to get to know the adult versions of them. This was nothing new for the Parker boys (there are three in total). But John was always treated a little differently. So much so that he suspected that he was adopted (or at the very least purchased from Irish gypsies). He didn't even look like either of his brothers or parents. John had his suspicions but little proof.

Mr. and Mrs. Parker have a vague idea of what their children were like and that is all they've ever really needed. On Sundays they have a barbeque and get together with their boys to discuss the weeks events. John is usually late having stopped by Jim Friendly's for his daily and often futile chat with Francesca.

They said you died alone

Chapter 2

It was Monday with the usual Monday headache. Like any normal Monday for John he had drunk too much beer at the barbeque the night before and spent the first thirty minutes of his Monday while he sat still in bed thinking about Francesca. You see, usually through the week John builds up his determination to ask Francesca out by Sunday and then Sunday comes and he loses his nerve and drinks too much beer while his family teases him about a secret girlfriend.

A neighborhood away Francesca spends her Mondays sleeping till noon when she has to get ready for work. She lives with her mother in a small three-bedroom one-bathroom house that's walking distance to Jim Friendly's. She sleeps comfortably in a tiny room that John has only heard about in passing.

John begins this Monday by combating the pounding, cheap beer headache with four cups of coffee and six generic aspirin. The morning countered by being blindingly sunny (even for Los Angeles) and two bus loads of high school students from a local Magnet school. The mob swarmed on the Religion and Philosophy department as soon as the store opened and the kids attack John with all manner of question on things like Thomas Aquinas and the influence Loa Tsu must have had on Confucius. For the first hour of the Magnet school siege John did his best to answer all the questions he could. It wasn't till one of the students surmised that John was little better then a community college drop out and then decided it would be better for John if he just stayed out of the way with his

They said you died alone

Five Years Part I

"found in the trash at a bus depot knowledge." On a normal day John would have at least put up a better fight but on that Monday his mind was elsewhere. He resigned himself to do inventory and catch up on back orders. All that having taken a total of forty-three minutes he joined every cigarette break he could until the students left. Despite it all John survived the inquisition and the belittling at the hands of high school students. At the end of his shift, John grumbled his goodbyes to he co-workers who called him Mark (he wasn't speaking to any of those who called him James) and made a beeline for Jim Friendly's. As was often the case when John ventured to go anywhere nothing ever was a direct route. Surviving the day instilled John the determination to ask Francesca out that he had always lacked in the past; he was going to ask Francesca out and that was that. He grew restless as he walked to the coffee chop. It was late afternoon and still hot, John drifted into a daydream as he walked along Ventura Blvd.

In the fantasy world John was some sort of apocalyptic adventurer in a torn and bloodied shirt, with a gun belt and a well used chainsaw strapped to his back. He would march into Jim Friendly's (which would differ little from reality save for the post-apocalypse mutants at every table though it was still better than the reality of the geriatric mutants that served as regular customers), Jim Friendly himself would greet John with a sneer and a playful minor cord on the piano (for whatever reason it was a grand piano strapped to Jim Friendly like a guitar). John would utter, "come get some" to Jim who would answer with a

They said you died alone

Five Years Part I

swinging piano attack and pithy musical quips. The scene would play out as John imagined it, something like Brian Depalma's "Phantom of the Paradise' with music by Paul Williams. Truly one of the worst films every made. John would skillfully dodge each swing and scoff at Jim Friendly. When John was through toying with him, he would knock Jim across the room with a single punch and then move on. John's next obstacle would be the swarthy Kobe. In reality Kobe Marx, who was born in Pamplona, Spain to unwed art student, was a waiter at Jim Friendly's and had once dated Francesca. In the fantasy realm Kobe would be dressed like a desert prince and swinging a curved sword[4]. Kobe would prance about the restaurant and as he did the feather in his turban would change color with every movement. Apocalyptic John would shake his head; remove his gun from his belt and fire. Kobe wouldn't fall he'd explode. Behind the exploded remains of Kobe the desert prince would be Francesca. She would be lying on her side on the lunch counter, dressed like Jessica from Logan's run (after Jessica and Logan escaped from the robot who froze everything for the sake of preservation). Francesca filled out the costume better then the movie Jessica. The display of force and violence made an impression on Fantasy Realm Francesca, she was breathing heavily, melting Apocalypse John with a piercing look. Her crimson lips shined from the light

---

[4] It should have been a Scimitar though it was shaped more like a Kukuri. A Kukuri was a tool employed by Nepalese farmers. It was used to sever the head of a buffalo. A Scimitar was the only appropriate weapon when it came to dealing with interlopers, infidels and wives who spoke.

They said you died alone

Five Years Part I

provided by the cowboy hat lamps that littered the ceiling of the restaurant. John looked toward her with a confidence he never had as she breathed; "Do you seek Sanctuary runner?" John began his stride only to be impeded by the sudden appearance of a parking meter that he promptly walked into. Knocking the wind out of himself brought John back to reality. It was back to the San Fernando Valley and it was ninety-three degree in February, John was still a coward doing nothing with his life and he had managed to injure himself and no one stopped to see if he was all right. In fact someone may have even laughed and in all honesty even John thought it was funny especially since he really didn't hurt himself. The run in with a parking meter did allow a moment for John to collect himself. He caught his own reflection in a shop window and shook his head at himself. He was a mess, hadn't shaved since last Wednesday, his hair, though short, was shooting off in every possible direction and to top it all off he was wearing a Smiths tee shirt[5]. Francesca was not a fan, and she had said so in a late night conversation with John that had started while they discussed the film Cool Hand Luke and the strangely hypnotic jiggling of George Kennedy's manbreasts. John knew he couldn't approach her like this; he needed to change or at least a shave. Maybe this was just the excuse to back

---

[5]The Smiths were a musical group from Manchester, England who achieved commercial recognition and mild success in the mid nineteen eighties. They were lead by a morose young man by the name of Steven Patrick Morrissey, who was known to perform with a bouquet of flowers in his pants. They developed something of a cult following with young people, such as John, who reveled in melancholy and poor choices in hair fashions. Additionally, it helped if you liked references to English taxes, Margaret Thatcher and the romantic poets, Keats and Yeats most specifically.

They said you died alone

Five Years Part I

down again. "What a loser," he muttered
to his reflection, if he needed a reason
to chicken out this was it. Try as he
might even the fierce inner coward inside
John wouldn't let him back down today. He
scanned the surrounding shops for a
solution. There was a tattoo parlor, a
vintage clothing store, a few appliance
outlets and pawnshops. John was feeling
bold and ran immediately for the tattoo
parlor.

They said you died alone

Chapter 3

Inside the parlor it was quiet, almost empty. The walls were covered in local art, some good some bizarre and some just plain crap (most of it was full of recycled new age ideas without a much in the way of individuality). Beneath the art, lining all the walls, were the sample tattoos for the often foolish and somewhat unimaginative kids who get a tattoo because they saw it on the popular but misunderstood person they admire. Aside from the eye candy it was fairly empty and smelled of antiseptic. John stood in the entryway where a counter separated the shop from the work area. On top of the counter was the appointment book, sticker folder and display case for lighters and knives. Also in the entry way was a couch and TV, the couch held the only artist in residence at the moment who was a heavy man-child by the name of Cory.

Cory didn't go by any cool nickname like Craven or Ascension like any of his fellow artists. Cory was his legal name and the nickname he preferred, even though the other artists had christened him with the perfectly suitable Baboon shitface, due in large part to his wholly unnatural howling whenever he would get tattooed or pierced. Cory was wearing his customary sleeveless tee shirt and shorts, which he always wore to show off his tattoos and multiple piercing. Only recently he had the topside of each hand inked to read "Cory Rulz", when he placed his fists together. As for piercings, he had four metal studs lining each eyebrow (having plucked, shaved and waxed the metal studs served in place of

They said you died alone

his eyebrows), each nipple pierced with as ten gauge bar he even laid to claim to an assortment of genital piercing that no other person could (or wanted) attest to.

Cory sat on the couch in the tattoo parlor eating a wok full of Star Wars cereal, which he had been hoarding (so it was at least three years old), mixed with teriyaki flavored beef jerky. Cory was upset and this was his comfort food, at least when he couldn't afford a pie, which wouldn't be till Friday (by pie it should be noted that it would be three Peanut Butter pies from Denny's that Cory would consume while watching the Sound of Music). Only last night had Cory been excommunicated by his Dungeons and Dragons group for being an ass and taking the game far to seriously and far too personal. Cory barely acknowledged John when he entered the parlor, but he did know John. This snub was common for Cory who only chooses to greet ladies, which was partly why very few came into the store. Cory knew John from the humanities class Cory took after he couldn't get into Anthropology/Witchcraft 202 in Cory's fifth year at a two-year college.

Cory and John's last encounter, which was at least seven months prior, nearly resulted in a fistfight. It began with an argument on the last days of the composer Liszt. From there it got as ugly and personal as Cory could manage. Cory peered into his marble notebook with a big "E" on the cover. It was his enemy's dossier in which Cory kept as accurate an account on all those who crossed him and it was alphabetized. Each individual grievance could be further cross referenced to match any other for

They said you died alone

Five Years Part I

type, trauma caused and humiliation
inflicted. Every entry earned a score
based on these factors. John's was 3.5
before Liszt. Symbols were added for any
extra grievances beyond the one that
necessitated entry in the enemy's book in
the first place. Below each name was all
the information that Cory had been able
to gather through basic observation.
These notes were to serve as verbal barbs
for whenever Cory felt he was under
attack. Even though Cory was the
sharpest, most cutting and cruelest wit
that he would ever acknowledge, Cory felt
he needed an edge. Next to the entry that
began "Parker, John" were a pair of
beige squares that signified the two
occasions when John beat Cory to the last
rice crispy squares in the schools
cafeteria. Such a slight would not be
forgotten. Under the name was perhaps the
briefest entry in the enemy's book
entirety. All it read was; "wears vans,
probably a drug user or an
environmentalist, possibly a skater? Only
at the moment of the "Liszt" argument
did Cory lament his own lack of fervor
when it came to avenging the rice crispy
treats, but he had to work with what he
did know about John.

"Ok Scabs," Cory chuckled
thinking to himself how easy it was too
slam John. Basing his first attack, Cory
was right about a portion of John's life
but only served to confuse John. Though
it was true that John had suffered an
assortment of non-serious injury due to a

They said you died alone

skateboard it had only happened once in his life[6].

Back in the class John volleyed the "Scabs" with; "You're an ass." Cory countered with "Cool out there stony, maybe your should get your munchies now," he accentuated with a swine like snort. The second shoe-based assumption was that John was a stoner (pot smoker if you prefer) and it was a dangerous remark for a fat guy like Cory to make. John answered with silence and a bit of head shaking; it was stupid even for Cory[7].

Cory was stunned and somewhat angrier. John hadn't jumped all over the food remark like he had hope and as so many in the past had done allowing for Cory to play the victim of a vicious attack. "I'm going to give you such a punch," Cory threatened in his usual whine. The weak crackling quality of his own voice always wounded Cory as he did pride himself on his own abilities as a verbal pugilist. Cory was such a sorry physical specimen that he would often be

---

[6] When John was nine years old his brothers wanted to break in a new skateboard. They surmised that with an initial blood letting it should be safe to ride. So they secured John to the board using two rolls of duct tape, and then proceeded to launch him down a steep hill. John slide down maybe twenty feet or so before he really began to roll. Being taped to the topside of the board John threw it off balance, which caused the board to flip over and tumble the rest of the way down the hill. He picked up quite a lot of speed as he tumbled. Rough pieces of asphalt tore into him and subsequently freed him from the tape and board. John lost momentum and rolled into a tree on the roadside. The board continued down the hill and into traffic where it was promptly smashed by a delivery truck. So in theory the board never did cause another rider harm and John would never get on another board.

[7] Having been part of this particular student body for five years (in a two-year program) Cory had been entered into the common vernacular of the school. 'Cory Stupid' was an act or state of astounding, baffling or otherwise amazing, moronic conduct. Some examples of this; consistently running into a plate glass window, tucking your tee-shirt into your underpants, farting whenever you ran (if you ran), expressing a fond desire to hunt and kill bears whilst being terrified the most vigorous of ground squirrel.

They said you died alone

winded after the daily struggle to open
his two-liter bottle of cola that he had
with every lunch. Fighting for Cory was
no easier then fencing was for a dead
squirrel. If you pinched Cory he would
squeal, run about three paces at top
speed and then collapse in a sweaty,
shaky heap. Cory wasn't morbidly obese
but he was in tremendously poor shape for
a man his age, which was thirty-one. He
was also mean, spiteful and selfish. In
defense of his own inability as a fighter
in the flesh and bone sense, Cory would
decry physical violence as the first
response of an imbecile. To add greater
injury this community college was Cory's
domain and to be challenged in his own
domain was incomprehensible, at least to
Cory. He readily abandoned his principles
and put on is best fight face. "You're a
complete jack ass," John answered
finally, "why don't you just sit down
and shut your mouth." Cory shook,
gritted his teeth and tears welled in his
eyes. "I hope you get face cancer and
your face falls off John Parker," he
screamed and then did a gypsy curse
maneuver with his hands before the
professor intervened and stopped the
fight. Cory would not forget this
altercation, but John would. Cory would
add a donkey and a skull and cross bones
next to the beige squares next to John
name in the enemy's book and his score
would increase to seventeen.

They said you died alone

Chapter 4

Back to the present Monday, Cory hadn't looked away from his cereal bowl.

"Do you have a razor I could buy?" John asked

Cory still didn't look up, "Razors are for customers only," he said with his mouth full spraying milk and jerky bits.

"Fine," John began, "then I'll buy something then," he retrieved his ATM card from his wallet, "do you take ATM cards?" Cory chuckled to himself; he had John where he wanted him. "Slow down cowboy, there's a ten dollar minimum on ATM purchases." Cory was sure as hell that a loser like John didn't have a job or even a spare ten dollars. Cory would really need to research his enemy's book far more thoroughly in the future. John moved over to the display case holding the piercing jewelry, knives and lighters. John immediately gravitated to the lighters. He looked over the mostly empty Zippo display, It held a Bettie Page lighter, a couple of Beatle album cover lighters and a few with skulls and naked Demon girls.

"I'll take the Bettie Page lighter," John said mush to Cory's astonishment. Cory's eyes twitched and his nostrils flared, "But that'll be thirty-three fifty plus tax," he muttered. Cory was beginning to realize how greatly he had underestimated John and John's ability to hold a job. Though to be fair Cory was amazed in this fashion on almost a daily basis, especially when an 'enemy' did not live up to the research and loser label that Cory had assigned to them. So often had the smug, superiority candy coating melt

They said you died alone

Five Years Part I

away to the bitter, resentful chewy
center. Cory was a little traumatized as
he got up from the couch, as he set his
wok full of breakfast food on top of the
counter he was almost ready to confess
all of his secrets to John. The fact that
he really wasn't a tattoo artist and that
he was only watching the shop while his
Aunt Julia was out. Aunt Julia only let
Cory pierce and only when she was
present. Or the fact that he still lived
with his mother, who continually threw
out his skin magazines and made him go to
confession for looking at naked ladies
and having lustful thoughts about them.
It was a fragile moment for Cory as he
dragged his feet back to one of the
supply carts to get a razor. Cory was
starting to feel like John could be a
friend, and friends were so hard for Cory
to make seeing as how he was an ass and
all.

"So what's the razor for?" he
asked as he shuffled back to the counter.

"Well I was walking to Friendly's
and I realized that I looked like some
kind of derelict and I can't look that
way tonight," John said.

"Meeting a special friend?" Cory
wondered aloud. Cory did truly want to
know; he was hoping it was a lady friend
so he was going to press for details.

"Well kind of," John began, "I'm
going to ask Francesca out, she's a
waitress there."

"Right," Cory leered, "she's gay
you know, wears logging boots like
everyday." Cory was once again revealing
his poor research skills and another
addition to the enemy's book, which now
spawned three notebooks.

They said you died alone

Five Years Part I

Cory had been rejected by Francesca not too long before today. He pressed his luck after a polite rejection, causing Francesca to be rather brisk with her second and third dismissal of Cory's advances. Cory then assumed she must be a lesbian and blurted out; "Dyke, Bitch, Whore" and was permanently barred from the restaurant and escorted out by a couple of the busboys with a boot print on the seat of his pants. Jim Friendly's joined a Burger King on Ventura and Tampa and eleven other establishments in the area surrounding Cory's house that would not let Cory back.

"I'll take my chances," John said. Cory chuckled and grabbed the lighter from the display case and took Johns card. "Do you wanna use our bathroom?" Cory asked.

"What?" John was not quite listening or really there, "oh to shave, yeah that would be great."

Cory led John down to the bathroom, giggled at John and then returned to his cereal. The bathroom had a toilet, a sink and a dirty mirror. The walls, ceiling and floor were littered with stickers, graffiti and 'Cory Rulz' in strategic places (though never above five foot three inches). The razor John held in his hand was a single blade disposable made by Bic. The razor was one of thirty from a jumbo pack. John snapped the white safety cover off and began to run warm water over the blade. John never liked single blades; they always caught on his skin leaving him with little scabs of exposed flesh. Double blades were always better, though John did prefer triple blades. John splashed warm water on his face. "Can't be precise today," he said

They said you died alone

to himself, "I don't really want to loose that much blood."

John began slowly shaving his face, the heat from the water caused the mirror to fog up. He grabbed a few paper towels from the wall dispenser that was covered in Dead Kennedys stickers and 'Cory Rulz'. The paper towels were like those common to a gas station, they were like poorly pressed sandpaper and surprisingly useless. Still John tried to clean off the mirror. A feat that, due to the apparent layer of filth and cigarette residue, had never before been attempted. It was something like trying to reorganize mud. With a murky reflection, John pressed forth. He shaved around his sideburns; at this point John had sideburns down parallel to his earlobe. He then shaved along the jaw line, leaving a trail of red spots on each side of his face, which John made worse by reversing the razor shaving his face upward. John gave himself a mock smile, tossed the razor into the trashcan and left the bathroom.

Cory's Aunt Julia had returned from her shopping trip, which must have ended with a trip to the corner liquor store. Sitting next to a pair of to-go boxes was a four pack of Heineken talls. Aunt Julia wasn't big like Cory; she was more like an Amazonian with a cartoon lumberjack's physique. She was well covered in tattoos and piercings and the tresses of her hair were shaved to show off the serpent that ran the length from one temple to the next. She was far more pleasant then Cory and that was mostly because they weren't related. The title of 'Aunt' was more honorific and served as a reminder that despite the fact the

They said you died alone

she could and often wanted to wail on Cory, she looked out for him instead. But today she was a little pissed off at Cory. It was Julia who as dungeon master (or DM if you prefer) for the game expelled Cory and all of Cory's characters (including Cory the evil Orc wizard and Cory the mischievous rouge half elf, but most of all the spiteful Corina a Halfling were-mongoose sorcerer) from future play.

"Hey Julia," John said as he made his way to from the bathroom.

"John?" Julia seemed a little surprised, that and she had a mouth full of combination number twenty-four which was a half lime seared chicken, carne asada, rice and beans, "Cory said you were back there but I didn't really believe him."

"Yeah, I needed a shave," John answered.

"That little bastard over there said you were going to ask out a gay waitress." Julie announced. Cory snorted with a giggle and shot milk through his nose. The word 'bastard' always made him giggle. "Well if it's Francesca over at Jim Friendly's," Julia paused to open her other take out box which contained a combination the restaurant made only for Julia it was slow roast pork and lobster soft tacos with extra beans and no rice, "she's not gay," she continued with another mouth full of food, "she may way army boots but she's not gay trust me."

Cory stopped smiling and John seemed to know the answer. Julia was a regular customer at the Book Silo. She was usually looking for books on witchcraft, tattoo art, Bettie Page and Varga Girls. Julia and John struck up a

They said you died alone

Five Years Part I

friendship that was at first based on
their mutual interest in Varga Girls[8].

"Asked her out then?" John
wondered. Julia nodded her head and took
another bite of her lunches. "So how did
it go?" John pressed. Julia swallowed
her food, "Wrote her a note on a napkin
when I paid my check one night," she
paused to suck down a beer. "And?" John
knew the outcome at least he thought so.
"And she's a bitch," Cory interrupted.
In the same breath Julia turned sharply
in her seat and fired an open packet of
salsa at Cory who squealed but couldn't
get out of the way.

"You shut your fat face Cory,"
Julia commanded, "just because a women
rejects you, you of all people, does not
make her a lesbian or a bitch." She was
staring through him now. Julia was really
getting tired of Cory's trash talking of
every woman he's ever met. "If you say
something like that again so help me, I
swear I'll skin you alive." This was
followed by an uncomfortable silence,
which Cory would break about a minute
later. His stomach began to rumble as all
the nervous acid mixed with beef jerky
and old cereal. Cory began belching. Then
he erupted with vomit all over himself.

"GODDAMMIT Cory go clean yourself
up," Julia laughed. Cory got up and ran
to the bathroom. "He is such a little
bitch sometimes," Julia turning back to
a very stunned John.

"Does he do that a lot?" John
asked.

---

[8] Varga girls were paintings done by Alberto Vargas
primarily as calendar girls and centerfolds for Esquire
magazine in the nineteen forties. They were provocative
for the time though still somewhat tame cheesecake
pictures. They were often painted on the sided of
American military planes during the Second World War.

They said you died alone

Five Years Part I

"Only when I yell at him," Julia
answered, "now where was I?"

"You wrote her a note on a
napkin," John said

"Yeah that's right," Julia began,
"she was really sweet about it, she
wrote me back a lengthy note telling me
how flattered she was but that she
genuinely wasn't interested." Julia let
out a belch as Cory reemerged from the
bathroom. He was teary eyed and
shirtless. His upper torso, which, was
not meant to be seen by his fellow man,
was as white as a sheet. Cory's man boobs
wobbled as he made his way back to his
couch and bowl of cereal as if the
previous incident never happened. Julia
was lost in thought as Cory waddled back.

"That girl does have a great
looking ass though," Julia finally said,
John nodded in agreement, "what a
fuckable piece of ass," Julia added
rather absentmindedly.

"Aye 'tis a fine ass," John sighed
in a sea salts voice, "well I have a
couple more stops to make so.." Julia
interrupted "What? you're still here,"
she belched again, "get going John."
John was frozen till he heard that even
then his movement wasn't too swift. Here
comes the fear again, the inner coward
tries to rear it's ugly head.

"Get the lead out, she's not going
to be single forever," Julia barked.
Cory giggled into his wok of cereal.
Someone else was getting yelled at this
time. "Shut it Cory," Julia snapped.

"Right then," John said. The
atmosphere of the parlor was once again
getting uncomfortable, "thanks Jules,
I'll catch up with you later." John
patted her on the back as he walked past.

They said you died alone

Five Years Part I

"Cory you stay out of trouble there tough guy," John exclamated that by shooting a finger at Cory. This was enough for Cory to begin loathing John again.

They said you died alone

Five Years Part I

Chapter 5

John felt good for the moment he walked next door to the vintage clothing shop to buy a shirt. It was one of the higher end vintage shops that carried it's own line of varied apparel. It still smelled like your average thrift shop though, which was something like stale cigarettes and lithium. Between the sweet and the stagnate there was the idea that most of the inventory came from either death, theft or some other depressed situation. Labeling themselves 'Vintage' allowed these stores to charge high prices for basically discarded clothes. John headed straight for the rack containing bowling shirts, grinning to himself. Francesca had commented on more then one occasion that John would really look better in a bowling shirt as opposed to his favored rock tee shirts. At the moment the closest thing he owned was a blue Hawaiian shirt that was currently occupying the bottom of Johns hamper. John didn't like shopping for clothes but he has a system for when he had to. It was simple, quick and painless. After a little research he found his size in jeans, shirts and even shoes in brands he liked. When he had to he would buy three of any particular item he needed so that he wouldn't have to shop for quite a while.

Consequently he owns six pairs of black Levis, three pairs of air walks, black with a white stripe, one pair of brown vans and six dress shirts, two gray, four black all long sleeves. The only exception was his tee-shirt collection, but outside of the style variety they were all large. John made

They said you died alone

Five Years Part I

his way quickly through the rack of bowling shirts looking for larges. Almost immediately he grabbed hold of a pair of shirts both large and identical in color, which was blue and black. They were both fifteen dollars. John cringed but it was not at the price so much as the sudden memory of a few months prior. It was during another of Francesca's 'what John should wear' speeches. Something about reds and oranges, but John didn't remember all that clearly. The gap in his memory was due largely in part to the fact that the evening in question Francesca was wearing a shirt that had shrunk in the dryer and couldn't be entirely tucked in. Accordingly, John was able to see the top of Francesca's panties[9] (that would have normally been hidden by a tucked in shirt) whenever she turned her back to him. So from that night all he remembers are panties (black), red and orange. Standing at the rack he started to agree with the memory and smiled at the thought of her panties. "That's a damn right," he said. It was the only thing he had said since entering the store. If it had been a busier day in a normal store it might have gone unnoticed. But this was a shop in a less then desirable end of the San Fernando Valley with only a handful of people in the shop. John drew stares and caused a

---

[9] It should be noted that when it comes to 'panties' there are two very different schools of thought on the subject. On one hand you have the women who wear them simply for the fact that they have to wear them (there are a strange lot, men and women, who 'go commando but that is entirely another matter). The other side of this is the men to whom 'panties' are more conceptual. 'Panties' are attributed with some quasi-mythical properties disabling rational thought (and in many cases basic motor function and general communication skills) at the slightest glance. Women, however, rarely have ulterior for 'panties' outside of the general need for underwear.

They said you died alone

mother to pull her child closer to
herself and further away from John.

      John wasn't paying any attention to
this. He was busy looking for orange and
or red bowling shirts. In the end of his
search, which had taken a total of six
minutes, John had collected one orange
and black shirt, one beige, black and
green and a red and purple shirt in
addition to the black and blue shirts he
found first. The red and purple shirt was
really the best find and the most
expensive. It had a name embroidered
above the left breast pocket. In shiny
purple stitching it read: Leon P. On the
back of the shirt it displayed an
embroidered bowling shark with an arch
above reading Inland Empire Bail Bonds.
This amazing shirt was priced at thirty
dollars. The other shirts lacked the
character of this one. They were a little
like blank canvas for a potential wearers
bowling related glory. They were actually
factory over runs and had never been worn
by anyone. Where as the Leon P. shirt
probably had such an amazing story behind
it, or at the very least an interesting
tale. The shirt itself was nearly
pristine with only one stain on the back
of the collar that could have either been
blood or coffee. John was fascinated with
the shirt and at the moment felt
determined to learn all about Leon P. the
least notable would have been why or
rather how could two men named Leon get
along well enough to bowl together? But
seeing as how the Sharks were from
Riverside and that traveling there meant
going through Orange county, which John
detested, essentially meant that John
would never investigate on his own,
though in another thirteen months he

They said you died alone

Five Years Part I

would learn the truth weather or not he
wanted to.

They said you died alone

Chapter 6

What did happen to Leon P., whose
name was actually Paulson, was strange
and fairly alarming. It would also change
the course of John life (along with
nearly the entire population). For better
or worse it was an irreversible. Leon
Paulson was John's age the summer he
died. It was almost a year to the day
John was buying the shirt (closer to
eight months for the sake of argument).

Leon was a father of two and a
relatively successful businessman. In the
beginning of May of that year he
developed what at first he thought was a
bad case of Hay fever. The illness
persisted and Leon thought it was just a
summer cold, so he ignored it for the
first week. The second week he cursed
while he coughed and sneezed, as much as
a Lutheran Pat Boone fan might, and he
drank plenty of water and orange juice.
The third and forth week he felt dizzy a
good portion of the time, stayed in bed
and missed quite a lot of work. The fifth
week he actually felt better, though he
still had a cough, which his wife blamed
on smoking. On Sunday of the fifth week,
Leon slept in missing church for the
first time since he was a boy. He got up
around ten to watch a baseball game and
as he walked into the living room the
fever returned sweeping through his body.
The dizziness returned with a blinding
heat pulsing behind his eyes. He swayed
about the room, gritting his teeth and
trembling. His family returned from
church to the middle of Leon's madness.
Leon was in the middle of the room
tearing apart the family dog. It had been
a border collie. The dog had done nothing
to incur Leon's sudden psychotic rage; it

They said you died alone

Five Years Part I

had just been the first living thing he
came into contact with. Leon had taken
the poor creature by the skull, dug his
thumbs into the dog's eyes and cracked
the skull in half. Leon was in the midst
of breaking the dog's chest cavity open
as his family entered the living room.

Leon, to this point in his life,
had never harmed another living thing,
but he was about to do harm to three
more. Leon had been startled by his
family's screams and leapt straight at
his wife. Maybe it was because she
presented the greater threat or maybe
there was some unresolved resentment
between husband and wife. There was no
time for explanation, Leon was moving too
fast for that. He tore her heart out in
less then thirty seconds. He crushed his
wife's heart as he let out a great,
almost primal scream. It wasn't victory
or the fact that he had just tore his
love apart, he was no longer able to
discern such an act. It was his eyes,
they had begun to melt from the inside
and he could no longer see. His children
were frozen in terror as he swung his
arms about trying to find them. He cooed
to them, as he was no longer able to form
words. It was a sickening call as he
sprayed blood from his mouth. This was
all happening to quickly for the kids to
react and Leon found them. He pulled them
close in what must have seemed like a
moment of mock tenderness. A blind,
murderous father consoling his children
over the body of their mother. But it
wasn't tenderness Leon wanted, as he
smeared his wife's blood on them, he
needed to feel them. With his last moment
of abnormal strength he tore each of
their throats out. They fell next to

They said you died alone

their mother where they would soon bleed to death. It was five past ten in the morning now. The sun was burning through the bay window of the living room illuminating the horrific scene in an almost heavenly glow. It was shining down on Leon as he stood in the middle of his undoing. The fever had robbed him of any remorse; any ability to ever fully comprehend what he had just done to his family. He was surrounded by blood that he had spilled and he hadn't a lucid thought in his head. He collapsed on to the pile of bodies as he twitched and convulsed. The fever had reached its peak. With a muffled snap Leon stopped moving as both his brain and eyes popped and tissue poured from his eyes and his nose.

The grisly incident would be discovered later in the afternoon by Leon's younger brother Arthur. Arthur had come in through the side gate next to the garage so that he could get a cold beer from Mrs. Paulson's secret stash. He would snap open the beer just as he entered the living room to discover his brother and family. He would scream and cry out. Then he would throw up and then finish his beer. Arthur grabbed another beer before calling the police. The horrific murders would go unsolved though unofficially blamed on a local Orange county chapter of the Church of Satan. Ironically this chapter had been inactive, so far as ritualistic killings go, for the last thirty-five years and at the time of the Paulson murders consisted of just three members. Earl and Francine

They said you died alone

Five Years Part I

Myers of Yorba Linda, [10]both of whom where sixty-five and sixty-six respectively and only really got around these days with the help of a pair of personal mobility scooters and a blue Dodge conversion van. The only link police had to the murders was Derek Wall. Derek was the only follower that the Myers had left. He was a recently paroled reformed skinhead formally of the once fearsome Black Luftwaffe. Derek was once a leader among skinheads all throughout California and parts of western Nevada. Derek had been sent up to Chino correctional for fifteen. He served six. Derek didn't find Jesus in jail, he found Earl Myers. For a number of years Earl had petitioned the wardens office to allow him to offer council to the soon to be reformed. Earl was a firm believer in giving a man a fair shot in life and to Earl that meant educating them. The prisons were always full of Christians, Muslims and God knew how many Jews, Earl would remark[11]. Eventually the warden relented and allowed Earl to hold weekly seminars. Earl was a forceful lecturer but only managed to reach Derek. Derek had felt betrayed by what he thought he knew and the people he had once relied upon, and Earl was able to show him another way.

Very little attention was paid to Derek upon his early release; he was

---

[10] Back in the nineteen seventies The Myers and their followers achieved an odd sort of notoriety when they organized the 'Satanists for Dick', a grassroots movement for church members who supported the reelection of then president Richard Nixon. The movement failed when as horrified Nixon saw a sign on a lawn in Yorba Linda. Nixon staffers secretly brought this to the attention of the local Church of Satan who then ordered the Myers to stop. 'Satanists for the Gipper' in nineteen eighty-three would get them effectively excommunicated from the church and the community in the greater South West.
[11] Earl was from a Jewish family from the same neighborhood in Patterson, New Jersey as Jim Friendly.

They said you died alone

certainly nothing special amongst a sea of skinhead parolees, one of a countless number throughout Orange County. But when Leon Paulson killed his family the Homicide detectives in charge of the case had nowhere else to turn but Derek. Let me explain; Paulson Brakes and Tires was a small, though successful chain of auto-maintenance shops run by Leon and funded by his father-in-law. Leon was by all accounts a good guy, a great father and a faithful and devoted husband. So the thought of him slaughtering his family in such as brutal manner was beyond belief.

So Derek Wall entered the picture despite there not being any more then the flimsiest of connections and no physical evidence. Derek was six foot six, two hundred seventy pounds and only with three percent body fat (which only made him look more like a no-neck goon). His arms shoulders back and legs were tastefully decorated in the emblems of his club (as tasteful as swastikas, S.S. skulls and other Third Reich emblems ever could be). After his release from prison, Derek was truly a better man though still very angry. Additionally his face was clean-shaven and he had hair growing on his head for perhaps the first time since he was fourteen.

Derek grew up in the San Fernando Valley. He went to school with John Parkers older brother Jeremy. Jeremy would pick on, beat up and just generally make life in Parkman Junior high hell for Derek. Derek was already six foot two in the seventh grade; he was also fifty pounds over weight with an unmanageable

mane of heavy metal hair[12]. Derek's
father, Conner Wall was a sergeant with
the Los Angeles. Conner had recently been
transferred to the Traffic Division from
Homicide after an interrogation beating
scandal that cost several senior
detectives their freedom, though in some
cases just their pensions. Conner was
hard on his son for very few justifiable
reasons outside of Derek being a fat
disappointment (but mostly Conner was
just a mean bastard). Before his freshman
year of high school Derek's parents
divorced and Derek and his mother moved
into a crappy, roach infested one bedroom
apartment in Santa Ana. It was the kind
of place with bars on every window and a
broken security gate at the front. Derek
slept on the couch in living room
listening to nightly arguments between a
spousal abuser and victim in the
apartment above and petty dealings of
local thugs. It was a less then desirable
neighborhood just north of Costa Mesa
Orange County. Derek and his mother had
gone from the mostly White Woodland Hills
to a mostly Hispanic Santa Ana. At
fourteen and a half Derek was faced with
the choice of continuing to be a victim
or of going on the offensive and
effectively becoming a bully.

---

[12] Not to be confused with 'Hockey Hair', which was a
more polite way of saying mullet. Heavy Metal Hair was
long, damaged and seldom brushed. It was made popular
by the musical outfits Metallica, Megadeth and Iron
Maiden. All bands that Derek was heavily into at the
time.

They said you died alone

Chapter 7

All Derek had really done was trade ideologies, Supremacist, which can be hateful for Satanism, which is ironically humanist while still being elitist. In any case Derek needed a job and having been a mechanic prior to his most recent incarceration applied for work at ever-applicable venue, including all three Paulson Brakes and Tires locations. On all three occasions of Derek's applying Leon, as was the case with every applicant, personally reviewed and rejected the application. The first application had the distinct smell of beer not to mention the spelling and grammar errors and numerous blank portions. Leon was a born again Christian who had sworn off beer and was personally offended that anyone still drank the devils elixir (it was Mrs. Paulson who hid a twelve pack in the refrigerator in the garage). With the rejection of the second application Leon sent a four page, hand written letter asking Derek to seek the forgiveness of Jesus Christ. It also included a photocopied list of biblical passages that included general summary paragraphs outlining how each might relate to what Leon felt might be helpful in Derek's salvation (also included was a twenty dollar gift certificate for the Book Silo with the explicate instruction that it be used for a bible). At that point Derek had only attended one week of the court appointed anger management class at the Riverside Adult learning Annex (he was also taking a knitting class to help deal with his idle hands). So Derek was still two weeks away from the classes that covered more constructive expressions of the wounded

They said you died alone

Five Years Part I

soul. Needless to say, when Derek
received the letter he was angered beyond
words, but not beyond writing a bizarrely
threatening letter. Derek professed his
desire to kill Leon, his wife, their
children and to bring an unholy suffering
down on any future descendents. Earl
Myers intervened before the letter could
be sent. Derek was a consummate
perfectionist. He had Earl read the
letter to check it for spelling and
grammar errors. Earl read the letter and
understood the angry his protégé felt. He
suggested, however, that they go to the
driving range and hit a bucket of golf
balls and then see if Derek still wanted
to send the letter. Golf was the key
learning tool that Earl employed in
teaching Derek patience. Earl would often
explain that if you lost you temper with
the game you lost control of it. The same
went for everything else. It was a
struggle, but Derek was learning to
persevere, he was learning not to stab
people in the throat when they dismissed
him. He applied a third time at Paulson
Brakes and Tires on the Friday before
Leon killed his family. It was a simple
matter that quickly became an ugly
confrontation. Leon was in the shop
discussing a new hire with the manager
when Derek filled out the application.
Just as Derek began, Leon approached, put
his hand on Derek's shoulder and spoke;
"The position has been filled friend, I
was just coming out to take the sign
down." Leon said this in his usual
friendly way. Derek's hands began to
tremble, knitting needles and golf clubs
were so far away. Derek had become
convinced that Leon was conspiring to
keep him unemployed. Derek knew Leon on

They said you died alone

sight (from the print ads that ran in every Sunday Orange County Register), and he was sure enough now that Leon knew him on sight as well. There was no conspiracy, Leon didn't know who Derek was and the position had been filled.

The letter that Leon had sent to Derek, though personalized and hand written, was a form letter that went out to all under qualified applicants. Leon did maintain a genuine interest in the salvation of his fellow man but he also had a business to run. As for Derek, the knitting classes were helping the anger management was not.

Derek snapped his pen and crumpled the application just as Leon was saying something to the effect that he'd be happy to keep the application on file. Derek clenched his fists; tears welled in the corners of both eyes. "I'm not going to forget this," he rumbled with rage choking him. Derek pointed at Leon and drew a line across his throat to indicate that he was going to cut Leon's throat. Then he turned and stormed out of the building. Less then a week later Derek would be arrested at his new job while he was taking the trash out, he would be fired when it was explained it was for a suspected, multiple homicide. The investigation would close a month later when they realized that Derek, nor any other 'cult' member could be placed at the crime scene. Derek, having already lost his job at Happy Burger (which was a poor knock off of Burger King), would look for another six months before finding another full time job. It would be as a security guard/janitor at the

They said you died alone

Five Years Part I

notorious topless bar "The Blue Blue
Kitty Gentleman's Club"[13] which sat in a
bad part of Long Beach (which is not
unlike being the ice sticking to the
inside of a freezer) on the corner of
Crenshaw and Pacific Coast Highway. The
collective possessions of the Paulson
family would pass through extended
family, thrift stores and church donation
boxes. The murders would remain unsolved
and subsequently added to a growing list
of equally bizarre and unexplainable
brutal crimes around the America's and
parts of Europe. These crimes would
remain mostly unconnected by any news
agency or criminal investigator outside
of the supermarket tabloid "The
Cyclops". The Cyclops steadfastly
maintained (after abandoning a far more
accurate tale of Nazi scientists and the
cloning of a secret army) that Satan
himself had unleashed the plague of his
seed on millions of unfaithful wives
across the globe. They would go on to say
that it was only a matter of time before
the world would be engulfed in
unfathomable violence at the hands of the
spawn of the devil. Of their theory only
this was true: it was simply a matter of
time.

---

[13] The Blue Blue Kitty was notorious for many things;
food poisoning, pregnant strippers, serving watered
down, economy brand diet grapefruit soda when they lost
their liquor license. Most notably, however, they
employed some of the most aggressively ugly women who
have ever been paid to take their tops off.

They said you died alone

Chapter 8

John Parker didn't know any of this. He never met Leon or his family. John did read about the murders, but they only received passing mention in the Los Angeles Times. The article John read briefly mentioned the brutality of the murders but the paper treated it as just another random crime in Orange County that was probably related to gangs, Methamphetamine, skinhead violence or a grocery list of problems "that we just don't want in our backyard". The paper used the article to attack the state governments lack of funding for education or a recent tax cut that it didn't agree with or nearly anything else that the paper didn't like about the current governing party.

What John did know was that he had a really cool bowling shirt that was his size. He didn't even mind paying thirty-five dollars for it. He strolled up to the counter, plopped down four out of the five shirts while he put on the "Leon P" shirt over his tee shirt. "I'm going to wear this one out, ok?" he said having already finished buttoning the shirt. The clerk really didn't care she smiled and nodded as she rang up Johns new shirts. John began drifting off into his post apocalyptic realm when the clerk mumbled the total. John handed off his card without so much as listening. The clerk really didn't give a shit; she was waiting to her from her agent about her last audition, which was a month ago.

The clerk was an actress you see. In total summation of her career: Sara Jeffries (the clerk) had appeared in the lead role of six of the last eight of her

They said you died alone

Five Years Part I

high school productions of Sleepy Hollow
Public. These included "The King and I"
as Anna, "Sweeney Todd" as Mrs. Lovett
and "The Sound of Music" as Maria.
Foregoing college Ms Jeffries took a
position at the prestigious Blueridge
Dinner Theatre in Danbury, Connecticut.
Which, consequently, was more famous for
their prime rib special or perhaps even
their chocolate/champagne cocktail then
the class of actors who had passed
through their doors. Feeling limited by
her location, and just being generally
good at being miserable regardless of her
situation, Ms Jeffries made haste to Los
Angeles to be (of all things) discovered.
With her families blessing and two
thousand dollars for headshots she began
her career in retail attending
approximately three auditions in a four-
year span. By the way a headshot is a
professionally orchestrated or rather
staged photograph setting the actor to be
in one of three poses or looks. These are
typically; the sultry pose, the playful
pose, and the determined pose. John has
seen this sort of thing though he'd never
seen those belonging to Sara Jeffries.
John's brother Jason was at one time an
aspiring actor. After having appeared in
a McDonald's commercial when he was
thirteen Jason Parker rigorously pursued
acting as a career till he was twenty-
three. Jason Parkers headshots were at
best comical. The sultry pose showed
Jason in a tuxedo posed like a catalog
model from the seventies, the playful
pose showed Jason in a tuxedo tee-shirt
in the exact same pose and the exact same
expression. The determined or "action
pose" showed Jason in a camouflage
jacket over the tuxedo tee-shirt with the

They said you died alone

Five Years Part I

same expression and the same pose which
was his right hand under his chin and
Jason looking straight at the camera as
if to say "Yes I'm sexy, have some?"
Jason was the subject to the cruelty of
heredity. At eighteen he lost most of his
hair, just as his grandfather on his
mothers side had done. At nineteen his
formerly flat stomach began to take on a
more Buddha like rotund appearance.
Coupled with his already stringy arms and
legs, often referred to as chicken legs
or Don Knotts syndrome, it gave Jason
Parker the most unfortunate silhouette of
a gangly boy holding a beach ball. At
twenty-three he entered semi-retirement
from acting, resigning to being a patron
of the arts (which was as a head waiter
at an exclusive restaurant after having
been rejected as an acting coach). He was
stricken with the worst case of Adult
acne that has been seen in the twentieth
century in any developed country. Just
the past week, for his thirty-second
birthday, he treated himself to braces to
correct his smile so that he could once
again pursue acting. So while John was
paying for his bowling shirts in one of a
thousand or so thrift stores that litter
the landscape of Southern California that
were staffed by the would be but
tragically lethargic artist, his brother
Jason was in Culver City, which was about
an hour or so away, one of five hundred
or so 'would be's' all in line for one of
two possible speaking roles in a feature
film. John would get to hear about it all
the following Sunday at the family
barbeque. Jason's tale of career woe was
always familiar, the studios would always
fear his talent, they would swoon at his
aggressive sexual nature and would pass

They said you died alone

in favor of a lesser man. It would all come back to the three years Jason spent at Anaheim City College, which is located in the heart Old Anaheim, which, is possibly the only pleasant looking part of Anaheim. Jason Parker was heralded as the greatest actor that the city of Anaheim would see in nineteen eighty-six perhaps even in eighty-seven. Jason would always over look the fact that as a working actor he'd been unemployed for the better part of eighteen years. In all this time Jason had forced himself to remain celibate so that the awesome, and somewhat fierce power would not over take him in his pursuit of the arts. In all truthfulness Jason was still wounded from the confession of his date to the senior prom. Connie Lewis had been his paramour for five months and it was at an after party where she had consumed six wine coolers she was finally able to tell Jason that in their time together, however brief, that she had become comfortable with the fact that she was in no way attracted to men. This being stated Connie left the party with the date of the football teams quarterback. The emotional scarring on the psyche of a seventeen year old was bad, almost as bad as the beating Jason received from the football teams offensive line for making their quarterback's girl "go gay".

John's own romantic exploits were nearly as limited but not nearly as sad or pathetic. He had a steady girlfriend throughout most of college. A young lady who worked at a vitamin shop, who John was always eager to please despite the fact that she treated him like shredded used tampons. Their relationship lasted a year, two months by her calendar. John

Five Years Part I

thought of her as a moon goddess, in fact
he hadn't been this taken with a girl
since Breanne Milo in the eighth grade
(which was thankfully for John a brief
tragedy). The love of his college life,
whose name was Lynn Green, did at one
time like John but always maintained that
he would have benefited from long term,
possibly interment based therapy. Lynn
officially ended the relationship a week
before John's twenty-fourth birthday.
John quit school and moped around for a
year or so. He spent that year hanging
out at a Japanese bar in North Hollywood
where his friend Ginene worked as the bar
manager (that wasn't her real name but it
was the name on her visa). She had come
to the United States from South Africa to
work as a writer, and she sort of fell
off track. She took it upon herself to
teach John how to seduce a woman, a
subject that John would never prove to be
a quick study on.

They said you died alone

Five Years Part I

Chapter 9

John marched out of the store bag in hand. Sara Jeffries wouldn't get the call she was waiting for and would sulk for the next several weeks. John was confident; he felt ready though the closer he got the more doubt crept back in to his mind. Rejection, that horrible word slowed him by half a step. Had he read all the signs wrong? He wondered. He didn't really know and it wasn't like he had the experience to know what he saw if she was showing anything. Ginene had told him what to look for. He began to ponder the 0potential disaster that he was embarking on and it slowed his pace to a crawl. John stared off down the street ahead and he began to feel just slightly foolish. The shirts did suit him well enough, but he wouldn't have bought them had he not thought that Francesca would like them. He was about to berate himself when he walked into another parking meter there by snapping himself out of his self-doubt funk. Why it was only a week ago that he had walked her home. His Eisenhower jacket still smelled of her perfume, he smiled and remembered the kiss on the cheek she had given him when he stuttered about having to go to work, declining an invitation to come in and watch Mash and have a beer. He wasn't going to give up again, not going to be a coward again. "What's the worst she could say?" he wondered aloud, "No", he laughed, "not like I haven't heard that before." He began his stride again, "If I fail here," he said renewing his solo conversation, "it'll be a set back that's for sure,"

They said you died alone

Five Years Part I

John smiled, "but at least it's one I've faced before."

About three and a half storefronts away from where John was arguing himself into a clumsy frenzy, Francesca was busy herself. It was an hour into her shift and she was the only waitress working until the seven o'clock shift arrived. Kobe was there but he sat at the lunch counter fighting off the tequila he consumed the night before. Kobe was in the midst of a self-destructive "I'm twenty-five and I've thrown the best things in my life away" faze. The self-medication was a combination of all liquors clear and dark, not to mention beer and schnapps and maybe some of the more exotic liqueurs. There were an uncertain number of things weighing Kobe down, but mostly it was his ability to sabotage any meaningful relationship he had, almost by instinct. Francesca, meanwhile, was busy with twelve tables and no help from the night manager Philippe who himself was busy snorting cocaine in the unisex employee bathroom with one of the day cooks and two of the busboys. Francesca was annoyed, but it wasn't the missing manager, the incapacitated Kobe or the fact that she was sweating all over her customers and they were still complaining that it was too cold in the restaurant. John was late, an hour late. To top that off there was some old man sitting at John's regular table. It was strange, the old man showed up at almost that exact time that John would have, the old man looked around, then ordered coffee and sat down at John's table. He looked anxious.

John was in front of Jim Friendly's now. He grabbed a copy of the

They said you died alone

Five Years Part I

L.A. Weekly, which was a free newspaper, from a red stand in front of the restaurant, and then strolled inside. It was chaos inside but a familiar sight to John. Francesca gave John a smile and an evil glare as she ran past him with a full tray. Without evening looking John headed for his usual table. The old man waiting smiled as much as seemed possible, which still seemed far out of character. John didn't see the man till he looked up from his paper when he reached the table and was about to sit down. "Oh, I'm sorry didn't see you there," John apologized out of instinct. "Don't be sorry," the man said with a smile that seemed to cause him some measure of pain, "just have a seat John." John was puzzled but he sat down slightly forgetting his mission. John set his paper and bag of shirts down. The old man took a notebook out of his pocket and made a quick addendum of it as it was out of character for John to shop from that particular thrift store.

"Do I know you," John began, "I'm sorry if
I do, I don't have a great memory for faces."

"No need to apologize my boy, you don't know me."

"But you know me?" John questioned sounding slightly paranoid, "is that what I'm to understand?"

The man nodded his head," Yes that's correct," he answered dryly.

"Well would you mind if I asked....," John began before being interrupted.

"Who I am and why do I know you?" the man laughed, which was nearly as unsettling as seeing him smile, "the why

They said you died alone

Five Years Part I

isn't important right now John." John
was never a big fan of mind games. He was
quickly growing tired of this and was
about to get up and leave when Francesca
arrived balancing three plates and two
pots of coffee. She was happy to see John
and had taken to worrying whenever he was
late. "You're late John," she said in a
tone that he'd never heard before, "I'll
be back with your coffee in a couple of
minutes, ok," she winked at him and
didn't wait for a response as she
disappeared back into the mob of patrons.

"She's quite fond of you John,"
the man said after Francesca left the
table. This drew another puzzled look
from John.

"Ok smart guy," John said, "if you
know me so well what am I going to
order?"

"You're not," the man began, "since
today's pie is lemon meringue you'll have
a slice and three cups of coffee each
with three packets of sugar that you'll
shake twelve times before ripping open
and pouring into your cup and two small
containers of half and half," John was
getting creeped out by this but there was
more, "you'll stir each cup five to
eleven times before sipping, the first
cup will be to hot causing facial spasms
similar to the time when Francesca put
cherry syrup in your coffee, you'll spill
a portion of the second cup while you
watch her work but it'll be all right
because she will have brought a stack of
napkins numbering somewhere around
twenty-five, and the third cup will go
cold usually half way through while you
try to work up the courage to ask her out
to a movie and possibly dinner."

They said you died alone

Five Years Part I

"And you are?" John asked this time a little more indignant.

"That's not the issue here John, we're here to talk about you remember," the man said.

"Right," John answered sarcastically, "so you're my stalker then?"

"No John."

"Well then would you lease tell me how you know all of that?"

"I know almost everything there is to know about you John, about a lot of people," the man answered.

"To a great degree that would bring us back to the stalker issue wouldn't it," John began to wonder aloud, "or perhaps you're some sort of deity." This caused the man to laugh again.

"I would hope," he said, "that if there were such a thing that he would dress better then I," he gestured to the lapel of his gray tweed suit, "but for the sake of argument I will give you the same sort of proof that Peachy and Danny inadvertently gave to the people of Kafiristan." The man proceeded to remove a small pin from the underside of his lapel and showed it to John. He then pushed the pin into his index finger drawing forth from the temporarily regressed skin a droplet of blood. He showed the wounded finger to John and then applied saliva to a napkin and held it on his finger.

"See," he announced, "no fire of the gods encased in the flesh of man." Francesca returned with a slice of Lemon Meringue, a cup of coffee and approximately twenty-five napkins.
"Who's your friend John?" she smiled pointing to the man across from him.

They said you died alone

"I was hoping you could tell me,"
he replied dryly. The man smiled again.

"Johnny was always a great kidder,"
the man said forcing a pleasant tone,
"Francesca it's nice to meet you, I'm
John's uncle George from Chicago."

"Well can I get you a slice of pie
George?"

"No I'm fine with coffee thanks,"
George said. It was then that he entered
a staring contest with John. John didn't
know why he wasn't calling the man a
liar, part of him wanted to see how this
was going to end.

"I'll be back with some more soon
ok boys," she said as she moved back
into the sea of customers.

"Uncle George?" John peered over
at the man, "from Chicago," he
mimicked.

"Well it worked for the situation
at hand," the man answered.

"So your only a situational liar
or was there some truth to that?"

"It's only true if and when it
needs to be," he answered.

"So your names not George?"

"No."

"And you're not from Chicago?"

"I've been there, I'm not from
there," George lifted his coffee cup to
take a sip, John looked at him, far more
puzzled then before, George could tell he
was losing John's focus, "if it will
make it easier for you to listen to me
then think of me as your friend George
from Chicago." John pondered this for a
moment. He took a bite of pie and washed
it down with some coffee. Today the
coffee was lime flavored. John swished
the concoction around in his mouth before
swallowing with a big gulp.

They said you died alone

Five Years Part I

"That was quite a flavor," he grimaced, "so for the sake of clarity you are neither from Chicago or a George?"

"That's mostly correct," George replied, "I have spent time there, though I never have had a permanent home."

"Ok," John began sarcastically, "I hate to be blunt but could you get to the point?"

"First go finish your business with Francesca," George smiled, "then we can talk." John was swept with panic for a moment mixed with the odd aftertaste of Lime syrup coffee and hazelnut half and half. The first people who knew his intentions today were Julia and Cory, and they only knew twenty minutes ago.

"Don't bother wondering how I know John, she's not going to wait forever you know that as well as I do."

John got up and looked around, even if George was a crazy old man he was right. Francesca wouldn't wait. "Wait a second," John finally said turning back to George, "how do you know what she's thinking?" George raised an eyebrow and gave John a discerning look. "Quit wasting your life asking why John," George sipped his coffee, "I believe she's out back having a cigarette."

John started to say something, only to drop it, turn and move into the restaurant. There was no sense in arguing with the man, John thought to himself, he is right. John wasn't too sure how to get to the back of the building short of going outside and around it, so he pressed forward with a sense of urgency matched only by the fear and nausea that rose in his stomach. This really can't be

They said you died alone

Five Years Part I

that hard, he thought, I just have to
find out where the smoking area is.

Kobe sat at the counter hating
life. He could feel the air around him
as it moved and it caused him to ache, he
could feel the vibration of the
electricity in the light bulbs over head.
Or at least so he would claim, Kobe did
have a tendency to exaggerate his plight.
He was, however, doing much better.
Coffee, greasy eggs and not moving very
much usually calmed, if not cured his
hangover. Kobe held his eyes closed, he
could feel the blood flow, his face was
still warm, he knew he shouldn't have
gotten out of bed this morning. Kobe
opened one eye as John approached. He
winked his bloodshot eye at John. John
was having a strange day, but this was at
least a familiar sight.

"Have you seen Francesca?" John
asked.

"She's in the back on a ten," he
sighed and stretched without opening his
eyes, "just go on through the kitchen
you'll find her."

"Right-o," John answered.
It didn't seem necessary to even ask if
he should, the prep line behind the
counter was all but deserted. John had
always been curious as to what went on in
that kitchen. He managed to find it
between the 'Blue Plate' crowd and the
dinner rush. Two cooks were busy playing
a game of quarters on one of the
stainless steel prep tables. The object
of the game was to slide, skip or toss a
quarter across the table, reaching the
very lip of the table without going over.
Failing to reach the lip at all was also
failure; it had to land just so. The

They said you died alone

proctor of the game was a jolly, but at the same time slightly sinister looking fry cook. He had one of his hairy arms elbow deep in a tub of Jim Friendly's famous coleslaw as he mixed it. The other arm he held a dirty wad of ones and fives. John nodded to the gamers and made a mental note to never eat the coleslaw ever again as he pushed through the back door. He was greeted by a waft of stink and stale cigarettes. Part of the smell was from the metal dumpster where during the day all manner of food refuse had cooked along with some more hazardous materials. The asphalt was coated in a mixture of baked garbage water, urine and cigarette butts. About seven feet away from the epicenter Francesca sat on a couple of milk crates. She had a pair waiting for John. She smiled when she saw John.

"You'll get used to the smell," she said.

"Thanks for the lime coffee," he smiled as he approached the milk crates next to her, "there was something I was hoping to ask you."

"Hoping? hmmm," she pretended to think it over, "pull up some crates and sit down." Francesca handed John a cigarette as he sat down then lit it for him. John took a drag and coughed, she smoked harsher cigarettes than he was used to. "Mighty flavorful," he coughed, "I've been meaning to take this up again."

"Right," she raised an eyebrow, "so John did you come here tonight to ask me to go out with you?"

This was too easy, or was a polite rejection looming on the horizon. Was this a trap? "No John that's stupid,"

They said you died alone

Five Years Part I

he thought to himself. Francesca was
looking at him, straight in the eyes with
her crazy eyes. By John's definition
crazy eyes were any shade of eyes between
pale blue to whitish gray. Francesca's
eyes were a pale gray with a faint hint
of blue. She was also a firm believer in
continual eye contact that could be a
little intimidating. One of three things
was possible with this sort of eye
contact; she was flirting, she was going
to kill you or she was really pissed off.
It was never very clear to John. The one
possibility that hadn't occurred to John
or many of Francesca's regular customers
for that matter was that most of the time
eye contact just meant that she was
looking at you, nothing else. Tonight it
meant flirting.

John was looking for something to
say, he did want to ask her out, he
wanted to know everything about her,
which amazing John almost did know
everything about her, though he didn't
know that he knew. Francesca was a
painfully honest girl; she liked horror
movies and American rock music of the
seventies. She loved to dance although
she claimed not to be very good at it.
John knew that every morning when she
came home she had a beer and watched an
hour of MASH before going to sleep. Her
favorite perfume was 'Knowing', she
preferred thongs to bikini cuts, and that
she wore her boots everywhere she went.
John knew of so many things and had never
strung them all together. John tried to
speak, but Francesca had more to say,
"Now don't lie to me John, I know when
you're lying and you're not very good at
it."

They said you died alone

Five Years Part I

"All right," he blushed, "yes I
would like to ask you out." Francesca
smiled and took one last, long drag on
her cigarette while she retrieved a well
wore piece of paper from her server book.
"Pick me up at my house tomorrow after
you get off work," she started to get,
John held the paper in his hand it had
her name and phone number written in her
cheerful waitress scrawl, "don't look so
surprised John, you had to know by now
that I'd be happy to go out with you."
John stammered for words that he didn't
have at that moment, "Meet me here
tomorrow night after you get off of work
ok John?" He blushed and stared down at
his shoes as she got up from the milk
crates.

"I've got to get back to work
darlin'," she said.

"Yeah I should get back to my pie
and lime coffee," John laughed, "this
time I'll go around front." Francesca
gave him a wink and went back through the
kitchen door. John wandered down the
alley. The stink wouldn't allow him to
daydream. He patted him self down for a
cigarette remembering then that he left
them at his table with the crazy old man.
Midway down the alley John found a
walkway between Jim Friendly's and a
neighboring launderette. It was cleaner
then the alley, but not by much. John was
still kind of detached from his
surroundings. He wasn't entirely sure
that what happened had actually happened.
He stared at the piece of paper in his
hand again and again as he walked down
the passage between the buildings. The
heat of the day had all but faded into a
cooler night, except for the space that
John occupied. On one side of him was the

They said you died alone

Five Years Part I

air conditioning vents for Jim Friendly's
and on the other side were the vents for
the dryers from the launderette. It made
the walk a bit surreal. John was already
a bit out of his head and his shoes were
still sticky from garbage residue. The
vents from both buildings pushed trash
back and forth. John reached Ventura
Boulevard with sweat on his brow.
Reemerging on the street as he did John
was met with cooler air that brought him
out of his daze like an unpleasant
sobering up. Suddenly John realized that
he had left his shirts unattended at his
table and he had made a date for the
night that his brother Jason was set to
make his theatrical return (albeit in a
one man show based loosely on the Led
Zeppelin film 'The Song remains the Same'
at the Glendale Playhouse) and John was
really feeling like he needed to at least
consider looking for a new job and was
that guy George still at his table?
John's courage began to wane as he walked
up to the front window. George was still
waiting, as was John's bag of shirts and
the lighter he bought so that he could
use a razor, it occurred to John then
that he could have spent less money if he
had gone to the drugstore that was two
blocks further down the street. In his
haste to meet Francesca he'd forgotten
but she had asked him out anyway so it
was ok. John went back inside to retrieve
his bag and say goodbye to Francesca.

"Well George it's been," John
searched for the would for uncomfortably
weird, "something, yeah it's been
something," he laughed nervously as he
grabbed his bag. He didn't want to upset
the old guy.

They said you died alone

Five Years Part I

"John there is something you need to know," George said.

"Right, well you know where to find me," John said.

"Did Francesca arrange the date John?" George asked.

"What?, were you hiding in the alley or something?" John looked worried, this was putting him on the defensive and it had to stop, "what do you want from me?"

"I want you to sit down and listen to me," he said, "we have very little time left for games."

"If you leave me alone after this," John said with a pointed finger and a tired expression, "then I'll stay but only for a few minutes."

"I've taken a great risk in coming here to speak to you tonight," George began.

"That brings me to my first question actually," John rolled his eyes, "why the hell are you here?"

"Let me ask you first John, do you read a the paper called 'The Cyclops'?"

"Wouldn't you know if I did?" John peered in mocking suspicion, "you seem to know everything else right?"

"Indeed," George said, "well let me cut to the chase."

"Please do," John smiled.

"Within the next five years the world as you know it will come to an end."

"So you mean no more internet porn and day old hot dogs from convenience stores?"

"All kidding aside John," George said sternly, "the next sixty months will see the world engulfed in such fierce violence that roughly ninety-six

They said you died alone

percent of the population will meet there end." John thought about that for a moment.

"You're serious aren't you?" John blurted out.

"Plus or minus four percent of course," George offered.

"What going to happen that will cause all of this?"

"It's complicated," George relented.

"Can it be stopped?" John asked.

"An effort was made," George said, "but it only managed to accelerate and increase the scope of the problem."

"So why do I have to know about this why is it important?"

"Because John you are part of the four percent that should be unaffected," George smiled, "so is Francesca." John wasn't sure what to make of this, George was obviously stalking the both of them or the world really was coming to an end.

"So you have evidence of this?" John asked.

George beamed with pride; he had taken great lengths to document everything. He produced a musky smelling, coffee stained scrapbook, opened it to the first page and turned it so that John could read it. On the first page was a weathered old clipping from 'The Daily Cyclops' as it billed itself back in December of nineteen sixty-one. The headline read; Fugitive Nazi scientists help secret U.S. agents build clone soldiers. John only glanced at the body of the article because the photo next to it caught his attention. In the photo were some men in Lab coats next to some preposterous machines. In the background was what looked like a young George.

They said you died alone

Five Years Part I

Georges' scrapbook spanned nearly forty-five years of Cyclops stories about a mystery plague, the Nazi clones and Satan's part in it all. Virtually every article was written by Walter Myers the older brother of Earl Myers the Orange county, excommunicated Church of Satan member. Walter dedicated his life to his work, most notably forty some years to the Nazi Plague, or as he liked to call it 'Hitler's last blight'. He never married, lost most of his friends. This plague had become Walters's life and the ruination of a one time promising career as a journalist. The plague itself became clearer through the years. It acted like a cold for typically five weeks the whole while it would ravage the nervous system. It would reach it's climax as the host body tried to defend itself, producing adrenalin at unheard of rates culminating in the liquefying of internal organs coincided by a violent outburst always resulting in death. The origin was unknown the communicability was unknown. All Walter Myers could do was string together unconnected homicides with wild theory. This was the proof George offered. His notes lined each article.

"A little young to be a fugitive Nazi scientist aren't you George?" John asked.

"We prefer to be called spooks," George whipped the grin away with a sip of coffee, "my title is not the issue though," he said setting down his cup.

"So what? like no finger prints, secret assassinations and shadowy conspiracies?"

"Sometimes," George answered bluntly, "now you understand that I've come here at a great personal risk," he

They said you died alone

paused to look John in the eyes, "are
you ready to listen?" John fought the
urge to roll his eyes and leave knowing
full well that he could get equally
entertaining paranoia at home.

"Sure thing pal," John answered with
a hint of condescension that was lost on
George.

"What you will first notice will be
an increase in violent crimes that will
not be connected and should be somewhat
isolated from each other," George
cleared his throat, "blaming an anthrax
outbreak in Lancaster, California
Marshall Law will be declared and
California will be cut off from the rest
of America."

"Anthrax?" John was getting caught
up in the story, "who's going to spread
that?"

"No one," George said, "it will be
the cover story for your governments
excuse to isolate the problem and burn
the infected bodies in the Mohave."

"Is it going to work," John asked
anxiously.

"Fifteen, maybe twenty years ago
maybe," George looked almost guilty for
a moment, "things have evolved, there
are far to many variables to calculate,
what we do know, what we understand is
the rate of acceleration through the
global population, based on that we
reached our time frame and well here I
am."

"Why tell me?"

"Good question," George said, "two
answers, the simplest is that there has
to be survivors John and that's partly
what you were designed for. The more
complicated answer is that the people I
work for will want to know why you and

They said you died alone

those like you have gone unaffected. They
may already know, but I'm not sure. This
may involve a vivisection." The mention
of the word 'vivisection' made George
seem more and more like a paranoid,
slightly demented old man.

"Well George, I'm going home to wrap
aluminum foil around my head to keep the
secret radio waves out of my head," John
said this as he got up from the table,
"watch out for moving shadows ok pal."
John waved to Francesca, who was busy
with her table; she smiled back at him
then continued back to work. George got
up from the table, hastily gathering his
things. He threw an odd collection of
matchbooks and money on the table and
started to follow John out of the
restaurant.

"John don't be a fool, there is so
much more you need to know." John turned
as he pushed through the outer door
leading to the street.

"I've got plenty of crazy at home
George thanks," he said.

Three blocks down, sitting in a
midnight blue sedan, two men were sitting
and waiting. They watched as John and
George spilled out of Jim Friendly's.
From where they sat it looked as though
the pair was arguing. In the breast
pocket of the suit each man wore, very
similar in style to the one George wore,
were photo I.D. cards from the N.S.A..
The man behind the wheel was Paul Davis
and in the passenger seat was Seth
Oliver. They were there waiting for
George to emerge from restaurant. They
were there, waiting, because of George's
standing order that anyone who breached
security and approached a subject would
be summarily executed.

They said you died alone

Five Years Part I

"Who'd a figured it would be the man," Paul said referring to George. Among his co-workers and subordinates George went by no name, he was not a man to be trifled with and his reputation negated the formality of a name. His orders weren't questioned, and only a foolish man questioned his motives, openly or otherwise. Seth had very little to add save for a grunt or perhaps even a 'huh'. Seth was not in the N.S.A. for intelligence, he was basically a sociopath with a government grant. He flashed Paul a quick smile, he was fidgety and anxious, it had been nearly three weeks since he had killed anyone.

"Patience my friend we move when we can prove the level of exposure," Paul chimed. Paul was vying for whatever it was that George really did. The conversation that they had been watching started to look heated. Seth nodded to Paul who started the engine. The sedan roared off toward John and George. The sedan paused long enough while Seth cocked his gun. Even at a distance it was a sound all too familiar to George. In George's line of work this was how a problem was dealt with. No safety meetings, no counseling or memos. Any flaw, any deviation, any threat to the security of the project would be dealt with at the end of a barrel of a gun. This was standard practice but it was the first time George had been on the receiving end of this resolution. George threatened his own project, he knew this was coming; he would not condemn his assassins. George was a changed man however, and was not ready to accept death. He spotted their sedan back in New

They said you died alone

Five Years Part I

York, he knew their orders, he wrote
them. He also knew that just about now
Seth and Paul would be semi-engaged in a
long-standing argument over generic eye
drops being better than a name brand
variation. George had removed his nine-
millimeter from its holster and at the
moment was palming it behind his back and
out of view. After John said something
about having to catch his bus he turned
to the sidewalk where the sedan appeared
and Seth was firing the first shot at
George. The first shot his John in the
shoulder instead. It pushed him back, but
much to John's surprise it didn't hurt
like he thought a gunshot was supposed
to, it didn't cause his nerves to burn;
instead they surged and pumped as if
activated for the first time. The rush of
adrenalin made John light headed as it
exploded in his blood stream. He was
suddenly wobbly and fiercely aggressive
at the same time. John staggered like a
wounded animal as George leveled his gun
firing three shots. The bullets flew
inches past John's head. One shot hit
Seth in his shooting hand, causing him to
drop his gun with a yelp, a sound
something like an insolent child being
caught off guard. The second shot hit
Seth's opposite shoulder, preventing him
from retrieving another gun. The third
shot landed in the headrest behind Paul's
seat. George hadn't missed it was the
only warning shot the pair was going to
get. Paul took it as such and threw the
sedan into gear and hit the gas. John was
hurt and moving kind of sluggishly; he
didn't really have time to react to
anything that had just happened. George
stepped back and fired one more round.
John heard the crack of the pistol and

They said you died alone

Five Years Part I

fell to his knees. He felt a cool stream
rush down his neck and down over his face
and then it all went black.

    This is where the story should end,
but it won't, not yet.

They said you died alone

Five Years Part I

They said you died alone

Part II
The Origin of the
Species.

Chapter 1

In the late summer of nineteen-eighty six John, his brothers Jason and Jeremy, Angela and Richard and Jeremy's girlfriend at the time, Tiffany Renee Shore took a trip to Disneyland for John's eleventh birthday. At this point in his life Disneyland represented a warm family gathering for John, or at least the impression of what one was like. As a family this was there second trip, the first for John. Up to that point John and his brother Jason (and to a much lesser extent Jeremy who felt he was far to 'adult' for this sort of thing though Tiffany made him go on this trip) measured time in units of Disneyland trips (for John his first ten years were to be referred to as the before time). Disneyland represented the idea of a 'Happy Place', some of the happier moments shared with family, those rather expensive moments of freedom for children. One would do well to only remember the highlights of the day and not the ugly, over heated 'just spent a hundred dollars on a meal that you won't eat' moments that tend to dominate any theme park trip. Dad would be wearing his sunglasses cause he would be hung-over and more than mildly aggravated that he had to get up early on a Saturday and drive two hours to Orange fucking County to go to the Happiest Place on Earth. The first line of the day was at the entrance to the parking lot, giving the mob of angry, hung-over, station wagon driving fathers an opportunity to acknowledge each others plight through a series of engine revving and not letting anyone else in the flow of traffic. John's father would ignore the parking lot attendant (once the outrageous parking fee was paid, and a thorough cursing of the minimum wage piss ants was expelled) and park in the furthest lot from the entrance to the park[14] (some Disney character no one had ever heard of). The main goal of this was to ensure that the family car could be found at the end of the day. At the time this meant a nineteen eighty-five Ford Country Squire station wagon, powder blue with faux wood paneling.

The passenger manifest of the family wagon read like this; Mom in the passenger seat (she never drove Dad's car), Jason and Jeremy in the middle of the vehicle (with Jeremy's girlfriend serving as the all important 'I'm not gay' seat buffer), and John in the fold out seats that sat in the very back of the vehicle. The seats in the back were too small for an average sized person, but they were perfect for John. Sure he was already too tall for them, but they were the perfect place to play with his action figures on long trips. Once at the furthest parking spot from the park, the family would pile out of the car and exchange a series of semi-generic theme park related declarations. These were usually things like; 'I'm going on Space Mountain like a thousand times', or 'We're going on Pirates of the Caribbean first' or the more popular 'Stay together GODDAMMIT". Having just arrived it was a little early for Mr. Parker to be irritated, but the drive and the potential of the day ahead had him thoroughly annoyed. From the parking lot the Parker family waited in line with

---

[14] The one to ensure that no inconsiderate bastard parked too close and scraped the food, which, Richard claimed was still in factory condition.

innumerable identical families (eager
children, pre-exhausted parents) for the
tram ride that would take them to the front
gates of the park so they could wait in line
again, pay a sizable amount of money so they
could wait in line for the next several
hours of the day. The front gate is where
John's birthday trip began to turn sour.
Holding on to the bitter memory of his own
childhood, in which he had to get a job at
the age of eleven [15], Richard Parker went
through the line purchasing five tickets for
the family excluding John.

          "You going to join us son?" Richard
said to his sleepy eyed son. For the months
leading up to the event John had saved every
penny he could get his hands on. Fifty-two
dollars and ninety-three cents worth of
lawns mowed, dishes cleaned cars washed and
dogs walked, of course this was minus the
protection that had to be paid to his older
brother Jeremy. Jeremy, surprisingly enough,
was the family bully but he was not the
family math genius (the Parker family on a
whole lacked such). Jeremy gave John the
family rate, which was not taking
everything, just ten percent. "An
investment towards future protection from
beatings by me," was how Jeremy explained
this reasonable expense. Though Jeremy's
lack of math prowess did lead him to believe
that ten percent of sixty was seven John
didn't offer
an argument; he still had bruises from
Gestapo[16]. This left John with fifty-three

---

[15] This was a matter of perspective. As a child Richard
Parker was an extraordinary prodigy with small firearms.
The job was a paper route that his father suggested he get
in order to pay for ammunition, range fees and the
occasional neighborhood cat that young Richard shot to
impress his friends.
[16] Gestapo was a game that Jeremy claimed to have invented.
Neither Jason nor John appreciated it. It involved Jeremy
approaching his target (usually Jason, John or some poor
friend of theirs who had come over and didn't know any

dollars till he lost seven cents when he had
to change hiding places the night before
Disneyland. This money had all been saved
for the largest collection of Donald Duck
merchandise possible. In John's mind, at
the time, his life would have been so much
cooler if he had a larger collection of
Donald Duck paraphernalia. Donald was an
ill-tempered pants less sailor with a big
feathery butt. John played off his fathers
with a mix of panic and nervous laughter.
'Of course he bought me a ticket,' John
thought to himself. "Good one dad," John
answered in a hopeful laugh. "Indeed," Mr.
Parker snorted, "we'll meet up with you by
the hall of presidents." The rest of the
family (plus Tiffany) turned and headed
toward the entrance to the park. "Good joke
Dad," John laughed again still hoping that
this was all an elaborate birthday prank.
"Better get in line boy," Richard said
without turning around, "don't want to wait
for you all day and those lines are getting
pretty long." And in an instant it hit
John. It was something like the like feeling
of standing on a train track facing on
oncoming train. You see the train coming,
but you tell yourself that it's not going to
hit you right up to the time when the train
hits you. So as John got back in the ticket
line he began to realize what an unpleasant
place Disneyland could be. He marched
forward with the other families wondering to

better) and then asking them if they wanted to play
'Gestapo'. When the target responded with a 'No' Jeremy
would shout a crisp and brief 'LIAR' and punch them on the
arm. Jeremy would then ask again and when the target
(thinking that maybe they had figured out this game)
responded with a 'Yes' Jeremy would scream 'Liar' and punch
them in almost the same spot on the arm. This would go for
what would seem like hours. This was mainly because when
Jeremy felt like punching there was very little chance that
he would find something better to do. The target could only
hope that Richard Parker didn't join in as he had done on
the rarest of occasions (who could resist a 'punch
monkey'?). Eventually, Jeremy would get bored and find
something to burn or possibly watch television.

himself why he came, like many of the adults
all around him. The other children in line
buzzed about like hummingbirds whose heads
were about to explode. Making his way closer
to the front of the line John caught sight
of the admission prices; at least it would
only eat into a third of the Donald Duck
fund so he was somewhat relived, for the
moment anyway. What did keep pace with the
day was the list of the closed attractions;
two of the three rides that John was looking
forward to were closed for the afternoon.
"Figures," he mumbled. John reached the
front of the line muttered his "One Please"
to the chipper gal inside the ticket kiosk.
From that line he got in the line to enter
the park. Twenty minutes later John was
inside the park sitting on a bench waiting
for his family to exit the hall of
presidents.

The Origin of the Species

Chapter 2

John woke up and heard rain. His body ached with pins and needles throughout his legs. He was sore and he couldn't remember why. The room he was in was dark save for the light that came in from the window. It was that that time of day with a cloudy sky when you couldn't really tell if it was early morning or late afternoon. John didn't even know how he got in the room in the first place. His head pounded as though his brain had come loose and it was then, with his head throbbing, that he became aware of the fact that the bed he was in was perfectly made considering his presence. The air in the room was stale, with the hint of cigarette smoke and tile cleaner. On the wall straight ahead of the bed was a single painting. It was small, maybe eight by eleven and a half, it looked old but John really wasn't sure. His eyes strained just to look at it. He couldn't tell if it was a seascape or a picture of Jesus. Aside from that he was getting the feeling that he looking at the world for the first time. He reached up to rub his head and discovered that his head had been shaved fairly recently. It only annoyed him mildly till he felt the scars on the back of his head though he still hadn't noticed then sizable scar on his shoulder. He pushed himself up though he still felt groggy. This worked fine till his muscles burned and screamed at his having spent enough time enough time out of use. He decided the best course of action was to remain up right till the burning in his muscles subsided. John was just beginning to hear things clearly when he drifted back to sleep.

The Origin of the Species

Chapter 3

Back in Disneyland eleven year old
John sat on the bench outside the Hall of
Presidents as the Main Street Ragtime band
marched by playing some inanely happy tune.
John and his brothers usually made fun of
this sort of music, but for now his brothers
were sharing a warm family moment that was
equal parts heart warming and education, if
you were four or a slow-witted manbaby
carrying your own blankie. John sat on the
bench stewing over what he wanted to say to
his father. Stewing over something and then
getting flustered when trying to vocalize
the subject of the stewing was a hallmark of
John. Though John was genuinely confused. On
one hand if this was another elaborate joke
then John's father was just a master of
evil, but if it wasn't just a joke then
Richard Parker was really the Overlord of
evil bent on destroying all the good of the
world. This began to remind John of his
eight birthday when he and his father went
to watch a dog get put to sleep. This had
been Richards present to his then eight-
year-old son. The explanation went like
this: "Yes my boy, this is why we can't
have a dog, because all things die."

Richard and the rest of the family
exited the Hall of Presidents. The bullish
one in the pastel shorts directed the rest
of the herd to the heart of the park so that
he could have a talk with his son (John had
watched entirely too much television most
especially 'Safari World'). Richard
approached with a grim smile on his face
(something like you'd see in a tin type
picture of a corpse).

"Let's cut to the chase my boy," he
began, "you think I'm a complete bastard
don't you?"

"No sir," John answered into his shirt.

The Origin of the Species

"Cut the shit John!" he declared, "I'm
going to clear the air between you and I."
Richard snorted then paused a moment to
track the flight path of a bee. He was
terribly afraid of bees, not allergic just
afraid. "Ok, here is how it is I don't like
you, and I know sure as hell that you don't
like me," he looked near his son, "am I
right?"

       "Yes sir."

       "Good, nothing wrong with that, I
hated my father just as much as he hated me
and look what it's done for me[17]." Richard
rubbed his eyes, pressing his thumb and
index finger on the bridge of his nose.
"You're probably feeling singled out,"
Richard cleared his sinuses and launched
phlegm to the pavement, "like the other
boys, your brothers get treated better," he
waited for his son to answer. "Yes sir,"
seemed to be all John could manage. Richard
turned and faced his son, looking him
straight in the eye, "I'll tell you
something John," he paused another moment
as he was distracted by something he had
found in his moustache, "it's all true
Johnnie, but with good reason." Richard
trailed off which drove John crazy. His
father was notorious for doing just that mid
conversation. He would trail off and then
pick up what he was saying halfway into the
next topic. It was a though someone was
turning Richards volume up and down at whim.
"And that's why they're weak," Richard
shouted much to John's confusion, "they

---

[17] At this point in time Richard Parker ran a bookstore in a
high- end strip mall in Woodland Hills. A suburb of Los
Angeles with few hills and fewer natural trees. The Strip
mall included; the second most expensive diner in the San
Fernando Valley (Jim Friendly's being the number one in
that category with it's dollar ninety-nine bottomless
coffee with a maximum three refills) a kid's hair salon, a
karate school, a bridal boutique, a laser disc rental store
and several empty store fronts. The bookstore was
legitimate though it rarely saw a profit and it only served
a greater lie, which for the moment, is beside the point.

The Origin of the Species

don't need to know the sort of things you
will face." Again Richard turned to face
his son, looking him in the eyes. "They're
soft John and you have to be strong," he
sprayed. John was beyond mystified and
usually was whenever he spoke with his
father. "This is my present to you John,
it's a gift of bitter disappointment and a
lesson in self reliance, you are now more a
man than those bastard prince brothers of
yours will ever be," Richard paused if for
no other reason than to clear his throat
again, "and I know you won't let me down."
He patted John on the leg, got up from the
bench and adjusted his belt, "Now don't
tell your mother about this, she thinks I'm
getting you a Nintendo." The mention of a
Nintendo, which at the time for boys of
John's age was similar to the Holy Grail,
raised John's hopes that his father wasn't
insane and perhaps this would be a good
birthday after all. The hope didn't last.
John stood up, next to his father. Richard
Parker put his arm around his son and
laughed. It was a good hearty mental patient
laugh[18]. John's father followed the laugh
with this; "your mother is some kind of
fool John," he looked at his son and
laughed again, "some kind of damn fool,
thinking that I was going to buy you, you of
all people a Nintendo." Richard Parker
laughed good and hard for maybe five
minutes, occasionally choking on the word
Nintendo. It was disturbing to John and
would fill a pattern for the next four
years. That was until John's mother caught
on and barred her husband from acknowledging

---

[18] It was a laugh that said; "I just met a squirrel that
speaks Chinese and he certainly made for an awfully tasty
curry." It was a laugh that John was all too familiar
with.

The Origin of the Species

John's fifteenth birthday in any way[19]. The
rest of the day at Disneyland, for John was
filled with watching the other patrons of
the park as they moved past him, watching
toddlers scream and older children getting
yanked out of line by parents exhausted by a
hot early day, too much sass mouth.

---

[19] For John's twelfth birthday his father paid several of
his classmates to beat him up. That gift, which Richard
titled 'You have no friends' amounted to a pair of broken
teeth and a bruised collarbone. For thirteen Richard had
Jeremy place several M-80's under John's bed while he
slept. That gift, titled 'Don't let people know where you
sleep', resulted in several skin grafts. Fourteen Richard
gave John a hunting knife with the explicit instructions
that when it came time for John to kill him and assume the
head of the house roll, he was to cut out his fathers still
beating heart and eat it so that he could absorb all of
Richard's power.

The Origin of the Species

Chapter 4

It started at six the morning following John was shot. Derek Wall had just finished his swing shift at the Hawaiian Gardens Casino. Derek had only recently been hired as a 'Maintenance Engineer', which was the casinos way of saying 'janitor'. Derek was tired and it was a three-hour bus ride back to his bed in Yorba Linda. His clothes smelled of garbage water, cheap alcohol and sweat. Derek had to take four buses to get back to the Imperial Highway. He traveled through Bell Gardens, Cypress, Buena Park and then Brea. This was his first full week on the job after a four-day training course. Minus the cost of uniforms and the introductory fee to enter the local union Derek had to fight it out with the local hobo's for discarded bottles and cans so he could pay his bus fare. At this point in the day he was too tired to care how he smelled, he only had to keep the casino job till there was an opening at Earl's delicatessen. 'Should be any day now', was cold comfort after a fourteen-hour day. The Myers' deli was on Beach Blvd across from the Buena Park Golf course. Earl and Francine used to make it out to the deli almost every day. When they where younger they ran the place. But now with Francine having lost a foot and three toes to diabetes and Earl was just plain lazy they didn't get around as easy as they used to. That's where Derek fit into the picture. Earl had no son and whatever family Derek had wouldn't speak to him.

Chapter 5

Derek was an angry man when he committed his last crime. It was all part of some grander scheme. Twenty-three liquor stores and small convenience stores had been scouted and carefully selected. Atm schedules were studied by Derek's club. The club called themselves "The Black Luftwaffe". From nineteen seventy clear through to nineteen seventy-seven they were the most feared Neo-Nazis on the West Coast. A point of truth however, none of them had ever been pilots nor were any of them of African descent, it was simply a matter of having a menacing name. By nineteen eighty-seven they were little more then a joke in their own community. The Atm heists were going to put them back on top. But it would take time, recruiting to shore up the numbers. This did give the club time for training, every conceivable escape route was planned and mapped, Law enforcement response times were measured down to the second. In time the numbers would swell from thirty-one members back up to the far more menacing seventy-five. The Atm heists were meant to fund the highly dangerous diamond cutters robbery (the idea had itself been lifted from a movie). There were six diamond dealers in the L.A. and Orange County areas that, in the same twenty four hour period would be in the possession of upwards of two to three million dollars worth uncut diamonds from an old Soviet holding vault. The stones would then be sold through a contact out of Argentina and the Black Luftwaffe would receive roughly forty percent of the diamonds value. The bulk of the money would be used to help improve the groups standing within the American National Socialists. At the time the Black Luftwaffe

The Origin of the Species

were an often-ignored splinter group
somewhat disgraceful even for Neo-Nazis.
They were fumblers who with few exceptions
betrayed their own principles if not their
own personnel if there was a chance to
profit or save one's own skin. Thirteen of
the original fifteen founding members were
serving hard time on charges ranging from
assault to felony possession of narcotics.
The diamond money would also fund the Black
Luftwaffe's most ambitious act in their
twenty-six year history. This was of course
to blow up the Federal Reserve in Colorado.
This was an act that all the members were
ready and willing to take full credit for.
Then there was Derek. Derek was a relentless
perfectionist. His boots were always shined
to mirror exactness and his goatee neatly
trimmed. Even his tattoos followed a very
regimented pattern and all stayed within the
same theme. For Derek, perfection was a
continual push. It meant streamlined,
Spartan living and always trying to
eliminate the margin of error. Derek had
spent much time training for the Atm heist.
Each member was assigned a new recruit along
with three shops to hit. The first of the
three would lead almost directly to the
third, which in turn would lead to the
second and then the third where there would
be a concisely mapped out escape route.

        Derek had been scouting out a Liquor
Mart in Santa Ana. It was not one of the
assigned locations but Derek wanted to use
it for training. It had the same basic
layout as two of the three shops assigned to
Derek and his partner. It sat in the back of
a large parking lot with a taco stand
providing a momentary blind spot at the
intersection. Derek had a rough time
estimate for attaching clamps and chains to
the door of the Atm and ripping the door

off, which was one minute forty seconds.
That would place him two minutes and twenty-
five seconds ahead of the fastest local law
enforcement response time. That didn't
bother Derek, it would be close, but it
wasn't impossible. What did bother Derek was
his assigned partner for the robberies.

Ian Yates was twenty-seven and a high
school dropout. He embodied all that Derek
felt was wrong with the movement. Ian Yates
was all about the self- preservation of Ian
Yates. He joined the Black Luftwaffe during
an extended stay in L.A. County's Twin
Towers holding facility. Ian was a meth
dealer (and more than occasional user) and
had been arrested while selling his wares in
the city of San Fernando. Ian had been
selling without the express consent of any
of the local gangs, most notably the North
Hollywood Boyz[20]. The N.H.B. and six other
gangs (including the once feared 18th street
gang) had sixteen members in the Twin Towers
when Ian arrived. They had all been alerted
to his activities and were prepared with a
unified front that should have eventually
resulted in Ian 'voluntarily' hanging
himself in his cell. Territorial disputes
had been set aside and a peaceful accord had
been reached that was to last until Ian was
no longer breathing. A deal was made on
Ian's behalf before he even cleared
processing. The resident members of the
Black Luftwaffe (three prisoners and two
guards) intervened to save a lost Aryan son.

They agreed to beat some sense into
Ian and having him apologize in a manner saw
fit by all concerned parties, in return no
harm would come to him so long as he never

---

[20] Methamphetamine, the sales and consumption there of, was
the only illegal activity not tolerated by any of the East
Valleys numerous gangs. Environmental concerns and the
despicable nature of the user aside this was primarily
because it cut into weed and PCP sales.

dealt or cooked any more Meth. Ken Burrows
was the senior member of the Black
Luftwaffe. He was also awaiting a transfer
to Folsom State Prison. Ken was facing
twenty-five to life and he felt he needed
the goodwill of the 'Latin Kings', who were
the largest and most powerful of all the
gangs of any affiliation in Folsom. Setting
Ian straight would do that. It would also
provide a much- needed recruit for the Black
Luftwaffe, that's at least how it would be
rationalized to his Aryan brethren.

Ian would be taken down within his
first two hours. Burlap sacks filled with
bars of soap always left bruises but very
little evidence. In the course of his
initiation and punishment, Ian had six ribs
broken and lost four teeth. When is came
time for him to join, he leapt at the
chance. To Ian it meant the beatings would
all but cease and he would be able to fuck
with nearly any gang member with little fear
of retaliation. Ian would be a good fit for
the group. He was reckless and careless and
still quite a bit immature. The last part of
Ian's initiation involved shaving his head
and branding him with an Iron Cross on each
shoulder blade[21]. Ian Yates would get Derek
to the breaking point, to where he would
choose the Church of Satan over white
supremacy.

It was at the Liquor Mart where Derek
and Ian were working to improve their time.
Derek was determined to get it down to two
and a half minutes. Ian was gleeful and
feeling very powerful while Derek tried his

---

[21] This differed greatly from how many other prison gangs
admitted a new recruit. This was most notable by comparison
to the Aryan Brotherhood (a more successful white supremacy
outfit), which required a 'blood in blood out' act of
loyalty. This involved the killing of a predetermined
member of a rival gang. The only way out was to die. The
Black Luftwaffe needed members and didn't have the manpower
to fight another gang if the initiation kill went wrong,
which for them it often did.

best to maintain a professional attitude.
During their practice run, Derek was busying
himself attaching the clamps and chains to
the Atm while Ian worked crowd control. This
was the biggest mistake. Ian was shouting
orders at the clerk, demanding the money
from the register while shooting around the
clerk's head. Derek made a mental note to
ensure that Ian's gun wasn't loaded with
live rounds for the real robberies. Derek
nearly had the door of the Atm off, Ian
chomped down on a fist full of beef sticks,
he screamed at the clerk; "Strip down ya'
camel jockey [22]." Derek ripped the door off
as Ian fired wildly at the clerk. Derek
swung around to see Ian in a near state of
panic. There was blood on the bottles behind
the counter and no visible clerk.

"I've never killed anyone before D',"
Ian stammered.

"Well you weren't supposed to start
now,' Derek turned back to the Atm machine,
"now help me empty this thing out."

Ian stood still. He dropped his
handful of beef sticks. "I can't go back to
jail D'," he said.

Derek hated being called 'D'. "No
one will have to go to jail if you would
just get your shit together, RIGHT NOW!"
Derek barked, "Check the clerk, see if he's
dead." Ian leapt over the counter. It was
the fastest anyone had ever seen him move.
"He's not dead," Ian called out. He hit 'No
Sale' on the register keyboard and started
to take the cash out, "but he's pretty
fucked up D'."

---

[22] The clerk was of Italian descent (though his 'Italia
soccer shirt may have been the only strong indication of
this) and he was born in Pittsburg. Ian was an idiot who
was always trying to impress people with what an awesome
skinhead he was. In his short time with the group he had
become infamous for his inability to produce an original or
accurate racial slur, or the proper use of a pre-existing
one.

The Origin of the Species

Derek finished emptying the Atm. He turned slowly; it's not that important, he's just a fuckwit recruit, Derek tried to quell his anger as he turned around.

"My name isn't 'D' GODDAMMIT, its fucking Derek all right meat," Derek was about to lose it.

"Ok 'fucking Derek'," Ian mocked.

"This has already taken too long, lets go," Derek gritted his teeth. Ian scrambled with his hand full of odd bills and pint tequila bottles. It was already too late. A police helicopter spotlight was already on the parking lot, sirens blared only moments away.

"Oh shit," Ian whined. He threw his hand full of cash down along with his pint tequila bottles and grabbed the most expensive tequila the store had. He cracked the neck of the bottle off on the edge of the counter and poured it straight down his throat.

"I'm not going down for this Derek," Ian choked on a warm tequila burn. The sirens stopped moving, they were right outside of the Liquor Mart.

"You weren't supposed to fire your gun Ian," Derek calmly replied, "you and I will go down for this, and we will say nothing about the operation."

Ian seemed to be thinking this over. The Police outside were blaring something that neither Derek nor Ian was paying any attention to.

"No," Ian muttered.

"What did you say?"

"No, fuck you man," Ian replied, "and fuck the Black Luftwaffe, it's a stupid fucking name anyway." Ian shoved the cash register in Derek's direction. It was a weak throw (like everything Ian did) though it was enough to push Derek over the edge.

The Origin of the Species

Derek flew across the liquor store, grabbed
Ian by the neck and began pounding on him.
Derek took the butt of his gun and began
punching Ian's face with it. By the time the
Police and the Sheriffs pulled Derek off Ian
had lost fourteen teeth, had both cheek
bones and eye sockets cracked. This botched
robbery would domino into a crushing blow
for the Black Luftwaffe.

Derek faced a lengthy prison term while
Ian was able to cut a deal the Feds. You
see: despite being a new member of the
group, he knew all the plans for the Diamond
Heist and the Federal Reserve bombing. He
sold out his comrades out for a new face and
a few years of Witness Protection.

It would be so many years later that
Derek would find himself sitting across from
Rachel Gilger on his way home. Rachel had
just picked up her paycheck from her job and
she was on her way home. Well at least to
her boyfriend's apartment, she was no longer
welcome at her parent's home. Her parents,
being fairly prominent members of the local
Mormon Church, were immensely humiliated
when she came home pregnant. She was thrown
out, found herself working at a grocery
store to pay rent while her boyfriend went
to school part-time. She was on the bus
across from Derek; completely unaware that
anyone was near her. Her breathing was
shallow, and sweat poured down her face and
was stinging her eyes. Inside her, life was
stirring, her unborn son boiled inside her.
Rachel Gilger's child was about to burst
forth.

The Origin of the Species

Chapter 6

John woke in the very same room, in
the same quiet still air, though this time
he felt very little pain. There was no
longer a needle in his arm and he no longer
felt weighed down by his own body. He
shifted his legs and he noticed that he was
in red pajamas and no longer in a hospital
gown. His feet hit the floor and suddenly he
felt weak, as though he hadn't put any
weight on them in quite some time. The
linoleum beneath him sent cold shivers
throughout his body. He stood up and the
weakness he felt turned into an off balance,
light-headed queasiness. The afternoon light
breaking through the curtains hurt his eyes
as he made his way toward the window. He
shuffled his feet a bit at first and they
stung with each step. As he walked he began
to sense a presence in the room. Maybe it
was a breathing he thought he heard or the
stale cigarette smell, but the light called
out to him. John reached the window and the
light seemed to get brighter before his eyes
adjusted. There was an odd cold emanating
from the window; condensation lined the
corners of the window.

Outside was an unfamiliar scene. The
window over looked a sparsely covered lawn.
There were a few benches that faced each
other, but they had been enveloped by the
over grown lawn. At the edge of the lawn was
a wrought iron fence where large piles of
sand hand collected. Years of salt air
erosion had taken it's toll on the fence as
parts were either missing on falling apart.
Beyond the fence was a white sand beach,
beyond that was a gray, distant bar of land.

John stood silently for a moment. He
wasn't sure what too make of this. Behind
him he heard the groan of an old chair as

The Origin of the Species

someone pushed up from it followed by hard
soled shoes on the floor. Each step drew
warmth closer to John. He didn't bother
turning to look; he had an uneasy feeling he
knew who it was.

"That gray bar you see in the
distance is the California coast line,"
George said breaking the silence, "and to
answer your next question John we're on one
of the Channel Islands."

"What is this place?" John asked.

"It was the Paul Winter Sanitarium,"
George began, "the Winters were a wealthy
Oxnard family whose son Paul suffered from a
multiple personality disorder," George
paused to take a drag from his cigarette,
"they built this for him in nineteen
thirty-two."

"Okay, so what are we here?" John
asked, slightly impatiently.

"I'm getting to that John," George
said patting John on the shoulder, "in
nineteen thirty-four Paul Winter died in a
murder suicide with himself and the Winter
family went Bankrupt, the state of
California took possession to help cover any
outstanding debts."

"Murder suicide," John paused to
think things over, "with himself how did
that happen?"

"Well, as the story goes, five of
Paul's six extra personalities conspired to
kill Paul in an effort to kill themselves,"
George laughed to himself, "it seemed that
many of them, the personalities that is,
weren't very happy with Sanitarium life, so
the five in question each wrote a brief
note, a statement of purpose, and well from
the look of the corpse they caught Paul
quite off guard."

"Dare I ask how you know that?" John
said.

The Origin of the Species

"With the last of their money the Winters set up a very informative and very thorough museum of sorts in the lobby. "

"I see, " John began to scratch the back of his head, he felt a smooth scar on the flat part of his skull underneath his hair, "so how long have I been here George? " George made an effort to avoid the question by paying attention to the scar.

"They should have done a better job then that, " He said.

"Yeah, what's the deal with that? "

"Well you're dead John, " George said.

"All right, not what I was asking, and a little confusing on many counts, " John turned to face George, "see, even though I've never been dead, I'm pretty sure this is not what it's like, not at all. "

George laughed and lit a fresh cigarette offering one to John.

"May as well, " John took one, which George promptly lit.

"Good to know you haven't really lost your sense of humor John," George exhaled a cloud of smoke, "but in order to clarify tings a bit, you're not dead in any conventional sense, " George scratched his nose, "Richard, your 'father' knew this, it was always part of the program. " This conversation was beginning to make John uncomfortable. "I think I need something to eat, does this place have a kitchen George? "

Chapter 7

Francesca was walking home from work. It was three-thirty in the morning. She was still trying to decide on her costume for Halloween. Francesca's enthusiasm for Halloween was similar to a child's while they waited for Christmas, and if that child was strung out on pcp and sugar, joyfully threatening to tear the ears off of anyone who tried to ruin the holiday.

Under her arm she carried a six-pack of Dr. Pepper that she would drink warm. A cigarette was hanging from her lips and as she walked, smoke filled her eye and the ash grew longer and longer. It had been a decent evening at work, tips weren't bad and the customers were almost human. She missed John; he wasn't there to make her laugh anymore. The air around her was cold and still. Ventura Boulevard was almost empty so her footsteps echoed off of the surrounding buildings.

About one hundred yards behind, Paul and Seth the N.S.A. who tried to kill John were following Francesca at a cautious pace. This time they were driving an orange sedan. They were men of little imagination when it came to being inconspicuous.

"Is that her?" Paul asked.

"URrr," was Seth's reply.

"Well she is one of them right?"

"Does that even matter Paul, you said I got to kill her so I don't see how that's really an issue," Seth whined.

"Calm down buckaroo," Paul patted him on the shoulder, "so is this going to be an accident or a suicide?"

"Boring!" Seth shouted. "We've done both of those so many times they're boring."

"Something fresh then?"

Seth again only grunted. He licked
his lips and reached in to his coat to palm
his gun. It had been almost a year since he
had killed any one and it was starting to
eat away at him.

About fifteen feet or so down
Ventura, directly in Francesca's path was
Frankie. Frankie was, in the best of terms,
a vagrant musician. He told wild stories.
Sometimes he ran with the Manson family,
sometimes the Hells Angels. The times were
usually mixed up and Frankie never could
keep his stories straight. He played a penny
whistle, that one of the Monkees gave him
'back in the day' and though he'd laid claim
to knowing any song he could only ever
manage one tune. It sounded something like
the Popeye theme. Frankie never caused
anyone any harm. The most he would ever do
was hit you up for a dollar, the worst he
would ever do is have one too many Bud's and
sing a little too loud.

Frankie was crouched down and
shaking. He clutched his penny whistle. He
was sick; it was the same sick that got Leon
Paulson. It was nearing its peak as
Francesca approached. He'd already bitten
through his tongue, and the blood was
streaming down through his beard. His was
the only blood he would spill that night.
Francesca drew closer. She wasn't alarmed by
the sight of Frankie. He was always a
familiar figure along Ventura Blvd at any
time of day. His beer belly was never
menacing.

Still at a cautious pace, Paul and
Seth took notice of Frankie.

"We may have a problem, " Paul began,
"the vagrant in her path appears to be
holding some sort of weapon. " Richard
stirred, "She's mine, " he growled, "I get
to kill her and no one else. "

The Origin of the Species

"Wait a sec', maybe he'll do the job
for us," Paul interceded.

"Killed while fighting off a mugger?"
Richard wondered. "It seems so cliché, the
old man'd never buy it, I know I can do
better."

"You're probably right," Paul
relented, "then we should intercept the
problem.

Frankie was going mad, his head was
pounding and blood was welling behind his
eyes. He could see Francesca approaching but
he didn't know her anymore. He had to make
it end; it felt like his brain was on fire.
He dropped his whistle, which caused
Francesca to stop a few feet away.

"Are you all right Frankie?" She
called out. He grunted and howled a response
spraying blood at her feet. He began tearing
at his face, digging his fingernails into
his cheeks. "Frankie?" Francesca said. He
turned to her and spat a piece of his tongue
at her.

"We may have a bigger problem then
her," Paul said. Seth looked up and saw
Frankie spraying blood from his mouth as he
staggered forth. "That can't be one of
them, they aren't supposed to reach this
area for another six weeks," Paul added.

"It is," Seth sighed, "the old man's
projection must have been off. Seth pounded
his gun into the dashboard. "Shit, shit,
shit," he screamed, which caused his voice
to crack, "this isn't fair, I've done so
much preparation for this one and now it's
all going to be wasted." Paul looked to his
partner and nodded his head. "I know this
is bullshit," he said. Seth, however, was
not done with his rant. "I filed down the
inside of my Glock, Jesus Christ Paul my
Glock," Seth thrust the gun into Paul's

The Origin of the Species

face. Tears began falling from Seth's eyes. "I even made the bullets myself."

"Did you really?" Paul interrupted with some genuine surprise.

"Yes," Seth's tears stopped and his tone of voice changed instantly, "do you remember that Metallurgy class I took at the Mamaroneck learning annex a couple of years ago?"

"I can't recall you being happier," Paul said.

"Well before I killed the instructor he showed me how to melt and mix my own alloys using a variety of unconventional source metals."

"So what makes these bullets so special?" Paul asked.

"Ok, do you remember the Geneticist we killed in Albany around the same time?"

"Yeah, so, he was a member of one of the original design teams for the project right?" Paul said.

"What, oh he was wasn't he," Seth began, "anyway do you remember all of the religious icons and crucifixes he had in his room?"

"Oh that's right, he was trying to seek Gods forgiveness," Paul answered, "wait you didn't.."

"Yes I did," Seth beamed, "not only did I melt down the gold and the silver, but all the base metals as well."

"There's something poetic to that," Paul smiled, "but there's something else isn't there?"

"You mean aside from the segmented tips of the bullets?" Seth asked.

"No, that's practically your trade mark Seth," Paul lamented.

"I'm sorry if I'm so predictable Paul, we can't all be perfect," Seth cried, "I do change the pattern on the tip you know."

"I know and they're very imaginative," Paul said quickly. He was trying to quell Seth's angst. Creativity or the apparent lack there of, was something that disturbed Seth immensely. Their discussion had touched on a sore point and for a moment they each sat in silence each searching for something to say.

In the meanwhile, Frankie had begun taking steps toward Francesca. In each hand he held large pieces of his face. Francesca stayed back, frozen where she stood. His eyes were bubbling up as they started to boil from the immense heat emanating from inside his skull. With his next step toward her there was a very audible pop. His brain had burst. He collapsed before her. Gray liquid began seeping from his ears and his eyes popped. Nothing Francesca had ever seen could have prepared for this, she had known Frankie for the last four years and now he just died in front of her. She turned to run back to Jim Friendly's only to find Paul and Seth standing almost directly behind her. Paul was smiling, holding his gun behind his back, Seth was pacing[23].

Francesca tried to say something, anything. She knew what she wanted to scream, but nothing came out.

"It's going to be ok," Paul Smiled. Seth had finished his pacing behind Paul and was preparing to dispose of Frankie's body. Seth was already dressed in emergency biohazard gear, which was standard issue for N.S.A. field operatives (this is at least what Paul had told him). It was a simple

---

[23] Seth was a Glock enthusiast. Everything he used, from silencers to extended clips, knives and even the crappy nylon holsters that fall apart with extended use, all came from the Glock website. Paul was more of a traditionalist in regards to weapons. He packed the old government standard issue Colt 45. There were, however, two variations to the standard; Paul's was nickel-plated and had mother of pearl on the handle.

outfit though it wasn't designed to prevent
infection from an airborne virus, but it
would prevent infection from collecting non-
volatile matter. It consisted of a
combination facemask/skull cap, hip boots
and gloves that went past the elbow. Seth
added to his 'official' gear with a well-
used leather butchers apron.

Francesca couldn't tell from where
she stood, but Seth was pissed. This was not
his favorite part of the job, though in
fairness, it was his turn. He grumbled as he
walked past Paul and then Francesca. In his
hands he carried a skull saw (modified to
hold a larger attachment) and a pair of five
gallon orange buckets.

"Miss we're going to need you to come
with us," Paul said.

"What?" Francesca said. There was a
distance in her voice, a certain level of
detachment like she was finished analyzed
what had just happened but was still
searching for the solution.

"Well miss we're with a local Haz-Mat
unit and we're going to need to take you
into quarantine."

"Quarantine?" She questioned. She was
regaining some of her composure and her body
was starting to put her on the defensive.
"And don't call me miss, call me miss again
and we'll have a problem, I'm over twenty-
five you can call me maam."

Seth walked past the pair again. This
time he was whistling. Whatever it was, it
was muffled by his facemask. He passed again
with a pair of empty buckets.

"Yes, maam, Quarantine," Paul
answered, "you've been exposed to a serious
bio-hazardous threat and we need to isolate
you so that it doesn't spread."

"You are so full of shit," Francesca
challenged, "if Frankie was such a threat

we wouldn't even be here to have this
discussion. "

"Well you see the bio... " Paul began.

"Holy shit if you're going to lie to
me you'd better have more to say then 'bio,
Haz-mat and viral agents', " Francesca
interrupted.

"I didn't say viral agents, " Paul
said. He didn't like being called on a lie.
All he could do was stare at her. This stare
down would have been completely silent were
it not for the fact that Seth had lifted his
mask so that he could sing while he cut up
Frankie and placed the parts in his buckets.
He sang in a high, screechy falsetto. The
singing caused Paul and Francesca to break
their staring contest and look over at Seth.
Francesca looked at Seth with a level of
disgust that Seth had long since become
accustomed to simply for being Seth, though
he was thankfully unaware of it this
morning. This is how the singing went:
"Roll out the barrels, " pausing to slice
through the left elbow, "lets get the blues
on the run, " pause again to slice the arm
at the shoulder, "Roll out the barrel, "
pause to slice into the neck, splattering
blood all over his apron. With the head
free, he kept humming as he picked it up by
the teeth and hurled it into a bucket. Seth
always sang the Beer Barrel Polka when it
was his turn to dismember a body. And he
always got some part the of the words wrong
but he didn't care, Paul never complained
anymore. It had been Seth's turn for the
last three years, though he hadn't yet
noticed that Paul had not done any of the
crime scene clean up.

Paul forced a smile. It was his way
of acknowledging that he had to employ
alternate measure to get Francesca. Seth was
still happily dismembering, still screeching

the wrong words. Paul maintained his smile, and took a few steps approaching Francesca. Francesca focused her gaze on Paul and then to Seth. She was stuck between them. She could make a run for it, off to the empty street to her left. The guy slicing up Frankie might be too involved to give chase. That only left the liar. He probably had a gun behind his back, she could smell the gunpowder but she didn't know why. Since she first saw Frankie this morning her body began producing an abnormal amount of adrenalin. It had just now reached its peak in her blood stream it was making her lightheaded and somewhat shaky. It was also altering her instincts. She was going to hold her ground and brace for a fight. She gripped her bag like it was a mace or a club. Her bag held a hardcover book, a change of shoes, a crushed box of tampons, a metal lunch box, a pair of handcuffs and twelve and a half inches of chain she had picked up to hang her heavy bag with. Paul showed his 45', very deliberately pushed the hammer back into place.

"I'm going to set this down right here," he said gesturing to a halfway point between them, "we can discuss this without resorting to that sort of thing," he said pointing to the gun. Francesca remained silent. She had stopped shaking and her muscles had visibly tightened. She wasn't going to run, she wasn't afraid. The only advantage Paul had was that she couldn't be prepared for any new abilities she might have. He had to assume that much.

"Now there has to be some way we can get you to listen to us miss," Paul said knowing full well what he was going to do next. Francesca made the first move, lunging toward Paul swinging her bag. The bag made contact with Paul's chest just as Paul was

trying to whistle to get Seth's attention.
Seth heard the partial whistle, dropped the
body parts he was working on in the bucket
along with his gloves. Francesca was busy
wailing on Paul with her bag. Paul had taken
a fetal position on the sidewalk and was
remaining still. This was part of his plan.
Seth grabbed a bucket and secured the lid,
he needed a weapon and he left his Glock in
the car. Seth ran toward Francesca and Paul.
Hearing the approaching footsteps Francesca
tossed her bag aside. She focused on the
sound as she kicked Paul. Seth was a foot
and a half behind her, raising the full
bucket up, when she swung around and cracked
him in the face with a high kick. The kick
broke his nose, knocked out six of his front
upper teeth and sent him sliding back on his
ass ten feet. In the same instance Paul had
gotten up and removed his back up from its
ankle holster. He ran up on Francesca just
as she kicked Seth and cracked the back of
her head with the butt of his gun. She fell
to her knees and was beginning to fade as
her body started to reset itself. Seth
bolted up and threw down his facemask. He
spat teeth and blood to the sidewalk.

"Sthon of a bith," he sprayed, "whath
hat sthee done to my bootiful facth?"

Paul looked at him. Seth had never
been beautiful, couldn't even call him
handsome, but now he was certainly
grotesque. His nose was smashed and a few
shards of teeth remained in his jaw line.
His chin was covered in blood and his face
was twisted in a blend of pain, surprise and
humiliation. Paul looked away and smiled. It
was his liar's smile that Seth knew well.
Paul looked at the ground, searching for
something to say. He spotted Francesca's
open bag. A pack of cigarettes stuck out and
Paul grabbed them.

"Do you mind?" He said to her, already having lit one for himself. Francesca could say nothing, she was fading out. The voice, the noises that surrounded her were growing distant. Blood trickled down her scalp and pooled where she lay on the pavement. Her breathing was becoming shallow and her heartbeat had dropped by half.

"Can I kill her now?" Seth asked indignantly with a lighter spray of blood, "cause you said I could and I want to, so let me kill her."

"Would you stop that I said no such thing," Paul yawned, "besides, we can't kill her now, we may need her."

"What do you mean?"

"If she's one of them she can keep us alive," Paul said, "the old man got himself a protector, I thought we could use one too."

"Well I wanna hit her, so you let me, 'cause I'm gonna do it, now," Seth demanded.

"No," Paul quickly dismissed, "she needs to heal."

Seth peered down at Francesca, who was curling up on the sidewalk. The world around her was slipping away. Her eyes were heavy her body was weak. She could make out blurry silhouettes that comprised of Seth and Paul, but they were becoming darker.

"So, how long are we going to have to wait?" Seth asked.

"Forty-eight hours, four months, the old man wasn't really clear on that one," Paul picked up his Colt, "I don't even know what generation she's supposed to be."

"But when she's done I can hit her right?" Seth asked with some excitement.

"You're more then welcome to try," Paul smiled.

The Origin of the Species

"Damn right," Seth shouted, "I'm gonna
kick her teeth in and break her collarbone
and..."

"Enough of that," Paul said, "pick her
up and put her in the car."

Chapter 8

It was October, some where in the middle of the month; John didn't care at this point. His birthday had come and gone but that's not what he cared about. John was sitting in the dining hall of the Paul Winter Sanitarium. It was had a formal, long dining table that sat thirty. Beyond that a large bay window showed the choppy sea beyond the small island.

The table John currently occupied had only previously hosted five people and that was back in the late fifties. They had been an Oxnard based Anti-Communist citizens concern that met weekly. They consisted of the retired Oxnard police chief, a prominent local banker and his secretary/mistress (bondage and pain, never sex), the local high school baseball coach and his sixteen-year-old protégé Roman Franco. They would meet, have frank discussions about the Soviet threats to the American way of life, then get drunk and watch the secretary torture the banker.

"I can't believe how hungry I was," John said as he dug into a whole apple pie, "John said with a spray of pie, "I don't even like apple pie this much."

"Well you have been out since February, I was getting a little concerned," George chuckled and opened a weathered, coffee stained folder, "that was when we last spoke John, it's the middle of October now."

"Yeah I think I missed my birthday," John shrugged, "so would you mind telling me what happened?"

"Your situation was compromised, in simple language, you were discovered," George said.

The Origin of the Species

"Right," John spiked his fork into his pie, "by who?"

"By whom?" George corrected.

"No I really think it's 'by who?'" John began, "but that's not what I'm asking."

"Of course not John," George smiled, "you were discovered by agents of mine who feared a security breach and followed the established protocol, which meant that they had to eliminate the threat to the project."

"Agents of yours?" John felt queasy, "and they were going to kill me."

"Well yes and no," George said.

"Yes and no they were going to kill me?" John asked.

"Yes they were going to kill you, but they couldn't really be called my agents, they were 'loaned' to me by the N.S.A. for the duration of the project and several years beyond."

"Right, what's that about then anyway?"

"I helped the N.S.A. find its direction way back when," George smiled.

"That's not what I mean George," John said.

"I know," George said as he sipped his coffee, "it's simple really, John Parker needed to be dead."

Chapter 9

John took a long drag on a cigarette.
On the dining room table in front of him the
pieces of a Berretta he had just stripped
apart minutes before. There was a small
stack of plates to his left and a few boxes
of nine-millimeter rounds and empty
cartridges were to the right. John stared at
the pieces he didn't immediately know the
names, but they all seemed so familiar to
him. John took another drag on his cigarette
and picked up one of the empty clips and
began loading it with bullets.

"Shouldn't I be worried about lung
cancer or maybe even emphysema?" He was
addressing George who was creeping back into
the room. He wasn't trying to be sneaky in
any way, it was just force of habit.

"Those are riddles that we managed to
solve in the seventies John," George said
setting down a pot of coffee, "cancer will
never trouble you."

John was about to say something, but he
wasn't sure he wanted the answer.

"So how's the Beretta coming along?"
George asked.

"It's kind's new territory for me
George," John shrugged.

"It'll come to you John be patient."

"What do you mean 'it will come to me'
you've said that a few times and I really
don't know what you're saying," John rubbed
his cigarette out in his ashtray, "and what
do you mean you solved cancer?"

"Well you understand that your D.N.A.
is a collection of synthetic proteins
right?"

"I'm still not entirely clear on that
one actually," John answered, "and please
don't tell me I will be." George nodded his

head and sat down. He took a cigarette from
Johns pack and lit it.

"Now, you know that we failed at
manipulating existing subjects yes? "

"You told me about that, " John said.

"Good, well yes it was a resounding
failure, " George laughed, "of the original
one hundred there are only two left alive. "

"Ok, so where does that leave me and my
supposed inherited knowledge? "

"You, and those like you were part of
the project that followed, " George smashed
his cigarette out in the ash tray, "having
failed with existing material we took a
radical approach to the problem which was of
course to start a human being from
scratch. "

"Makes sense I suppose, " John offered.

"But we had limitation, and many
unforeseen problems with the very first
generation, " George slurped down some
coffee.

"Of course you'd have difficulties, "
John said feeling somewhat lost in the
conversation.

"Indeed, " George smiled losing a moment
to thought, "oh yes, we had the damndest
time synthesizing the human embryo so at
first we used existing eggs that we wiped
clean of their genetic material, or so we
thought anyway. This group yielded little
beyond a learning experience. Only one
subject survived infancy and she died when
she reached puberty. We gained so much from
her death; we made gender designation
obsolete for the next generation and the one
that followed that by eliminating
reproductive functions. This was partly a
defensive move, I mean god forbid our own
creation turns on us and begins breeding. "
George laughed. This made John uneasy, a
family was far from a consideration, but not

being able to have one at all made him feel
as though he'd been cheated at the very
least.

"What made the second and third
generations special was the acquisition of
the Hydro-accelerator chamber.

"The what?" John's question was nearly
automatic.

"The Hydro-accelerator served as an
artificial womb, it was developed in Japan
in the late nine-teen sixties well ahead of
its time."

        George rifled through his papers and
produced an old tattered photograph. In the
photo, George was wearing a nearly identical
suit; hair cut and concerned expression on
his face. Next to him was what appeared to
be a large blue globe sitting atop support
frames and attached to an odd assortment of
wires and cables. Next to the machine, on
the opposite side of George stood a young
Japanese woman in a lab coat.

Chapter 10

The lady scientist in the photograph that George showed John was Kazahira Kono. She was born and raised in the northern Japanese city of Sapporo. Both of her parents worked at the local Sony factory. Hideki, her father, was a humorless foreman, while her mother was in accounts payable. Kaz was raised to be different from any other child. At an early age she showed herself to be something of a musical genius. By the age of ten Kaz had composed thirteen piano concertos and three operas, two in Italian and the other in German. By age twelve she had abandoned music for mathematics. At fifteen she had began the work that would guide the course of her life: Genetics. At seventeen she produced a workable, however theoretical, model of a flawless D.N.A. sequence some twenty years before it was supposedly first coded. Kaz looked at D.N.A. like it was a musical composition. She reasoned that one could arrange the code in the right sequence to garner whatever result was desired. Further, she theorized, that genes could be programmed, or even fabricated to the end that a human could be designed for any purpose. These ideas frightened the scientific community. Quickly they resolved to ostracize her. By twenty-two Kaz was a community pariah and only those who openly sought the ruination and dishonor of their families would dare speak to her. It was in her isolation that she made her greatest discover and subsequent contribution to the future of the project. This was of course, the Hydro-accelerator. It was a very simple design for a very complicated matter. It was a large spherical chamber that acted as the

womb in which Kaz would construct life as
she saw fit to create.

In November of nineteen sixty-eight,
as Sapporo was preparing for it's winter
festivals, Kaz was on the verge of creating
her first engineered life. For the previous
summer and fall Kaz had volunteered at
numerous Women's Health Clinics and
hospitals. She was gathering the materials
and essential blueprints for life. The eggs
she 'gathered' she was going to clean of
their original patterns so that she could
program them how she liked. This would prove
to be Kaz's brilliant mistake and one that
Georges group had already made (and would
make again). The eggs could never be
entirely cleaned of their origins, but given
the technological limitations of the time,
there was no way to prove that physically.
Kaz proved on paper that she could replicate
an embryo, however she had been unsuccessful
in her attempts to do this. So she was left
with attempting to use existing materials
which she could never prove conclusively was
ready. This perturbed her but she proceeded.
The erasure method would leave between seven
and forty percent of the existing D.N.A. in
the modified embryo. This created several
problems. The first three of Kaz's
'children' exploded upon their first
exposure to fresh oxygen. The fourth would
live for a week before his heart collapsed.
This was proving to be frustrating to Kaz,
but the fifth would prove her right, well
mostly anyway. Tomu Go (Tom five)[24] would
prove all that Kaz hoped and feared. He was
strong, as strong as twenty men, but he
lacked the mental capacity of one man. The

---

[24] Like all of his predecessors he was named for Kaz's
favorite singer Tom Jones. She wanted all she created to be
as dynamic as the real Tom Jones down to the chest hair and
the cocky swagger.

neural pathways didn't seem to connect
properly, perhaps too much assigned memory
and knowledge. The brain function still
proved a bit of a mystery for Kaz and again
she was felled by her own flawed equations.
However, Tom fives growth and regenerative
properties were as unprecedented as was his
aging, which was as relentless as it was
swift. By the end of his first week Tom had
the appearance of a large hulking fifteen.
Tom was proving incapable of learning or
even of using any assigned knowledge. He was
aggressive, but slowing down as the weeks
progressed. On a Tuesday evening in Toms
fifth week he staggered out of Kaz's'
laboratory while the doctor was away at
dinner. He had the outward appearance of a
man of seventy-five, though he was still
quite strong. As he walked, his heart pumped
rapidly, adrenalin surged through his blood
stream; he was reaching the peak of a
chemical imbalance. The closest businesses
were the ramen bar where Kaz was having her
dinner (noodles and curry with extra chili)
and a massage parlor. The rest of the area
was comprised of a number of shipping houses
and storage that were mostly quiet for the
evening. The parlor also had a karaoke
lounge. It was full of various businessmen,
though mostly factory foreman like Kaz's
father. Hideki Kono would never be among
them. He felt that that sort of behavior was
dishonorable and demeaning to a man in a
position of authority. The men who were
there were the ones willing to pay the two
drink minimum to 'talk' with one of the many
hostesses. The guys singing were usually the
ones who either out of fear or poverty
wouldn't talk to a hostess. Public singing
was another subject of scorn and shame for
Hideki. For that matter so was smiling, so
was his daughter.

The Origin of the Species

The parlor was buzzing as Tom five
lurched near. He was dressed in a hospital
gown and looked like an old body builder
who'd suffered a stroke. The din of the
conversations about quotas, management,
mechanical negotiations for backroom sex,
timid pleas for affection from inexperienced
men and the blaring of off key singing to
tin music, these were the things that filled
Tom fives ears as he burst through the
doors. Kaz was four doors down enjoying her
complimentary dessert of fruit slices in an
orange cream sauce. Tom fives entrance drew
stares and a little laughter, but no one
paid him any real attention. All it looked
like was that someone's grandfather had
wandered away from the hospital again. This
happened all too often in this area for
anyone to care when they saw an incoherent
old man late at night. The security at the
geriatric ward was lax to the point of being
negligent or even non-existent. The only
thing anybody would do was call the hospital
and try to keep the old guy from hurting
himself. Usually, in this parlor, that
wasn't much of an issue. The old guys would
typically just stare at a hostess, drool and
mess their pants, if they were wearing
pants. It was cheap, cruel amusement. Tom
five started to growl. This amused some of
the closer patrons. What they didn't know,
what Tom five most certainly didn't know and
what Kaz would later discover was that Tom
five was the genesis, the ground zero of a
new highly communicable virus. It would
appear to be and operate just like syphilis
only faster and with a higher fatality rate.
It would fry the nervous system, cause the
adrenalin gland to swell to four times it's
size and cause to brain to boil in it's own
chemicals till it burst.

The Origin of the Species

Tom five was in the last hour of the virus's cycle when he reached the parlor. He started to convulse and the laughter and the multitude of voices and sounds confused him and made him angry. He never developed linguistic skills in his five weeks of life so he just growled louder. It was loud enough to annoy the man signing karaoke, loud enough to halt many of the conversations in the parlor. The singing man, whose name was Ren Johjima, had just transferred from a plant just outside Osaka. He didn't appreciate being interrupted in his efforts to make friends with his new co-workers. Ren marched over to Tom and began to berate him. Tom could never really understand the language, but he did understand tones. In fact the only part of his brain that did function properly was a canine like understanding of tonality. Ren persisted and pointed, his indignity was great and he wanted the old grandfather to suffer for it. "Stupid old man," he screamed and poked Tom five with the microphone he held in his left hand. In Rens right hand was an hours old Scorpion. The ice had melted and the cherry sat at the bottom of the glass swirling around in the watery liquor. Ren sloshed the drink around like he was waving a baton before a band of drunk and horny men. "Couldn't find you pants old man?" Ren mocked and tugged at Tom five pajamas. The pajamas were a powder blue two-piece with red cosmonauts and green dogs with space helmets. It was the largest size available three weeks ago when Tom five reached physical maturity and they were too small even then. Ren laughed at the pathetic old man, and he waved the rest of the bar to do the same. Tom fives left eye began to bubble as he thrust his fist through Rens neck resting his grip on Rens spinal cord.

The Origin of the Species

Ren was dead in an instant. The laughter had
changed to screams. Tom five swung Ren
around by the neck. One of the braver men
sitting at the bar got up and broke a chair
on Tom fives back. Tom five threw his free
arm back at the man, breaking his nose and
sending him flying back into the bar causing
the man to break his neck on the counter
top. Tom five howled in pain. He loosened
his grip on Ren, who dropped to the floor.
He staggered toward one of the hostesses.
Both his eyes began to bubble as he reached
her. Reddish fluid started to leak from both
of his ears. Tom five was trying to find the
hostess though he could no longer see her.
Four doors down and across the street from
where her creation was wreaking havoc she
strolled with a hop in her step. She hardly
noticed the four police cars racing toward
the massage parlor. It was just that sort of
thing that occurred nearly twice a week. The
police would drag out some belligerent, half
naked businessmen, just to show that they
were aware and were tough on such illegal
activities. These episodes never took place
on Wednesdays, that's when the local police
captain and his buddies went to the parlor.
      Her head was filled with music and her
thinking fuzzy from too much sake for her
too care too much about which businessman
would be humiliated tonight. The Sapporo
riot police burst through the parlor doors
as Kaz stumbled a bit and tripped on an
uneven bit of pavement. Tom fives eyes
finally burst spraying the hostess who had
taken a fetal position at Toms feet. A pair
of officers threw their shields down and ran
to tackle Tom. His brain burst through his
skull just as they made contact. Searing hot
gray matter splattered all over the
officers. But Tom five lay dead where he
fell. The police now had a sort of

The Origin of the Species

unpleasant mystery on their hands. They had
three dead men on their hands. Two could be
identified, but the third, the older man had
only bills and letters that were addressed
to a local where house stuffed into his
underpants. The letters were stained by
sweat and a few more bodily secretions that
no one really wanted to think about. A good
majority of the letters were addressed to
Dr. Kazahira Kono. There were letters from
her mother, bills from the electric company
urgent and unpaid for weeks. The most
intriguing piece of soiled mail was an
official reprimand from the medical board.
The summation of which was as follows; "In
light of your continuing ethical violations
and your persistence to pursue genetic
research that could only be tantamount to
you original cloning project we are hereby
forced to suspend your medical license as
of..".

     The morning that followed the parlor
murders Kaz awoke with a pounding headache.
She had already made her coffee when she
noticed that Tom five was not waiting for
his breakfast. He wasn't pounding the table
with his fists clenched around a spoon (he
was never able to use chopsticks). There was
pounding however. She couldn't quite place
it but there was definitely pounding
somewhere. She got up from the table
grabbing her coffee and closing her robe.
She tried to follow the sound. Her legs were
shaky and her steps unsteady. "Aha," she
said. The sound was coming from the service
door to the warehouse. The door was a long
aluminum panel that ran twelve feet long and
was seven feet high. It sat on a track so
that it could slide to one side to allow
room for large equipment into the warehouse.
The lower left hand corner had a smaller
door cut into the larger door so that Kaz

didn't have to slide the large door herself.
The pounding was enhanced by the fact that
the door was barley an inch thick. The
knocking resonated through the nearly empty
warehouse like chambered thunder. "All
right, all right," Kaz said. She never
announced her presence to curiosity seekers
or the random passersby. Her work was such
that it required tremendous secrecy. She
slapped her hand over her mouth but it was
too late. They must have heard her. Kaz was
awake in an instant, "and where was Tom,"
she wondered. She looked up at the monitor
above the door. She saw a pair of men
dressed in cheap suits. The men were
accompanied by a quartet of uniformed
policemen. "What do they know," she
whispered and sweated, "what could they
know, I can't let them in here." She
approached the door without realizing what
she was doing. "Maybe this should end, but
what about my mother and my father, I've
caused them so much shame already." "Dr
Kono are you there?" One of the policemen
called from outside the door. Kaz stopped at
the door and fell to her knees in front of
it. She stared back into her lab. The police
outside kept pounding on the door and Kaz
said nothing.

. . . .
. . . .

    "So what happened?" John asked. His
Baretta was reassembled and a cigarette
burned down to the filter in the ashtray in
front of him.
    "Dr. Kono was placed in my custody,
Japan wanted nothing too do with such a
scandal so in exchange for their complicity
I gave Sapporo the nineteen seventy-two

Olympic games and they made the story go
away. "

    "So what happened to her and her lab? "

    "She spent her first three years under
a close guard at an air base on the edge of
Okinawa and her lab mysteriously burned down
a few weeks after she came under my
employ. "

    "So it wouldn't be too much of a reach
to think of her as my mother, of sorts
anyway. " John said.

    "Yours and so many more like you, "
George smiled, "come on, there's more for
you to learn. "

Chapter 11

Russell Franklin was a liar and not a very good friend, or person for that matter. He would have been a cheat had he ever been clever enough. He bummed cigarettes off of anyone, despite the fact that he was always quitting. He never had any money, due mostly to his regular relapses with Meth. It was an addiction that guided Russell's life and was the source of most of his problems. As was often the case with Meth addiction it would be things like heightened aggression, erratic sexual desire these hit Russell like any other jittery fuckheaded tweeker, but with Russell he was naturally aggressive, Meth made him worse and, well, sex was another story. As for sex, Russell was never better then a pity lay at best. Genetics had a lot to do with it. Esthetically speaking Russell was the ugliest combination of his mother and father. He had a simian slope to his balding head and almost no chin to speak of, to the point that he had a very pronounced, almost exaggerated overbite. And from all appearances he didn't look like a Meth addict. His skin was clear of the scabs so common with his fucktard brethren who picked at their own skin, his teeth were pearly and white, though due to his overbite he was almost constantly drooling.

Russell's story was a simple one, or at least the end of it anyway. It began a week after John Parkers funeral. Russell didn't know John terribly well, save for a few cigarettes he bummed and threats he offered in high school. Russell attended the funeral to score some 'sweet, sad chick ass'. She didn't have to be hot; she just had to be ready to 'ride the Russell train'. Including Russell, there were ten people outside of Johns family, in attendance.

The Origin of the Species

Most, only really knew him from yearbook photos though, and were there as sort of a reunion. Of course there was Summer Leann Mason. She was the only one there with a low enough opinion of herself and a low enough IQ, who would succumb to Russell's charms. Summer was devastated, or so she would tell and re-tell to anyone who would listen to her. If only she had told John how much he had meant to her, things might have turned out different, at least for Summer. Maybe she wouldn't have been fired from her exotic dancing job (which was at the Blue Blue Kitty a club famous for it's ugly, sometimes pregnant dancers). Summer had only been the 'constantly late, assless wonder who wasn't very sexy naked', that was how the manager put it when she got fired.

Losing someone as important as John, however imaginary the connection was, someone who could have made her life so much better, made Summer feel better about everything. Though, in reality, Summer never spoke more then a few words to John, and she hadn't even bothered to bum a cigarette from him when she did. Russell leapt at the 'booty' opportunity that she represented. He consoled her, and they agreed to have lunch the following weekend, and only then because she wanted to get over her cold first.

Russell had passed through a tough week before lunch with Summer. He was currently clean, but very hard up. Summer was well known for being easy. In fact at least seventy percent of her high school and college classmates could attest to this[25].

Russell was peeing. He was shaking, he was a little angry that he had had to wait a

---

[25] Of Summer's seventy percent, four percent was comprised of same sex encounters, sixteen percent were teachers and nine percent were the fathers of various classmates. On the whole a whopping sixty-three percent of them considered her to be a 'bad lay'.

week and to top that off she ordered the 'Veggie Mexi-Platter' which meant that not only anal was out of the question, but that was like nine bucks plus the diet cola she was drinking, that meant he was spending at least eleven dollars on skank. Yeah sure, he was having the Mammoth burger loaded with two patties, bacon ham and two eggs and he was having a beer and a cola but he was a man. Come on.

Russell didn't really care about cost at the moment he was getting some. He bounced out of the restroom without washing his hands, which he never did. The restaurant was quiet, but Russell didn't notice, it was almost frozen. There was the hum of dreadful lite seventies pop music as Russell hopped past a bus station back to his table.

Awaiting Russell was the cause of the silence. Summer was standing in front of their table. Blood ran down her legs and had soaked through her dress. The waitress who had come with drink refills lay twitching at Summers feet. Part of the waitress's throat rested in Summers hands. Russell didn't catch the detail, ran up till he was a foot away from Summer. "Damn baby, you okay?" He paused to look at the situation in front of him. "What the fuck skank?" Summer dropped the piece of flesh she was holding and smiled, revealing her blood stained teeth. She tried calling Russell closer, but only managed to spray him and several of the closer patrons. This was all happening so quickly, that none of them really had time to react. "Are you on the rag?" Russell asked as he stepped closer anyway. He seemed to be trying to showcase his ugly nature, which was by no means difficult. But Summer hit first. Her eyes burst launching hot particles of eye onto Russell's face. "What

the fuck is your problem Summer? " Russell
cried. Summer thrust her blood strained arm
out and into Russell's crotch. Russell was
confused; arousal and fear filled his mind.
Before he could speak, Summer tore her
fingernails through to the soft flesh under
Russell's jeans and tore away his testicles.
Summer collapsed on top of the waitress as
her brain burst inside her skull. At the
same time Russell fell back, and for the
first and only time in his life, he
experienced real pain.

The Origin of the Species

Chapter 12

John sat on the edge of his bed. It was past Halloween past a birthday and he still hadn't set foot on the mainland since the night he died. The room he sat in was slightly more personalized, a stack and books and c.d.s sat on the dresser and a small gym bad that John had started to pack. The door the hallway was slightly ajar. The scene outside John's window had changed very little since John woke from his coma. Though the sky and the sea were the same color at the moment as it rained fairly steadily. John stared out at the sea, if what George said was really happening then everyone I know is probably dieing, everything is going to be different, I know I am, John thought.

Next to John on the bed was a pair of Berettas that George had given him as a late birthday present. These were the tools of his trade George explained. They were chrome with white mother of pearl handles. The novelty of owning his own firearm had yet to wear off. John remembered that growing up at the tale end of the cold war, he and his brothers would often tear through the neighborhood playing spies. Jeremy and Jason were always F.B.I. agents and John would always be the Russian spy that they were always out to get. The three brothers each had fairly realistic cap guns (this was before all cap guns were cheap plastic with orange tips) and cheap vinyl trench coats from Halloween costumes from years past. Bottle rockets and firecrackers were always employed as interrogation tools when the evil Russian spy was caught. John's pistols reminded him of the broken cap gun that he had been allowed to use by his brothers. It had chipped silver paint and as broken

The Origin of the Species

hammer that made 'kills' impossible because
it couldn't fire any caps.

John sat lost in thought as George
crept in the room.

"My folks are dead aren't they?" John
inquired.

"No," George said, "not yet anyway,
but what does that really matter?"

"Well as surprising as this may sound,
I am a little worried about them."

"You need to let go of that John, they
were care takers at best, but not really
your parents."

"Right," John scratched his head,
"we've covered this haven't we."

"Not all that well I suppose, but we
have touched on it," George fumbled with a
folder while he lit a cigarette, "this does
bring me to your first assignment John,"
George tossed the folder next to John on the
bed, "and let me cut the dramatics John
it's Richard and Angela Parker."

"Well then," John sighed, "you're not
insane are you?"

"Of course not John," George laughed
like he'd heard a good joke, "it's not like
I'm asking you to eliminate your flesh and
blood relatives these are just people who
you once shared a connection with."

"You've been trying to get that point
across haven't you," John continued to look
out to sea, he yawned, "and what do you
want me to de about them."

"Well Richard Parker was always a
potential problem and with the current state
of affairs we can't have him loose."

"Okay, what about my mothe..Angela
Parker?"

"She has no knowledge of the project or
even of your true nature, you should only do
what is necessary in her regard, lethal
force if warranted."

The Origin of the Species

The truth was that Angela Parker never really knew what Richard did for a living. She did know that John was not her real son and that he was adopted. Though she was always under the impression that they had adopted John through a Russian agency based in Leningrad. Angela Parker raised her little communist son feeling that she was doing a great service for John and America by taking one more innocent child away from those commie bastards. Angela Parker was always a fierce patriot.

The geographical truth was something John would learn about later. Each group was produced in a different country to maintain absolute secrecy. John's group was produced in a lab underneath a ramshackle seaside amusement park in Blackpool, England. So if anything John was English by birth.

Angela didn't know this. She also didn't know of Richards fondness for forgery, a rather unhealthy fixation really, that allowed Richard to provide his wife with John's Russian passport, birth certificate (Sergei Zupov was John's Russian birth name) and pictures of his Soviet parents. Angela accepted him as Russian. There was even a crude family tree (Richard had to learn Russian through a book for this) that linked John to Lenin himself. Truly a victory for America.

The Origin of the Species

Part III
No Distance left to
run...
Chapter 1

Derek Wall was a fugitive. This was the first in his life he ran from a problem. Sure he'd been in trouble before, but he'd always taken what was coming too him. Right or wrong he always stood up to face it. This was different.

So many months had passed since Rachel Gilger and her baby died in his arms. What happened on that morning was this; Derek had just finished the first of his graveyard shifts at Hawaiian Gardens casino. He was suffering from the sort of auditory hallucinations that could only be explained by sleep depravation. It was accompanied by cottonmouth, a caffeine headache and nausea. This was the norm for Derek for the past two weeks. Even Earl had suggested quitting, knowing Derek was too stubborn to listen to reason. Besides, the work wasn't all that degrading, the docked pay wasn't all that humiliating these were things Derek felt he owed, to make things right, he'd never back down.

Derek stood, waiting patiently for the first of three buses that would get him back to Yorba Linda. The gray sky above was a typical Southern California overcast morning. It was as though someone had dropped a gray sheet over a sun lamp. The light peaking out from the clouds and haze caused Derek's eyes to ache.

Rachel Gilger had gotten on the bus at the previous stop. She had dropped by her work, which was as a checker at a Safeway, to pick up her last paycheck before she started her maternity leave. Rachel was sick, worse yet she'd passed it on to her

No distance left to run...

unborn child. There was never any firm data
on the viral effects on children in-utero.
It was the one bit piece of data that George
didn't bother to study or challenge the
theories there of. The general consensus was
that unborn children were an acceptable
loss. Further, many at the agency had wished
that the virus were controllable when they
saw what it could have meant to population
control. Unfortunately, as it stood, when it
became clear that data was needed on unborn
victims it was equally clear that; a. the
virus was still primarily communicable
though bodily fluids and b. that it had
become time to accept the worse case
scenario with the highest fatality rate in
the history of the planet. This conclusion
had been reached some twenty years before
Derek Wall and Rachel Gilger shared a bus in
the early morning hours in Hawaiian Gardens.
The data that Derek would not be privy to
would have told him that any fetus exposed
to the virus before the end of the first
trimester faced a sixty percent chance of a
still born birth, while still thirty-seven
percent would simply liquefy in the womb.
The remaining three percent would be born
with severe to moderate chromosomal defects
(fused fingers and toes, no eye sockets,
mental retardation and so forth). After the
first trimester the effects of the virus
would be similar to a full-grown adults
response. However, the fetus will always
develop a symbiotic relationship with the
embryonic fluid and consequently, the fetus
explodes when introduced to an oxygen rich
environment. The common characteristics
among second and third trimester exposure is
as follows; accelerated growth, swelling of
the pituitary and adrenalin glands (similar
to that seen in exposed adults) and extreme
protein based growths. The protein need is

No distance left to run...

so severe as it continually exhausts the
available supply leaving the host weak and
emaciated. The immediate side effect of that
was that the fetus will grow long and thick,
however, patchy hair and finger and toe
nails as strong as bone.

This growth was going on inside
Rachel's womb as Derek got on the bus. The
bus itself was sparsely filled with the
usual early morning commuters. In total
there were six housekeepers, three from
Mexico, two from Columbia and the sixth was
from Chile. The six ladies worked in the
same gated community in Brea, and their
husbands and children were all friends. But
the five South American ladies always choose
to ostracize the Chilean lady when working.
When Derek got on the bus he passed
unnoticed by the five South American ladies
who were busy chatting in the front most
sideways seats. Only the Chilean lady,
Emilia Paz looked up. She recognized Derek
right away. She remembered the articles in
the paper (it was from when she was learning
English) and all the investigative report
shows that analyzed, reanalyzed and labeled
Derek Wall the worst man alive in America.
He was an evil mastermind. The news magazine
show 'Insider', which at the time was Emilia
Paz's only American news source, ran a three
part expose' on the evils of Derek Wall. It
included well-constructed testimonials from
former Black Luftwaffe leaders who laid out
the concept that Derek was "the best and
most heinous qualities of Hitler, Stalin and
the entire Khmer Rouge." Ken Burrows and
Ian Yates both contributed greatly to the
vilification of their former comrade. They
in turn were both very well compensated for
the potential endangerment. Additionally,
whenever they appeared on screen their faces
were blurred and their voices were

No distance left to run…

distorted. This was due to (as was explained
with every appearance) the fear that were
Derek Wall ever again on the outside of a
prison the reprisals for their betrayals
would be both swift and vicious. This was
done despite the knowledge that Derek was
only in prison for fifteen years and had
neither publicly of privately vowed any
manner of revenge. It was done to show Derek
as a monster, as 'the' monster. The
promotional clips for the shows had footage
of Hitler making a speech, which would then
cut, to Derek nodding sternly, then it would
cut to Stalin looking menacing and then back
to the Derek nodding footage. The promo
would end with Derek superimposed on a field
of skulls that spelled out monster. That was
the image Emilia Paz had in her head. She
crossed herself as he passed and began
muttering a prayer under her breath. It was
a prayer she had composed if she were ever
to run across the people she feared. It went
like this: "My God, my savior please strike
me from this mortal vessel before Derek the
monster can have his way." So really, it
wasn't about all she feared, just Derek.
Mrs. Paz was a rational woman, save for her
fear of Derek. This fear out weighed all
other fears in her life, the common fears of
a woman with low self-esteem like that her
husband was cheating on her and that her
daughters secretly hated her just like she
had hated her own mother. She muttered her
prayer and clutched her picture of Jesus. It
was a moving picture that when turned to the
left Jesus closed his eyes and raised his
hands in prayer; back to the right he opened
his eyes and lowered his hands.

Derek passed Emilia Paz as she
repeated her prayer. Derek understood he had
some notoriety, people retreated from his
presence, spat on the ground he walked but

No distance left to run…

this was the one he always liked, when
someone prayed against him. It was some sort
of notable accomplishment that someone would
use their relationship with their own
loving, forgiving God to wish themselves
harm in order to save themselves from you.
It would have brought a smile to his face if
he hadn't been so tired. Derek made his way
to the back of the bus where the only other
person was Rachel Gilger.

No distance left to run...

Chapter 2

Derek had only noticed Rachel as he sat down. She was pretty, despite looking sickly and sweaty, but she was pregnant, which automatically told Derek that she probably wasn't single.

What could he say to attract a lady, he often thought to himself. "Like to come back to the garage I live in, it's in Yorba Linda," he shook his head at this thought, "we could listen to my Wagner collection or watch public television on my thirteen inch black and white set." These things made Derek realize that presently he had very little to offer a woman. He didn't know who he was anymore and at thirty-seven he knew that wasn't very attractive.

Fifteen years ago he was a feared and respected leader. They betrayed him, sold him out when things went wrong. Seeing the pregnant Ms. Gilger threw Derek into a daydream. It was the same sort of thing he'd been having since Earl Myers first started counseling him in.

Derek would return home from a hard day at whatever profession fascinated him at the time, he would return to his palatial ranch style spread.
The fantasy homes would usually be on a river somewhere with it's own jetty and a powerboat tied up at the end. His children, sometimes two, sometimes as many as eight would be marching in unison on the lawn wearing matching black uniforms. The elusive portion of the daydream was Mrs. Wall. There was never a specific model, though she would be waiting dutifully on the porch. Her appearance would waver between a ravishing blonde who showed no physical signs of childbirth to a gorgeous red head who showed no physical signs of childbirth. Both

No distance left to run...

versions would be curvy, radiating sex and conservatively dressed. In more recent versions of the daydream, Derek reaches the porch and his beloved wife cracks him across the face with a two by four.

It was at this point in the dream that Derek became aware of a problem. Across from him Rachel Gilger was shaking violently. "Miss, are you okay?" This being said was against his better judgment, as this was definitely a problem. She started to hop in her seat and spray blood through her teeth. Derek knew he should have backed off then and there. He should have, but he didn't. He leapt to her side and tried to cradle her, to stop her from shaking. This was, he thought, an act of contrition, the way to make amends for all the wrongs he's done in his life. It wasn't just Rachel on the bus, Derek had made a point of inserting himself where ever he saw an opportunity to help. He held Rachel because he wasn't sure what to do. Her belly trembled and she sprayed more blood through her teeth. The other passengers did their best to ignore the noise from the back; Emilia Paz was too scared to see what the Monster was up to. The driver was off in his own world, playing a hand of blackjack on a pocket casino every chance he had, not just at stops.

Suddenly, Rachel swung her arm around and grabbed hold of Derek's shoulder. Her finger felt like steel cables trying to tear through his flesh. Even though she was only in her third week of the virus, the accelerated growth of her baby had pushed the fever to its peak. Rachel's belly began expanding; eight small lumps appeared to be pushing their way through her stomach. This caused her so much pain, her grip on Derek's shoulder weakened.

No distance left to run…

"Hey, you're going to need to pull over," Derek called out to the driver. The driver had just split a pair of aces and received a three and a two respectively. "What are you talking about?" The driver sounded annoyed. Here it was a full week before his Vegas trip, and he had to be ready, and this was just bullshit. It was bullshit till the driver looked up into his rear view mirror to see Derek cradling a bloody Rachel in his arms. The driver panicked and hit the brakes. This caused the back end of the bus to screech forward at an angle, partially blocking traffic in the other direction. There was a silent moment as the passengers tried to collect their breaths it wouldn't be long. Within seconds two of the vehicles that followed the bus collided, a cargo van hit a police cruiser. That combined energy hit the side of the bus that Derek and Rachel occupied. The force of the crash was enough to throw Derek across against a window, cracking three ribs. It threw all the cleaning women forward and the driver smashed his head against the steering wheel. In the process he managed to break his pocket black jack. Rachel's baby pushed off her spine, causing a very loud frozen celery cracking sound, and through her stomach. Rachel was dead even before the massive blood loss could be accounted for.

The baby jumped out at the first person it saw, which was a very startled and hurt Derek. The baby screamed and howled. Fresh oxygen was causing it to swell as it tried to attack Derek. The baby didn't have all that much longer. Each passing second caused the baby's fragile skin and internal organs to swell a bit more, Derek put his hands on the baby just as the other passengers became aware of Derek, the baby and dead Rachel. The house keepers screamed

No distance left to run…

and the driver started cursing (although
that was mostly for his broken pocket black
jack)

"Shit, this is not what it looks
like!" Derek called out. This only managed
to produce more screams and more cursing.
Emilia Paz looked up just as the baby
screamed and then exploded in Derek's hands,
splattering him with searing hot flesh.

No distance left to run...

Chapter 3

In the present, John Parker sat on the back of a powerboat headed for Catalina. For his first assignment he had to travel back to Woodland Hills, to the home he grew up in to 'eliminate' hid parents. The only real problem to this was that in July the Federal Emergency Management Agency declared Los Angeles, greater Orange County and San Diego County as lost causes. By mid August evacuation sites were established in Ventura, CA, Primm Valley Nevada and the U.S./Mexico border. The original plan to establish Marshall law had failed to the extent expected. The idea had never been containment, without a cure that was never going to happen. The plan had always been to slow the spread of the virus wherever possible.

John knew this; he also knew that his parents weren't in any of the evacuations sites. As of twelve-thirty the previous afternoon satellite photos showed a pair of heat signatures inside the Parker family home. Only forty minutes before the satellite photos were taken, Richard Parker's Discover card had been used to purchase three cases of twelve gauge shot guns shells. They had been purchased at Roy's Sportsman Emporium on Saticoy and Canoga. Roy's was an all-purpose store started in the mid sixties by Roy senior then run by Roy junior. They sold rifles, pistols, ammo, bows arrows crossbows and bolts, knives, whetstones, new and used military gear, lures, tackle, rods and reels. If you could hunt it, shoot it, stab

No distance left to run...

it, or lure it out of the water, Roy had
your gear[26].

---

[26] Now, granted, Richard Parkers purchase was well beyond
failed Marshall law and the evacuations, but Roy was a
survivalist who refused to close (he his in the store room
with steel shudders covering every possible entry way). Roy
was a veteran of two wars, decorated and honorably
discharged by the Marine Corp. He'd been waiting for the
end of the world for some time, that would be his time to
shine. Of course, at this point the North Koreans had his
left eye and then Viet Cong had his right hand.

No distance left to run…

Chapter 4

The cold night air felt good on his face, though John didn't like being on a boat. He didn't mind the occasional sea mist he just didn't like boats.

Another discovery John made was the day before was the 'Jason Variety Show'. Apparently Jason had stunned his critics, several weeks after John was shot[27], so much so that he'd been given his own federally funded show. Part of this was that there were an increasing number of well-established, popular and successful actors who were very suddenly unavailable for work.

The Jason Parker Variety Show, a showcase of comedy, drama and musical theatre, quickly evolved from a thirty minute format, to an hour then two, followed by three until, in a mater of weeks the show was evacuated to Las Vegas and reached it's six hour running time. The show included; Jason's all girl dance squad, which an awkward but well endowed dance troop comprised of the waitresses from the Hooters in Long Beach that Jason used to frequent. Providing the music was the Luther Cole Experience. The Luther Cole Experience was a Chicago based jazz and blues quintet that saw it's day in the early seventies. Luther Cole was a bus driver, Cubs fan, and a ding-dong and Michelob enthusiast. Luther arrived in San Diego for his Daughters wedding some thirty-six hours before the official declaration of Marshall Law was made. And the lead of The Jason Parker Players was Ms. Sara Jefferies a former San Fernando Valley

---

[27] It was supposed to be Jason's one-man show version of Ringo Starr's "The Magic Christian". Jason dedicated the show to his dead baby bro. "Johnny, bro we miss you," Jason cried before the first curtain and accentuated this with a poignant look to the heavens with a hand over his heart and tears in his eyes.

No distance left to run…

based thrift store clerk and aspiring actress. This was the most popular show on the air. This was due largely to The Jason Parker show being the only six hours of non-emergency, non-government broadcast allowed by the F.C.C..

John did have another brother who was officially missing. There were no reports on his whereabouts, nor was he listed in any of the evacuation site registries.

The missing brother, Jeremy Parker, headed for South America at the first sign of trouble. He loaded everything he could, including his girlfriend Misti (an exotic dancer and aspiring Adult film star) into his nineteen eighty-seven Chrysler Lebaron. Misti and Jeremy made it as far as the inland border town of Lajunda. It is believed that in Lajunda they met with one of several Mexicali death squads. Nothing is known of Jeremy or Misti beyond Lajunda[28].

---

[28] These squads were made up of several well-armed Mexican and Californian survivalists. Many similar groups popped up throughout much of the America's. Often they were deputized by local, overwhelmed law enforcement; sometimes they were working on their own initiative. Their main purpose was to exterminate sick people, reclaim or protect land and drink beer.

No distance left to run...

Chapter 5

John could see Catalina in the distance. It was probably another thirty minutes to the shore. From there he'd have to get on another boat, most likely a military transport to get back to the mainland.

Catalina was now an offshore military hospital. There was no civilian traffic on or off the island. Normally, this would have brought up the matter of proper credentials. That had been resolved before John left when George informed him that he was now an active agent for the N.S.A.. This awaited all of John's extended family were they to be activated, they were to serve their purpose, not necessarily their country.

In his right breast pocket, John had a new leather billfold containing his N.S.A. ID card. The picture had been pulled from D.M.V. files so it was of an eighteen year old John. His clearance level was such (although John didn't quite understand yet) that it gave him almost as much authority as George (one level below), and as George put it would be alarming to anyone who knew what it meant.

John was traveling fairly light for his mission. He had his Berettas, six cartridges of standard ammunition and six of armor piercing, a change of clothes, cash (as needed or applicable) and two cartons of cigarettes.

The Pacific rocked the boat back and forth. The last time John was on a boat was a family fishing trip when John was fourteen. Uncle Dan had arranged this trip; he was Richards's crazy brother. Uncle Dan arranged almost every outdoor trip. This particular trip was to Castaic Lake near Moorpark. Castaic, as John recalled, was a

No distance left to run...

dirty, still body of water surrounded by a
scorched earth looking shoreline.

Jeremy brought his girlfriend at the
time, Amber Lynn Collins. Amber Lynn dressed
for the occasion better then any of Jeremy's
previous girlfriends, white canvas sneakers,
no socks, Daisy Dukes and a white tube top.

They took two cars. The family wagon
piloted by Richard and Uncle Dan's project
car, a seventy-three El Camino. The El
Camino was a paycheck away from its sweet
paintjob, so it was primer gray with the
crude outline for the skulls and flames that
were to adore the car. Uncle Dan did spring
for the tiny chain link steering wheel
though and chrome naked lady mud flaps and
fuzzy dice that he'd ordered from a Playboy
magazine catalog.

Jeremy and Jason usually rode shotgun
with Uncle Dan for these sorts of trips. It
was a privilege that wasn't extended to John
till the Castaic trip.

Having reached Moorpark, and having
driven for a silent two hours, Uncle Dan,
Jason and John stopped at the only open shop
at the edge of the ghost town like section
of Moorpark. "Gotta grab some smokes and a
piss," Uncle Dan said as he moved toward
the poorly lit grocery store, "Jay be sure
and goose the gas a little so she don't
stall." Uncle Dan always called Jason 'Jay'
because it rhymed with his favorite insult
for Jason. 'Gay Jay' and 'pillow pirate'
were as clever as Uncle Dan ever got. For
this trip, however, Uncle Dan behaved,
trying to focus all his hate on John.
Though, until the grocery store stop he
hadn't said a word. He couldn't think of a
good rhyming insult for John. It had only
been monosyllabic grunts until Uncle Dan
started to nic-fit and had to stop for
cigarettes. Uncle Dan didn't like John

No distance left to run…

because he was convinced that John was going
to kill him someday.

At least that's how his brother Richard
explained it to him. Richard told Dan that
first John would kill a neighborhood dog and
paint his body with the dogs' still warm
blood. Dan always responds to this with a
slack jawed "Motherfucker." "Yes, but
there's more," Richard would sigh as if
revealing a deep dark truth. This story
would be told numerous times at family
barbeques. It was usually in told in the
garage, with gusto, beer spray and hushed
tones. The story would continue with the
wild speculations of the potential super-
human abilities that John might acquire from
the dogs blood. "You know the legends,"
Richard would say. "Yeah I read that
somewhere[29]," Dan would belch. "Right,"
Richard would say and squint for dramatic
effect, "in his dogs blood war paint the
little heathen bastard will creep into my
bedroom, which happens to be the biggest in
the house." Richard would always pause long
enough for Dan to be impressed. It was four
times the size of Dan's studio apartment
that rested above a carwash. "He'll have a
knife that he will have stolen from my
extensive collection." Richard would then
gesture toward the plywood storage cabinet.
There was no knife collection in there. It
was mostly Richards's forgery supplies,
blank passports, birth certificates and such
the like. On a lower self, next to the
pornography, was Richards war time
scrapbook. It told, rather loosely, what he
really did during the Vietnam War and
several years beyond. For security purposes,

---

[29] This was, in fact, a very well known lie. Danforth
Francis Parker was hardly even a functional illiterate. Had
he not played football he may never have received his high
school diploma.

No distance left to run...

and perhaps a little leverage Richard had
three additional copies hidden throughout
Los Angeles. One in a bowling alley locker,
one in a safety deposit box and one hidden
in a public library.

The plywood cabinet was secured by a
rusted padlock. The hinges on the doors were
bent slightly from various people trying to
peak inside. Though it's remained unopened
since nineteen eighty.

Richard did keep a small weapons cache
hidden within his bed frame with a voice
activated lock release. Within seconds of
shouting "horse feathers" Richard would
have two handguns and throwing knives.
"That bastard will leap n me and try to
catch me sleeping," Richard would continue.
It was typically at this point that Angela
would interrupt to tell Richard that his
coals were ready. Richard held two barbeque
truths over all others: 1. Under no
circumstances to you ever stray from
charcoal and 2. Keep your goddamn grubby
hands off his barbeque.

Uncle Dan only ever got to hear the
end of the story once. In the end, at the
cost of an eye and a pinkie finger, John
would finally win. He would crack open
Richards's chest and feats on his heart,
screaming like a howler monkey. This tale of
patricide always made Dan afraid of a boy
who was never better then a third his size.

Dan kept his eye out for an opportunity
to catch John off guard on the trip up to
Castaic. He kept waiting for John to do
something on the trip, any excuse to stop
the car. Nothing happened and then Uncle Dan
ran out of cigarettes and had to stop.

No distance left to run...

No distance left to run…

Chapter 6

John was smoking the last cigarette from his current pack. It was his lucky cigarette, the ninth cigarette in the pack turned upside down when John opened the pack and spelled out 'Francesca'. He'd also gotten George to do the same thing, though for George it was the eighth.

John wondered if the cash George gave him would really do him any good. George did tell him that the Army lifted its smoking ban so cigarettes should be available at nearly any outpost. Beyond quarantine areas the government would be doing it's best to ensure that life and commerce appeared normal. Even if that meant soldiers at grocery stores and Haz-mat teams visible in every major city.

John was at least more comfortable in his current vessel then the last time he voluntarily got in a boat. The last boat was an aluminum dingy that he, Jason and Uncle Dan had paddled out to the middle of Castaic Lake. That boat was almost thin enough to feel the water underneath.

Uncle Dan decided in the grocery store that this was how he repay his brother. Richard had bailed Dan out of trouble so many times, some literally involving bail money, that he felt he owed it to his little bro' to kill "the monster" (which was Uncle Dan's pet name for John). He was going to shoot John, dump his body in the lake and then they would all go to Casa De Pizza and celebrate. That was Dan's plan. He especially liked the Casa De Pizza part. Jason was also going to get pushed into the lake. But that was because he was gay and it would be funny. Killing John, however, was serious business. Even before he had a concrete plan he had gone to great lengths

No distance left to run...

to prepare for this, which involved getting videos at the library and not returning them[30]. By shear coincidence, and on a complete whim Uncle Dan had purchased a very shiny revolver, a thirty-eight caliber, also known as a Saturday night special. Dan had purchased this gun at a great discount, despite how shiny it was and how cool the handles were, at Roy's Sportsman's Emporium. The handles were black resin and part of the custom design of the gun. One side showed a phoenix rising, the phoenix had garnets for eyes and the other side held an S.S. skull and lighting bolts done in silver[31]. The last specification was the smooth interior of the barrel. This severely compromised accuracy, but made the gun nearly untraceable.

Uncle Dan didn't know the history of the gun it was just a bad ass little gun with a sweet skull and cross bones.

The plan had worked perfectly so far. Richard was on the shore with Angela, Jeremy and Amber Lynn. Dan had placed the revolver in the bottom of his tackle box. He handed John and Jason their fishing spools, which were just large plastic rings in day glow colors and fishing line wrapped around them. They were home made based off of something

---

[30] The entire Parker family had received the rare distinction of receiving a lifetime ban from all services and borrowing privileges at all Los Angeles County libraries. Dan Parker had to use a neighbor's card, Angela Parker used an assumed identity and the rest of the family simply didn't bother.

[31] The revolver had been a special order by Clemintine Joanne "C.J." Burrows. She was the ex-wife of the former Black Luftwaffe leader Ken Burrows. It was going to be his forty-fifth birthday present, which was interrupted by his lengthy trip to Folsom. C.J. had the pistol on her when she was arrested after leading the Highway Patrol and L.A.P.D. down the P.C.H. at one hundred fifty miles an hour. The speeding added to then parole violation as well as three counts of manslaughter, one count of felony possession with intent to distribute (nine kilos of cocaine), two counts of endangering a minor (her sons were her coke mules) and six counts of contributing to the delinquency of minors. C.J. got life plus forty years and the gun made its way from a Malibu County evidence locker to the showcase at Roy's Sportmans Emporium by way of a trade with the Evidence locker sergeant.

No distance left to run…

Dan saw in a magazine, they didn't work very well.

About an hour into the silence and the staring at the water with bugs and fish scales floating at the surface, Dan put his plan into action. He sprung up, rocking the boat, and swung around to knock Jason in the water. In the confusion that would cause, he'd shoot John, pizza and beer weren't far off now. Uncle Dan knocked John in the water by mistake. John had been rifling through the tackle box and took it with him into the water. The tackle box, with the hidden revolver sank to the bottom. Uncle Dan freaked out. Suddenly this was all Jason's fault and Dan turned to the boy with a burning hate in his eyes. Meanwhile, John, who was not a very good swimmer was panicking, cold, and swallowing more lake water then would reasonably be considered good for you (.02 ounces).

Uncle Dan was trying to wring Jason's neck, cursing and spraying his anger till he couldn't see straight and there was a dull ache in his left arm. John's panic subsided when his feet brushed the bottom of the lake. They'd only gone out about fifteen feet but in the unnerving moments of swallowing water and not being a strong swimmer he wasn't really paying attention to where they were. John dog paddled till it was a bit more shallow and then walked to shore.

Uncle Dan looked up; he was out of breath and no longer trying to strangle Jason. Jason was teary eyed and holding his neck. Dan made eye contact with Richard on the shore. Richard shook his head, the operation was over, and Dan had failed him. There would certainly be no pizza and beer now.

No distance left to run...

. . . .
. . . . . .

    John reached what was supposed to be a
secret dock on the back of Catalina. It was
starting to rain again. The lights from the
military encampment on the front of the
island gave off a kind of halo. On the dock
there was the silhouette of a lone figure
waiting for John.

No distance left to run...

Chapter 7

About eleven hundred miles north of Los Angeles County, Francesca was waking up in a now all too familiar room in Southeast Portland. It was a small room, not all that uncommon in older Portland homes. The room itself was a study in organized chaos. In one corner was a basket of clean, unfolded laundry, which was completely undistinguishable from the basket of dirty laundry next to it. Francesca hated laundry, putting it away, folding it whatever was entailed with it. Across from that was a dressed that was supposed to contain her clothes. In the drawers of the dressed were several boxes of .45 caliber ammunition, DVD's and a spare boot polishing kit. On top of the dresser were several more boxes of ammo as well as a couple of precariously stacked piles videos that seemed ready to fall at the slightest provocation. Next to the videos was a TV, VCR, DVD combo. On the floor next to the dresser was the only sense of order to the room. There were two pairs of boots. Both pairs were black leather, size eight steel toes. The pair closest to the dresser was well worn and held together in many places by fishing line (eighty pound test). The other pair, Francesca had yet to really break in. On the wall above the dresser was a map of greater Portland metro adorned with forty-two red pushpins marking various points in and around the city. They represented forty-two kills performed by Francesca. Twelve were part of her on the job training. They had been the first twelve people to piss Seth off when Paul, Seth and Francesca first arrived in Portland.

The advantage to the Portland killing ground was very simple. No one noticed. Many

No distance left to run...

different factors contributed to this. Many rival gang members had been released from prison, but mostly Portland had been hit pretty hard by the virus. Local law enforcement was overwhelmed as it was and they didn't have the personnel to investigate twelve extra deaths. The government would be stepping in soon, sooner then was originally planned.

Francesca was a federal employee now. She had the same clearance level as John, much higher then Seth and Paul.

Francesca sat up in her bed. She'd cut her hair short shortly after she first woke up in Portland. It was still long enough for a ponytail, but more manageable. She looked at her map, giving it a faint smile, though she couldn't clearly see it yet, there was still a lot of sleep in her eyes.

Fifteen of the kills that followed her training were strictly business, orders from Washington. The fifteen that followed that were people who have inadvertently crossed either Seth or Paul.

She threw her blanket to the side and shuffled to the edge of the bed. She lit a cigarette and rubbed her eyes with her free hand.

"Wake up sunshine princess," Seth hollered from the doorway, "we got a new assignment." Seth finished with a spray. He still bore many scars from the beating he suffered at her hands. He never did get his revenge or any dentures to replace the teeth she knocked out.

Consequently Seth spoke with an angry sort of lisp. He had the appearance of a fiercely barking dog in retreat.

No distance left to run…

"Fuck you Mighty Mouse, where's Paul?"
She responded with a cloud of smoke[32].

Seth had no respect for women of any
variety. Grandma Oliver had always told him
that they were no good parasites that would
cheat him, hurt him and not love him like
Grandma Oliver. Francesca had hurt him and
she continued to do so. This was so much
like his childhood with the humiliation, the
deep hurt and the sandwiches.

Seth stood in the doorway, frozen in an
angry daze. He'd been in the kitchen making
lunch for himself and Paul[33]. The lunch
consisted of grilled cheese sandwiches
(Seth's comfort food). He'd been burning his
own sandwich when the assignment arrived.
Paul had always presented the assignments,
Francesca would go kill someone and Seth got
to clean house. Seth was starting to resent
this arrangement and his lack of
involvement. As a housekeeper, Seth had
neither been thorough, effective or
efficient. HE broke the vacuum cleaner in
their first Portland week. The broom that
Paul replaced the vacuum with remained
untouched. All manner of dust and small
refuge collected near the bottoms of all the
walls, giving each room a slight curved
look.

"Paul went for coffee stupid," Seth
chuckled as though this were common
knowledge. This was his chance to take
control, make her sweep the floors and do
the laundry.

---

[32] It was never a wise idea to engage Francesca in any form
of conversation before her first cigarette of the day had
been extinguished.
[33] Conveniently, Seth always forgot about Francesca when he
made lunch, which had been his daily chore since they
arrived in Portland. It was his way of saying "Fuck You
Whore'. This slight had gone entirely unnoticed as
Francesca hadn't regularly eaten any sort of lunch since
she was eleven and hadn't gotten before noon since she's
been college and even then it was only when she had to.

No distance left to run...

"Seeing as how I just woke up fucktard, how was I supposed to know that?"

Seth didn't have a good response for this. He did give it some thought, though the best he could come up with was a series of nasal sounds attempting to mimic what Francesca had just said[34]. Francesca simply looked on with disgust.

"Paul said he'd be back in twenty minutes," Seth whined. He then threw the report as hard as anyone could manage to throw a single, unfolded sheet of paper. The paper smacked itself back against Seth. Francesca smirked, tears raced to Seth's' eyes. Just as this was all about to reach an ugly climax, three things happened to break the tension. First, Francesca's alarm clock went off[35], which had been set to two forty-five (continuing the unsettling trend of Francesca waking up just before her alarm), second and coinciding with the alarm clock, Paul burst through the door, having returned from getting coffee. The final tension breaker was Paul. He was singing, at the top of his lungs and quite badly. He was happy and he shouldn't have been, the world was falling apart and he had a job to do. Paul was seeing a young woman by the name of Serenity. She was a cashier at a Vegan cafe on Hawthorne.

Paul hadn't brought home any coffee; he had a brown, recycled paper bag full of

---

[34] Seth R. Oliver had always had trouble maintaining friendships. In fact most people who had any association with Seth were co-workers who blissfully avoided social interactions, beyond of course, daily encounters. This was mostly due to the fact that he was a complete asshole, though many (including most recently Francesca) theorized that Seth suffered some sort of fever related brain damage.

[35] The alarm clock was purchased by Francesca at an Asian market on Sherman Way in Van Nuys, near the dead center of the San Fernando Valley well over two years ago. The clock was cheap and sat inside a shiny red apple. On top of the apple was a pink-segmented worm with wide eyes and a sinister moustache. At the preset time he danced to a tin sounding version of "The Girl from Impanema" with increasing speed to the music and the dancing as the hour wore on. Mr. Happy Burt Dance Shoe was his name.

No distance left to run...

leftovers from the picnic lunch he'd
'enjoyed' with Serenity in Laurelhurst Park.
Today's menu included Sweet and Sour tofu
stir-fry and gluten free rolls. Paul
launched the bag into the garbage so it
could join the other lunches he and Serenity
had shared over the past week. Paul was
singing, as he always did, "The Summer
Wind". This was a sore point for Seth,
whose own singing had been a source of
ridicule, mocking and intense scrutiny.

Above the butchering of "The Summer
Wind" Seth and Francesca shifted their
mutual animosity from each other to the
absent Serenity. That and Francesca wished
that Paul would, at the very least, learn
one new song.

"This has to stop," Seth sniffled,
"it's not fair, we're here to do a job."

"Seth don't be a dick," Francesca
smiled, "on one hand she's too stupid to
still be alive, besides you hate all women
anyway."

"Most, SO?"

"So, you're jealous."

"NO," Seth stomped and snorted.

"Yes, yes you are," Francesca lit
another cigarette, "Paul is happy and
you're not, and you can't stand it."

"No, IT'S NOT TRUE," Seth protested.

"Yes it is, look it's even making you
cry," Francesca said.

"Fine, you're so smart, what are we
going to do about it?" Seth couldn't hide
his tears anymore. The answer Seth had been
pining for, resting all his future happiness
on was a fantasy construct; "I'll tell you
what WE'RE going to do, you and I will have
so much loud sex, that will be so sexy, that
it will wake the dead, and then you'll punch
my front teeth out." This was his fantasy,
despite the fact that he hated Francesca; he

No distance left to run...

only really wanted her willing submission. That sort of submission would take an unholy miracle[36], but Seth had viewed far too much pornography to realize this. Francesca would answer with "fuck", however, it would not be in the context Seth had hoped for.

"What we're going to do," Francesca began, "is this, you're getting the fuck out of my room and I'm going to get dressed."

---

[36] On a previous discussion regarding the future of humanity, Francesca lamented that it was sad that the human race could potentially end with the three of them. She went on to add that there wasn't enough beer in the world to make procreating with either Paul or Seth appealing, palatable or even possible.

No distance left to run...

Chapter 8

Fall in Portland meant rain. Of course so does summer, spring and winter. Francisco Ricardo was one of the more successful independent landscapers in the greater Portland Metro area. Which, honestly, was never saying very much given the shameful lack of full sized yards. Ricardo Landscaping was cash only business with a small but loyal and effective crew of six men.

As a citizen Francisco was a native of San Diego, born to immigrant parents who hailed from El Salvador. He paid his men well, better then most but never extravagantly and paid his taxes on time. He only the briefest of criminal histories including but not limited to drunk and disorderly and driving without a license. The only real problem is that Francisco Ricardo is not a real person. The greater majority of the time he exists solely on paper. However, on three occasions he has been known to manifest himself in three different forms. Perhaps this warrants some explanation.

Nine months before the most recent appearance of Francisco Ricardo, and by shear coincidence the morning after John Parker was shot and exactly two weeks before Francesca would disappear, Derek Wall would become a fugitive. His position as both the most feared and hated man in Southern California (which is by no means a small feat) would be reaffirmed and secured for a long while.

Rachel Gilger would posthumously attain modern sainthood (the kind of sainthood attributed to those whose only contribution was a horrendous death) and Carl Jr., as the baby was named, would be

No distance left to run...

compared to Jesus Christ and Albert
Einstein. This was, at least, how Rachel's
mother and the father of the exploding baby
would speak to the press.

Back to the morning in question, this
notoriety was hours away. It would be at
least three until Derek would be seen on the
bus. A lesser man would be swept up in
panic. Covered in blood and having no
immediate means of transportation Derek
leapt out of the bus and broke into a run.
He had to get off the street, he knew he
couldn't make it back to Yorba Linda, the
best he could hope for was the Deli on Beach
Blvd. Earl should be there by now, about
halfway through quitting the New York Times
crosswords by now. Earl would have a plan
beyond the Deli; he had to, Derek thought.

Derek put himself on a direct path to
Cypress Community College. Sirens screamed
as Derek ran, he knew he had to get off the
street. Soon enough there'd be news and
police helicopters overhead. He couldn't
face that again. It wasn't prison it wasn't
even the press. He couldn't go through be
hated all over again. There wasn't time to
get caught up in this; he thought to himself
have to keep moving.

Lucky thing for Derek was that it would
only three and a half hours from becoming a
villain again. By that time Derek Wall would
have already vanished, a phantom, just
another reason for parents to walk their
kids to school. Another piece of luck was
the direction of the police response. It
came from a station to the south of the
accident, Derek headed east.

Helicopters were overhead by the time
Derek had ditched his shirt and jacket while
jogging down an alleyway. Even though the
work shirt and jacket had cost him sixty
dollars combined, he knew that the Police

wouldn't necessarily be looking for joggers. He'd been able to wash off most of the blood and bits with a garden hose at the edge of the alley.

Back at the crash Derek was momentarily forgotten, what with the multiple car crash and the exploding baby. The scene was swarmed by a mix of police and reporters, though details were sketchy, the hint of carnage had the press salivating. Emilia Paz remembered what she thought happened though. Although her state of shock and religious babblings bought Derek enough time to run down the alley. When she was able to speak all she could say was "El Monstruo!"

No distance left to run...

Chapter 9

The Monster made it all the way to Cypress Community College. He was out of breath. The campus before him was laid out much like a city of the future as envisioned by low budget nineteen seventies cinema would create it. Desolate but functional, with curved support columns covered in white and beige tiles. There were no trees in sight on the quad except for a concrete monstrosity that sat in the middle of an island surrounded by dark, murky water[37].

Derek passed the little island as he made his way across the quad. The fountain was not running today, and hadn't been in month. Derek was covered in sweat. He tried to keep up the jogging, nodding to oblivious groundskeepers and the foolish students who had early morning class. This had been a bad morning and it wasn't even seven forty-five yet. Derek made his way to the athletic department. There he might be able to steal a shower and a change of clothes. He heard the sounds of a team dragging themselves out, probably football, as he entered the locker room. Derek stood still for a minute; the only quite he might get for a long time.

---

[37] At the base of the concrete tree was a dedication plaque from the class of seventy-nine. It was dedicated to the class of two thousand and the people of Cypress who were going to need to know that there was a time when trees did grow in Orange County. It was in the shape of a palm tree, which was supposed to function as a fountain. It sat in the middle of its own island surrounded by still water. Incidentally, the leaves pointed up instead of down. The original intent and design was of a mushroom cloud with a dedication to the class of two thousand and any other survivors of the great nuclear annihilation that the class of seventy-nine expected by the year two thousand. The dean reasoned that there would more likely be no trees left in Orange County then there would be a nuclear holocaust. Subsequently, this was the last dedicated art allowed or accepted by any departing class.

No distance left to run…

No distance left to run…

Chapter 10

Francisco Ricardo lasted appeared in San Jose, CA from nineteen eighty-two to nineteen eighty-seven. Kurt Franklin Lowell was a Seminary dropout he had issues with celibacy. Shortly after that he served his country in a most unremarkable fashion as was discharged as honorably as an Airforce base assistant grocery store manager could be. Coincidentally, so serious effort was made on the part of the Airforce to get Corporal Lowell to reenlist when his service neared it's conclusion. From the Airforce, for his service he received money for college, which Kurt put towards his teaching degree. From teaching his troubles began. Mr. Lowell got his first job in the city of Portland, OR. It was in Portland that he found he really liked teenagers, so much so that it became a problem for Kurt, in regards to not having sex with as many of his students as possible. Kurt was never terribly good looking, but he was charming and could buy them beer and cigarettes.

While still an airman, Kurt made friends with many fellow grounded airmen who happened to be Satanists. Kurt took to the Church of Satan like a Vegan takes to burning down a burger joint. This wasn't really a problem, granted Kurt was an arrogant, loud mouth but arrogant loud mouths were (and still are) found among the faithful in any religion. Kurt's arrogance only became a problem when he got his teaching job in Portland and rumors began circulating about his involvement with students. So in the late winter of eighty-one local Satanists intervened and Kurt Lowell vanished while on a skiing holiday to Mount Hood. In March of nineteen eighty-two

No distance left to run...

Francisco Ricardo appeared for the first
time in San Jose, CA[38] to start his
landscaping business. The rest of eighty-two
and most of eighty-three were uneventful. As
'Francisco' all Kurt had to do was make the
occasional work site appearance and work the
phones. That was it.

In spring of nineteen eighty-four, the
scandal that Kurt and his fellow Satanists
thought had been averted finally broke.
Three of Mr. Lowell's former students (and
former sex party participants) graduated and
ran into trouble with the law. The first was
a high school wrestler Joseph Peter Marney.
Marney, nineteen at the time and a super
senior as he was returning for a second try
at senior year, robbed a liquor store[39]. Joe
was wearing only a clown mask with green
nylon hair on top and a pair of Converse
All-Star. The robbery had a two-fold
purpose. Joe needed two bottles of Cinnamon
Schnapps for a graduation party that he
wasn't invited [40] to and to scare the
immigrants that ran the store into "going
back where they come from". The immigrant
family had a son graduating in Joe's class.
This was a possible third reason. The naked
robbery went as well as naked robberies
usually went. Joe was apprehended within
minutes of snatching the bottles and
screaming off a few racial epitaphs.

---

[38] The very first appearance of Francisco Ricardo occurred
in nineteen seventy-four in Victorville, CA. Matty Franco,
the eldest son of Roman Franco, ran down his would be prom
date in his fathers Cadillac. This incarnation would be
gone by seventy-seven.
[39] A rather draconian Oregon state law delegated the sale of
liquor to specially designated shops there-by making
idiotic teenage pranks and drunkenness rather difficult.
[40] Having failed in his first go round as a senior, just as
he had as a freshman many would have reasoned, correctly
that Joseph had no place at any kind of graduation related
celebration. His presence would (and had been the year
before) inappropriate at best. However, Joseph reasoned
(mostly to himself) that it was never a real party unless
they had a 'Super Senior'.

No distance left to run...

The local police had figured that a naked ride home, followed by a very loud announcement in front of Joes house would be humiliating enough for a dumb kid who just swiped a couple of bottles and wasn't going to graduate this year anyway. What did stir the trouble was the police brass and municipal hierarchy felt a need (election year) to appear more compassionate and progressive in regards to troubled youth, such as Joseph Marney. They were going to have young Marney assigned to both community service and therapy. He would be their poster child for a more caring local government, no need to vote the other guys.

Joseph fell apart in the back of the patrol car. Having refused a blanket on the grounds that they were covered in bum puke, he sat naked. He began crying and shaking, shouting horrible things to the family standing outside their liquor store. He rambled about sand niggers, sex parties and Mr. Lowell.

By this time Sarabeth Rachel Keenan and Tiara Leeann Ryan[41] were already in the back of a patrol car, not for the body jewelry that they had just shoplifted, nor was it because Joseph Marney was crying in the park of a patrol car one hundred blocks away, calling out their names. They were named as regular participants in Mr. Lowell's parties, but that wasn't why they'd been picked up. A body was found in the reeds by the Columbia River near Airport Way and 181st. Sarabeth had been called in to identify the body.

It would turn out to be her father. Sarabeth was terrified so she insisted that

---

[41] Tiara was a chubby faced girl who always wore extra large 'Tinkerbelle' sweatshirts to hide her voluminous breasts that she was ashamed of, as her family said she should be. Sarabeth was a pale, sickly looking girl who didn't know how to wear make-up.

No distance left to run…

Tiara came along. Sarabeth wasn't a suspect, there had been far too many pissed off ex-girlfriends and ex-wives and not enough evidence to place anyone at the scene. Sarabeth did it though she shot him.

In short, Sarabeth and Tiara had become close friends and occasional lovers during and after their parties with Mr. Lowell. One afternoon when the pair was watching TV, Sarabeth's father stumbled in to the living room. He was drunk and had struck out with his most recent girlfriend. He decided to solve to problems at once when he announced that "Daddies gonna fuck the gay right out of the two a ya." This was not received well by the girls. There was a struggle, and then Sarabeth got his gun and shot him till he stopped moving. Tiara grabbed a blue tarp; they rolled him up and dumped him into the river.

Sarabeth and Tiara got to the station shortly after the naked Joseph Marney. Sarabeth was sent off to identify her father; Tiara was pulled in to answer some questions. Sarabeth would be when she finished pretending how upset she was, though she didn't have to be very convincing.

The girls did confirm Joseph's story, and helped to clarify things a little bit. There had been no coercion outside of the promise of beer and schnapps, which had been delivered. No illegal drugs were ever involved, as that would have conflicted with Mr. Lowell's religious beliefs. It was just about sex and a good time. The trio, Joseph, Tiara and Sarabeth remembered Mr. Lowell fondly, he was a little weird about Satan, but that was about all they knew about that. They couldn't tell the police his current whereabouts, they really didn't know. This is where the case went cold. As it turned

No distance left to run…

out, Kurt Lowell had been missing for five years. When it was investigated further, he's never returned from a winter holiday, but wasn't reported missing until the following spring. What little evidence there was pointed to a violent end for Kurt Lowell. Though it wasn't conclusive, it was good enough for the police.

It wasn't good enough for Jeremiah Marney, Joseph's father. When the story broke Jeremiah was so repulsed that he threw Joseph out of his home. Joseph would stay on Sarabeth's couch till she and Tiara tired of his rotting feet and surprisingly proficient wind breaking.

Jeremiah was angry and more focused then he'd ever been. But all he had was a mental picture of his queer son and a yearbook photo of Kurt Lowell to go by. He was smart enough to realize that he needed to be cautious in seeking his revenge. Jeremiah tried to track Kurt Lowell though American Legion Post, knowing that Kurt had served in the Airforce. He wrote letters to every post he could, sent them photos, saying he was looking for his old buddy. Nothing came back. Kurt Lowell was gone, dead. And he would have stayed that way had he listened to what he'd been told by the Satanists who'd set him up in San Jose. The most important part was to never have or maintain a public profile. In the span of a week, Kurt blew it. He won a regional dart throwing contest, was awarded a "Channel Fours Alert Samaritan of the week" tee-shirt and gift certificate for putting out a brushfire near a rest home[42] and he'd on a seat on the city council. This attached

---

[42] The rest home was across the street from an all girls' Catholic high school. Kurt started the fire when he dropped a cigarette watching volleyball practice.

No distance left to run…

enough recognition, at least in San Jose, to Francisco Ricardo to be problematic.

One of Jeremiah Marney's letters finally did get a response. The response came in the form newspaper clippings that referred to Kurt Lowell as Francisco Ricardo. This would be it; he had to be Kurt Lowell. A note accompanied the clippings stating simply; "you'll be glad to know that the Sarge is doing great here in San Jose, CA. "

Within a week Kurt Lowell, a.k.a. Francisco Ricardo, would disappear for good. Few questions would be asked. Coincidentally Jeremiah was selling home made dog food at a Saturday market in Portland about a week later.

No distance left to run...

Chapter 11

"Will Mrs. Myers be all right?" Derek asked. He was riding in the passenger seat of the Myers nineteen eighty-six Dodge conversion van.

"Ah hell Derek, Francine's been wanting a week off from the two of us for a while," Earl chuckled, "she'll be fine."

It was nearly two in the morning as the van made it's way through greater San Bernardino County. They were taking the long way to the interstate. It was time for Derek to get out of California and Earl was always a fan of road trips.

"You'll have to let your hair grow out," Earl said, "be too easy to find you with a shaved head."

"Right, so what's the plan Earl?" Derek was always more comfortable calling Earl by his first name then he was calling Mrs. Myers by hers, he never wanted to seem to familiar with any woman.

The plan was put together after Derek called Earl from the locker room at Cypress Community College. Earl told Derek to hold tight and he went into action. The first course of action called for was a wardrobe change. This meant changing from TV watching blue boxers and old stained California Angels tee shirt to "Action Stations Earl". This was also everyday Earl. This uniform consisted of artic pattern (blue, white and gray splotches) camouflage pants held of by what he called his official church suspenders[43]. He topped this off with a black tee shirt and a red Angels mesh cap that sat never sat right on his head, and the brim

---

[43] Earl made this joke about his suspenders because they were bright red. Very few people who heard this joke knew that Earl was a Satanist, so, consequently, very few people got the joke. Those who knew Earl through the church wish they didn't.

was almost perfectly level. His choice of
shoes was limited by his fallen arches so he
put on his New Balance sneakers.

The second course of action dictated
that Earl march over to the recliner
adjacent to the telephone. He dug up he old
phone book and began making some calls. He
called in favors, a lot of favors, swallowed
some pride and spoke to people he hadn't
seen in nearly twenty years.

"Well the first thing we're going to do
is stop at the Denny's in Baker and have
some pancakes," Earl smiled. This was his
favorite part of any road trip, which was
without a doubt, eating.

"Are we really going to have time for
breakfast?" Derek sounded confused. He knew
of Earl's love affair with pancakes and
crappy diners but this really wasn't the
time.

"Of course we will," Earl defended
himself, "granted, those Jack-Booted, no
offense, thugs are most likely looking for
this sweet machine but waiting at the
Denny's in Baker is the friend of a guy I
know."

"So?" Derek growled.

"So, the friend is going to take my van
and hide it out in Henderson and he's going
to leave us a van to drive off in."

"Okay, where we going from there?"

"We'll know when we get there my boy,"
Earl patted the steering wheel.

"Great fucking plan Earl, some friend
of a guy you know, fucking great, and why
does it have to be a van?"

"I like vans," Earl offered. He really
didn't have a good answer for Derek. They
drove in silence for almost forty-five
minutes.

"How about some tunes?" Earl finally
broke the silence. It wasn't so much that he

No distance left to run...

was asking, he was going to put something on
the stereo and if Derek didn't like it he
could always rip the tape deck from the
dashboard and throw it out the window. Derek
simply nodded which was validation enough
for Earl. In Earl's van you had a choice of
two formats; eight track of stereo cassette.
Earl had steadfastly refused to buy into
compact discs, until such time as the greedy
bastard car corporations joined with those
lying sack of shit record companies and
whittle things down to one format that Earl
could carry in his pocket. But they never
did answer his letters.

Earl's musical library was also
severely limited. Martin Denny, Don Ho, the
Samoan children's choir, all parts of Earl's
lifelong desire to live in the South Seas.

The dream was squashed when dreams
should be. It was May of nineteen sixty-six
and a vibrant and a mostly unfettered Earl
and a charming and handsome Francine were on
their honeymoon. "It was just before the
world would try to break me," Earl would
add to the story with a hollow sort of
laughter. The honeymoon didn't go according
to plan. Francine broke her ankle getting
off the plane and the airline lost Earls
bag. "Who's needs clothes on a honeymoon,"
Earl would chuckle, "lucky thing for me, I
hadn't lost my paperback," he'd finish with
a dismissive shrug.

Their first dinner in Honolulu
Francine discovered that she was allergic to
Poi and she developed a rash from head to
toe. Earl took it in stride, sure he'd have
to wear the same suit for the duration of
the trip and Francine was scaly and
irritated and he could nothing for her
except get her the occasional tomato juice.
Earl was in Paradise. And it rained in
paradise for the next five days. So Earl

No distance left to run…

helped Francine brush up on cribbage and he took the couples hula dance class that they'd signed up for as part of the honeymoon package. He had a teriyaki, pineapple burger for lunch everyday and shark steak for dinner. Earl enjoyed what he could of island life.

On the sixth day, when it was time to go, it had stopped raining and Francine's rash had cleared up, Earls bag even showed up. She would eventually forgive Earl and Hawaii and they would never set foot off the mainland again. Earl would dedicate his den to his lost Polynesian dream and that's pretty much where it would stay.

No distance left to run...

Chapter 12

The sun would be coming up in the next two hours. Derek was fighting off sleep as Earl drove. Martin Denny's The Quiet Village had been playing for the last thirty miles; the music was helping put Derek to sleep.

Baker and the rendezvous Denny's were on the horizon and Earl couldn't wait. He wasn't allowed out for pancakes these days. A trip to Denny's would entail a short stack, three cups of coffee, two sides of sausage links and some pie, maybe a whole pie.

"Hey Derek, we're there," Earl said slapping Derek on the arm as they pulled into the parking lot.

It wasn't quite light yet; the sun was just peaking over the horizon. When they stepped out of the van there was a startling heat, somewhere near ninety degrees[44].

Earl and Derek made their way inside. There wasn't another van in the parking lot and this was a concern to Earl. He was told that there would be a van. Instead there were two highway patrol cars, a station wagon and a Cadillac but no van.

"Who are we looking for?" Derek asked as they stepped inside. Earl didn't answer right away. He'd become fixated by the crane toy machine that sat in the lobby. He fished out some change and popped it in the coin slot and began working the joystick control. He was trying to win some ridiculous purple bear. There was nothing special to the bear; Earl liked to have props for his analogies. It was his intention to set the bear on

---

[44] Baker at noon would hover near a hundred twenty or more. There were few trees, few permanent structures aside from a gas station with a Taco Hut in the lobby and Denny's. Baker had the appearance of a desert outpost that could vanish at a moments notice.

No distance left to run...

fire, but Derek's question made him lose his
train of thought. The bear dropped from the
weak crane arm, Earl sighed and turned to
scan the restaurant. The restaurant itself
had few patrons and fewer staff even
considering the location and the time.

    The cook and the waitress were having a
friendly conversation that would result in
the same decision as the past several
hundred such friendly conversations which
was this; No, she wouldn't sleep with him,
have a three way with him and his wife or
his girlfriend nor could he watch her with
her girlfriend since she was obviously a
dyke because she wouldn't sleep with him.

    The four highway patrolmen were busy
telling stories about drunks and half naked
women they'd pulled over on the interstate.

    Sitting at the counter was the only
paying customer. His name was Roman Alistair
Franco. He was sixty-two. He was thumbing
his way through the Las Vegas Morning Star.
The front page of which had a decades old
mug shot of an angrier Derek Wall with a
headline that read; The Monster Returns.
Roman was trying to find the sports section
so he could check the baseball news. As a
younger man Roman played first base for the
Montreal Spirit and later for the Kinsetsu
Buffalo. He was still in what he considered
playing shape though more recently he had
started to look like the aging body builder
that he was, flabby skin hanging off of
taunt muscles. Roman never married, had two
sons, one estranged, one dead and a
daughter.

    Roman had sweat beading on his
forehead. He was generally a sweaty man. His
hair was slicked back, giving it a helmet
look. It was dyed black with very deliberate
streaks of gray at his temples for a more
dignified appearance.

No distance left to run...

In front of Roman, on the counter, was a black and white shake and an untouched plate of sourdough toast.

Earl spotted Roman, a man he hadn't seen or spoken to in twenty years or so and he suddenly wished that it wasn't Roman Franco.

Twenty years prior Roman had orchestrated the excommunication of Earl and Francine. This had affected Earl much more then Francine. Earl missed the social aspects of the Church of Satan, the interfaith intramural softball that Earl himself had organized, the pancake breakfasts. So many thing that he hadn't done in twenty years.

"Something wrong Earl?" Derek asked. Earl cleared his throat and sighed. He looked at Derek; he had so much potential he shouldn't get involved with Roman's bunch. Earl then turned to Roman, who was still engrossed in the paper and hadn't noticed them yet. Earl began to remember all of the revenge fantasies he'd imagined for Roman, but given the unfortunate realistic nature of Earl's imagination all the revenge fantasies resulted in Earl getting pummeled into a gooey pile by a bloodied nose, but triumphant Roman. Earl had a low opinion of himself as a fighter.

"Roman," Earl said as he approached. Roman looked away from his paper. His eyes widened with pleasure but little surprise.

"Earl you old briny bastard, how the heck are you?" Roman bellowed in his most jovial baritone. He sounded like a pleasant old radio announcer. Earl suppressed his cringe, he hadn't been called briny in some time. Roman was still making a dig at Earls Polynesian dream after twenty years.

"How's, oh what's her name?" Roman pretended not to remember.

No distance left to run…

"Francine," Earl said, "she's fine, lost a toe to diabetes, but other then that....."

"That's terrible," Roman interrupted with a hint of mockery. He paused to take a very exaggerated bit of his toast.

"Aren't we a little pressed for time Roman?" Earl asked.

"Earl, you of all people should know that there is always time for pancakes," Roman laughed and reached out to pat Earl's belly, "why, you're a living example of a life devoted to breakfast and related pastries." Roman laughed again and continued to pat Earls belly vigorously.

"What about my van? What about the police?" Earl asked in almost a whisper. He didn't want to draw the attention of the nearby highway patrolmen.

"What about your van indeed," Roman gestured to the now empty parking spot that the van once occupied, "there is no need to whisper, the highway patrol over there is with me, and your van is sitting on the back of a flatbed tow truck headed for an abandoned ranch outside of Henderson."

"But what about the plan?" Earl seemed worried; he didn't like to deviate from any plan.

"Circumstances changed, as did the plan," Roman paused for more toast, "ever so slightly though, now have a seat and lets eat."

No distance left to run...

No distance left to run…

Chapter 13

Morning in the desert can be harsh,
quite and blinding. Little to see except for
horizon and highway. Earl, Derek and their
new driver Roman Franco were rambling down
the highway at a near Sunday drive pace.
They were traveling in Roman's ninety-two
Cadillac El Dorado. It was a dark red, a
custom crimson paint job, not the factory
maroon. The red crimson velour interior
would have made for uncomfortable seating
had Roman not insisted on keeping the
windows closed so he could keep the interior
temperature at sixty-two.

"I know what you're thinking Earl,"
Roman finally said breaking the talk radio
silence. Earl wasn't entirely sure how to
respond to this. "You're thinking, why
velour and not leather right?"

"Well now that you mentioned it, I was
going to say something," Earl stammered his
lie. Really, he didn't give a shit what he
was sitting on he was worried about
Francine. Earl wasn't there to wake her up,
she was going to sleep through the alarm and
miss her game shows. The she was really
going to be pissed. She might even notice
that Earl and Derek were gone.

"You remember my fondness for skinny-
dipping don't you?" Roman asked this with a
disturbingly impish smile.

"No sir, I can't say that I do," Earl
had wanted to say that the image of a wet,
naked Roman would have been burned
permanently into his retinas, thereby
rendering him legally blind. But seeing as
how they were past the official middle of
nowhere portion of the desert he kept his
mouth shut. "Now that you mention it I seem

No distance left to run...

to recall something about it, skinny-
dipping, sort of familiar. "

"Yes well, you see, leather seats would
only burn my skin, " Roman smiled again, "If
we weren't in such a hurry I'd show you just
how bad I got burned before I switched from
leather to the rich velour you're now
sitting on. "

Derek was in the backseat. He wasn't
sleeping, though he really was tired enough
to sleep, he stayed back and listened and
tried to conserve his energy.

"So that's the young man who has
brought you back to us, eh Earl, " Roman
said as he glanced up in his rearview
mirror.

"What's the change to the plan Mr.
Franco? " Derek asked as he leaned forward.
This trip was trying his patience. He was
uncomfortable in any car. It wasn't so much
his size, which didn't help matters much, as
it was an untreated neurosis of
claustrophobia. Buses and really big trucks
were his preferred method of travel; he did
like motorcycles, but could never afford
one.

"Is he always so direct? " Roman said
addressing only Earl.

"Most of the time, he is learning to be
more patient with people though, " Earl
defended.

"Bah! " Roman answered.

"So what is the plan? " Earl pried.

"First let me tell you what we learned
as it did dictate our course of action, "
Roman cleared his throat, "now some of this
might be quite shocking, you don't shock
easy do you Derek? " Roman chided.

"No sir, " Derek answered.

"Of course you don't, a baby exploded
in your arms and you still had the piece of

No distance left to run...

mind to get away, May of nineteen fifty-
seven the N.S.A., National Security not your
old pals the National Socialists Derek,
secretly arrested an old German doctor in
Argentina and seized his lab and research.
This quack, Mengele I believe his name was,
was trying to clone your old buddy Hitler,
who knows maybe he was close to succeeding
with that," Roman laughed. He often laughed
at inappropriate times and most often when
there was no humorous content to a given
situation[45].

"What does any of that have to do with
us?" Earl asked.

"I'm getting to that Earl," Roman
snarled, he wasn't fond of Earl, name
calling surely wasn't far off, "the N.S.A.
wanted to make the perfect killer only with
Dr. Mengele's advances it was still fairly
limited and suffered some miserable
failures."

"How miserable?" Derek asked.

"Well many believe that these United
States entered the Vietnam conflict for the
very purpose of testing a battalion of
chemically enhanced, modified soldiers."

"Okay, so..." Earl started before Roman
cut him off.

"Nineteen sixty-eight The N.S.A.
stepped in and seized the lab of a Japanese
lady scientists," this caused Roman to
pause and nudge Earl as if to silently say a
lady scientist, what a laugh indeed, "this
lady doctor had actually been able to code

---

[45] Roman Franco would also apply laughter in numerous other
ways; whenever he didn't understand something, when he was
uncomfortable with a situation, after repeating something
said to him followed by "you don't know?" But the most
unsettling laughter came from Romans private time. This
consisted of watching snuff films, in the dark, with the
sound off whilst listening to Lithuanian pop music.

No distance left to run...

and isolate D.N.A. and had created a near
completely inorganic life."

"Near complete inorganic what?" Derek
said.

"Yes my boy, truly a miracle of
science, you see her limitation was having
to start with an unfertilized egg, that she
cleaned of its trace D.N.A.."

"That's just crazy talk Roman," Earl
said.

"Is it?" Roman sneered, "or is it the
sanest ever talk falling on crazy ears?"

"No it really sounds like crazy talk,"
Derek added.

"So be it," Roman sounded wounded,
"but somewhere between Argentina and Tokyo
Rose two astounding things happened a plague
was created and they may have created a new
race of men."

"What evidence do you have of this?"
Earl asked as Derek leaned in.

"Well until our young friends bus
incident, we had stories which reminds me
Earl we have a surprise waiting for you at
the compound." Reflexively Earl choked back
his almost immediate disgust at the idea of
a Roman Franco special surprise. Roman had
always been a man with a stunted and
severely limited sense of humor[46]. Earl's
mouth felt dry, his eyes twitched recalling
the Roman surprise of boiling sea salt and
vinegar to the face.

"Really, a surprise Roman, you really
shouldn't have gone to all the trouble,"
Earl finally managed.

"Well maybe surprise isn't the right
way of saying it as it is really more of a
reunion, though probably still a surprise,

---

[46] Past Roman Franco surprises included; replacing Earls
standard Aqua Velva with gasoline, substituting goat urine
for orange juice at numerous pancake breakfasts, throwing
non-lethal, however, still venomous creatures at Earl
during many California Church of Satan wilderness retreats.

No distance left to run...

so there you have it, it's a surprise
reunion," Roman seemed rather pleased with
that and himself, he felt he knew best what
his surprises meant to people[47].

Derek was still doing the math on the
story spun by Roman about the N.S.A.,
Argentina and Hitler clones, well not so
much clones anymore.

"Wait a minute, "Derek shouted, "what
the hell do you want me for." This shouting
caught Roman off guard. He slammed down on
the brakes, Earl and more so his gut slammed
into the dashboard breaking open the glove
compartment and spewing forth it's contents.
Earl in turn spewed forth his contents onto
the dashboard. The car fish tailed to a stop
and fell silent. Roman boiled, Earl wiped
his mouth with his tee shirt and Derek
rubbed his forehead. Roman shook with anger
as he turned to speak to Derek.

"Damnation you have got to know right
now..." Roman froze with that last word as
he saw what was on his blazer sleeve. He let
out a high-pitched scream when he determined
it to be Earl's rejected breakfast covering
a good portion a three hundred dollar
blazer. Roman burst from the vehicle. Earl
and Derek exchanged a glance as Roman cursed
and danced on the pavement trying to shake
loose the vomit.

"Earl you boob!" He screamed, "this
was a Botany 500 why I...," Roman spotted
more on his pant legs, "you fat filthy son
of a BITCH, you got it all over my trousers,
Lucifer's great red beard," Roman then
stripped down to his underpants[48]. Roman

---

[47] When Roman Franco Jr. shot himself, the note he left was
a detailed thirty-page report about his father and the
variety of surprises he shared with people. The report
included pictures, diagrams and testimonials.
[48] Roman's underpants were a blue snakeskin pattern of a
cut best described as a banana hammock and typically
favored by male strippers. Worse yet this style only
supplied a thin strip of material between his cheeks. This

No distance left to run…

marched in his skimpy underpants, sock
garters and orthopedic oxfords to the
passenger side door.

"What do you suppose he wants?" Earl
chuckled, trying to make light of the
situation. Roman seemed ready to burst with
anger, or as Earl pointed out to Derek, into
some kind of interpretive dance routine.
Roman was not amused and very flustered
until he realized that the doors weren't
locked. This was something that had escaped
Earl and Derek as they sat in relative
comfort mocking Roman.

"You silly bastards," Roman shouted,
"you are certainly having a jolly good
laugh at good old Roman. This started to
make Earl nervous. Roman was on to
something. He tried to tell Derek to get
something to use as a weapon but it was too
late.

Roman swung the passenger door open.

"Get out of the Cadillac, both of you!"
He demanded. Earl obliged and scrambled out
of the car. Derek struggled but couldn't get
hid door open no matter how frantically he
yanked on the handle. He threw himself back,
raised his feet and kicked the window out.

"Great, now I'll never get the tint
right for that window," Roman said as he
absentmindedly rubbed his ass.

"Excuse me?" Derek said from the broken
glass frame of the door.

"The tint was custom made for me and my
Cadillac," Roman found what he'd been
searching for, examined it for a minute by
rubbing it between his fingers, "not really
something I can replace all lickety split
sonny," Roman finished. He looked up at

---

did, however, enable anyone unfortunate to see this to
satisfy even the faintest of curios as to what a flabby old
bodybuilders buttocks looked like, which was similar to
gray sacks of ground beef.

No distance left to run...

Derek and the broken window and twitched his
nose as if to indicate he smelled something
he didn't really like. Derek was doing his
best to contain his anger, which entailed
flexing his neck muscles and taking a series
of deep breathes. Earl busied himself by
rolling pieces of tinted glass under his
shoes. Roman slapped his partial dentures up
and down against the roof of his mouth with
his tongue. He stared at Earl with a mixture
of disgust, sadness and proactive thought.
He looked at Derek, though still annoyed
with him, he was also hopeful. Derek was the
future, their future.

"Right," Roman bellowed breaking the
silence, "Earl, take off your shirt."

"What?" Earl stammered.

"It's covered in vomit Earl, take it
off," Roman stopped a moment to adjust his
sock garters, "Derek clear the back seat of
broken glass," He grabbed the door handle
and opened Derek's door, "perhaps I should
have mentioned it sooner but the child
safety locks were on."

No distance left to run...

No distance left to run…

Part IV
In the field where I
died.
Chapter 1

    John Parker stood on the mainland for
the first time in about a year. The world
George spoke of was beginning to take shape.
There was a very noticeable and heavy
military presence and this was only Ventura.
Gun towers seems to be as common as palm
trees and there was no visible civilian
traffic. Much of this was clear from where
John got off the last boat. He walked up the
jetty and into a plaza where he was the only
person not in a uniform. Though, no one paid
him too much attention as he made his way
through.

    It all had an atmosphere of an
occupation not civil defense. Recruitment
posters adorned the windows of most of the
closed shops in the plaza. Most of the
soldiers congregated at or around the patio
of the 'Papaya Plantation', which in it's
time had been a marginally popular and
mildly successful bar and grill. Most of its
customers had been guests of the hotel that
it shared a plaza with. The house specialty
was teriyaki chicken on a bed of sticky
rice.

    At the moment John was walking by it
was the Officers club and the hotel was
their headquarters. All unnecessary along
the West coast had been prohibited for
several months so there was no need to
maintain the tourist trade here.

    It was a sea of olive green and khaki
but the pimply-faced teenagers appeared to
out number the grizzled veterans.

    One of the young shoulders did take
notice of John. His name was Kevin Bishop
and he was nineteen. There was almost a

In the field where I died.

pleasant round quality to his face that was always betrayed by his permanent sneer and unibrow. He was in the process (and had been for the last two months) of trying to grow a moustache to give him a more authoritative look. Through a combination of dumb luck and a general lack of qualified personnel Kevin had risen quickly through the ranks to the point that after last month battle for Los Angeles[49] Kevin was given a field promotion to second lieutenant. Kevin had R.O.T.C. experience in high school so he felt he was entitled to an officer's position and power.

He didn't like the look of John, "he must be a civilian," Kevin mumbled to himself. Kevin was often looking for ways to improve his command status among his subordinates, many of whom he was still trying to impress.

"Hey you," he shouted from his table, "it's past curfew!"

"Excuse me?" John replied without impeding his step.

Kevin stumbled out of his chair. This drew a few looks from the surrounding tables, but it really wasn't anything new, Kevin was always trying to throw his weight around. John stood still while Kevin scrambled to his feet.

"Gonna' need to see your papers," he said, straightening out his uniform.

"Papers, right," John sighed, "afraid you've lost me there pal."

"Hey asshole I ain't your pal," Kevin said as he drew his pistol, "I'm an officer

---

[49] The Battle for Los Angeles was somewhat unexpected though to call it a battle is, at the very least a gross exaggeration. At best it was a quasi-pathetic skirmish between the Skinhead army under the command of the Shogun of Van Nuys, the Mexican Mafia of North Hollywood, the Vietnamese Thug Cult of Northridge and the Russian Jewish gangsters from Tarzana. At the time the San Fernando Valley (where the battle really took place) was considered an acceptable loss so only troops from the National Guard and the Army Reserve were sent in to deal with the factions that refused to evacuate. It did not go well.

In the field where I died.

and I need to see your papers." Kevin liked
to hold his gun, especially when he got to
point it at something other then a mirror.

"Well all I have is this," John offered
his N.S.A. id. Kevin squinted, he didn't
know what he was looking at, nor did he
really care. It wasn't a set of travel
papers and that meant Kevin detain without
question, or was it shoot without question,
Kevin was having a tough time thinking about
this. Only as recently as yesterday Kevin
had been introduced to Martinis, which he
reasoned was the only suitable drink for an
officer, even if it did taste like rubbing
alcohol. He was on his fourth of the evening
when John walked up.

"You C.O. is expecting me," John
interrupted.

"IS that so," Kevin snatched away
John's id and swayed, "Special Agent
Parker, John D."

"Yes it is," John answered, "and time
is really a factor here so I'd really
appreciate it if we could move this public
power trip along okay." John finished with
a quick smile.

"Really?" Kevin was using his best
sneer.

"Yes, really," John answered.
Kevin started to turn his back only to swing
and try to pistol whip John, which in turn,
John caught before it hit him. "Cut that
out," John said. Kevin was furious. That
move had worked in everyone of Kevin's
carefully mapped out scenarios. John still
had a hold of Kevin's pistol hand. Kevin was
sweating, 'alcohol and anger were sabotaging
his awesomeness' this third person thought
made Kevin want to cry. He often referred to
himself in the third person. John didn't
give him a chance to try anything else. He

In the field where I died.

wrapped his hand around Kevin's wrist and twisted his arm around his back.

"Now I don't like to use threats to get things done corporal so how about a demonstration?"

"That's second lieutenant, what?" Kevin whined. John smiled and tightened his grip on Kevin's wrist until there was a muffled crack. Kevin screamed out.

"You fucking broke my wrist," he cried.

"So can we go see your commanding officer now?" John asked in a pleasant tone.

"Fuck you man, I'm in pain here," Kevin blubbered. John sighed then he gripped Kevin's forearm and bicep and bent his elbow in the opposite direction breaking it with a loader snap. Kevin fell to the ground, vomited from the pain and bawled even louder.

"See what you made me do," John said. It was then that John took notice that there wasn't a soldier who appeared to be under thirty in sight. Another soldier, a giant in camouflage pants and a green tee shirt, approached with clenched fists.

"You know, it takes only eighty pounds of pressure to break bones right?" John asked the approaching giant (who was six foot seven). This halted his stride long enough for him to seem confused.

"Now, before you make me break something else, pick up the lieutenant and lets go see you commander."

In the field where I died.

In the field where I died.

Chapter 2

The Commanders office was on the top
floor of the hotel. It occupied the entire
top floor, which was the rotating restaurant
and piano bar.

The company commander was himself a
recently promoted veteran of the Battle for
Los Angeles. Lieutenant Colonel Dennis
"Denny" Wall, he was a first cousin of
fugitive bus baby killer Derek Wall, but
that was all they had in common.

Denny had been comfortable as the c.o.
of a battalion of reserves and when the
senior officers went down in the battle
Denny leapt at the chance to take charge of
nine such battalions.

These battalions resembled the German
army toward the end of world war two. They
had been a mix of the very young and the old
reserves. Through a combination of desertion
and summery execution (due to disciplinary
problems ranging from looting to
insubordination) helped thin the ranks of
the older soldiers.

Denny was a micro-manager and tended
to insert himself in nearly every possible
aspect of his command and his troops. Right
down to the way they folded their socks and
the brand of apple juice they drank with
their lunch, Denny had his hands in it.
Denny worked best amongst chaos and at the
moment that was the state of his desk. He
was feverously making notes about tomorrow's
mess hall menu when his phone began to buzz.

"What?" He hollered at the phone. He
didn't like interruptions and had and will
continue to issue numerous memos on the
matter.

"Sir, Lt. Bishop and a corporal are
bringing a civilian to see you," the voice
on the phone said.

In the field where I died.

"Why in the name of all holy hell is
that fuckwit bothering me with a curfew
issue?" Denny screamed, though he really
couldn't wait for a reply, "we've had this
discussion so many times before GODDAMMIT,
Bishop used to be able to make up his own
mind."

"Yes sir but...," the voice tried to
cut in.

"That boy hasn't been the same since I
caught him naked in front of his computer,"
Denny shook his head, "he was all sweaty
and shaking his baby wand around, some sort
of chat room thing, you know."

"Afraid I don't sir," the voice
answered.

"Really?"

"Yes sir, lost interest in that sort of
thing when I was fourteen."

"Right, right me too, a little too
much information I suppose, on Bishop I
mean."

"Quite a bit too much yes sir."

"Right, well what is the civilian
matter all about then?"

"Well it seemed rather important sir,
the civilian broke both bishops elbow and
wrist on his right arm."

"Sweet Mississippi Jesus really?"

"Yes sir."

"Well send them up immediately," Denny
sounded excited.

"They're already on their way sir."

"Very good then."

With that said the elevator bell chimed.
Denny scrambled to load his pistol. The
elevator doors opened to the host stand of
the restaurant with a half-pipe partition
separating it from the rest of the room. The
host stand was one of the few places that
had remained untouched since the army
commandeered the facility. There was still a

In the field where I died.

partially full waiting list, dusty menus and
a bowl of thin chocolate mints.

    Kevin spilled out of the elevator, he
was crying and clutching his broken arm.
    "Bishop, pull yourself together," Denny
barked.
    "But he broke my arm," he blubbered
with a snot bubble coming out of his nose.
    "But he broke my arm, SIR," Denny
called back.
Denny tucked his pistol into his belt and
went up to the half pipe to see the
civilian. The corporal followed Bishop out.
He had an arm behind his back and he was
grimacing in pain. John was behind the
corporal holding his arm by his thumb with
the understanding that if the corporal tried
anything else John would break his thumb
off.
    "And what's your ailment soldier?"
Denny said to the corporal.
    "He broke my thumb, SIR," the corporal
answered.
    "Really, why?"
    "Because I tried to hit him on the way
up, SIR."
    Denny looked over the corporal. He was
massive in comparison to most any other man.
He appeared to be ready to burst from his
uniform at any moment. Denny then carefully
looked behind the corporal. John didn't seem
to be straining himself in any way. He had
the corporal subdued, he hadn't broken a
sweat and he was holding a duffle bag. John
looked like a Mormon missionary. He was
wearing black pants, black shoes a white
shirt and tie and a gray hooded track
jacket.
    "So you're some sort of ass kicking
Mormon kung fu master?" Denny asked John.

                In the field where I died.

"I make no claims to any religious affiliation, come to think of, my family was Catholic, but I can't say we ever went to church," John said.

"Okay, so you're some sort of ass kicking quitter who is also a kung fu master?" Denny said this revealing some of his very limited imagination. Denny had always feared that one day shadowy forces would send a kung fu master to bring him down, so he made a habit of questioning every new person in this fashion. He gripped the side of the partition that he was still partly covered by, bracing for an angry, possibly kung fu response.

"What? no, no stop that," John said, "hang on a second admiral," John handed the corporal his thumb back, "all right, hold onto this, and if you think about hitting me again break it," John moved away leaving the corporal to ponder his hands, "Special Agent Parker with the N.S.A.," he said flashing his id.

"The National Socialists, I didn't know you guys were so organized, say did you know my cousin he was a Nazi?.... and it's Lieutenant Colonel not admiral."

"Right-o, I'm with the National Security Agency," John smiled.

"Really, national security, can't say I'm familiar with you guys," Denny said.

"Well, think of us this way we're the FBI, the CIA and Internal Affairs with more authority and broader jurisdiction," John finished and scratched his nose.

"Really, that's fantastic," Denny said nervously, "say, Agent Parker, would you mind holding on for a moment?"

"Be my pleasure Colonel," John smiled. Denny dashed around to his desk and grabbed the phone. John, meanwhile, pulled out his Baretta, chambered a round and returned it

to its holster. Kevin Bishop stopped his
wailing and looked at John with terror in
his as to what the pistol might mean. The
corporal was still bewildered by his own
thumb resting in his massive hands.

    "What can you tell me about the
N.S.A.?" Denny whispered into the phone.
    "National Socialists or National
Security?"
    "The security one."
    "Seriously?" The voice sounded
concerned.
    "Is that bad?" Denny really wasn't
sure[50].
    "Did you see an id?"
    "Yes, wait, he didn't have a badge,
shouldn't he have a badge?"
    "No."
    "Well fine, what am I suppose to do?"
    "Get him whatever he needs and get him
out of here as quickly as possible."
    "Why is that so important?" Denny
asked.
    "These sort of agents are never this
visible unless someone is seriously
fucked," the voice paused, "and if we're
very lucky it's not one of us."
    "Right, so whatever he needs?"
    "Yes, and hurry."

---

[50] For the last fifteen years Lt. Colonel Wall had been
employed at Whyte Hardware on Saticoy and Woodlake in
Canoga Park, in the northeast San Fernando Valley. Whyte
Hardware was on of the last of the family run stores in the
area. Even though he wasn't family, he was regarded as such
and had been promoted to assistant manager shortly before
the declaration of Marshall Law. As for his military
service, one weekend a month and two weeks a year he was
Captain Wall and got to play army. That was until Marshall
Law blanketed Los Angeles, Orange and San Diego County and
all local reserve units were called into active duty. He
has only been Lt. Colonel Wall for the past few months
after the regular army company commander (as well as the
greater majority of commissioned officers) fell in the
Battle for Los Angeles.

In the field where I died.

Chapter 3

The floor overhead creaked and little particles of dust and light fell through the cracks. Seth stared up at the floor above him. He heard a pair of muffled voices, laughing and talking. One of the voices was high pitched and it was a voice that caused Seth to shiver with disgust. He shuffled about the basement floor trying to follow the movement above him. In his hand he held his Glock 17 with an extended cartridge expanding the capacity to thirty rounds. He wasn't going to bother attaching the silencer; he wanted them to know what was coming.

"Seth, are you down here?" Francesca called out from the top of the stairs. He didn't answer; hoping that she goes away and he could finish the job. He heard the door close and the intrusive light disappear. He licked his lips and returned his focus to the task at hand.

In the room above music started to play. "Dammit," Seth muttered, "Sergio Mendes and Brazil 67 that means they're going to have sex." Seth raised his Glock to fire.

"Seth?" Francesca called out. He leapt back; he did not like being caught off guard.

"Fuck!" He whispered, "don't sneak up on me like that, I thought you'd gone to the kitchen."

"No, what are you doing down here anyway?"

"Paul's up there with Serenity and they're having sex again."

"Ewww," Francesca, "you were just going to shoot them weren't you?"

"Yes I was," Seth answered defiantly.

In the field where I died.

"Bad Seth, " Francesca smacked him upside the head, "Serenity is pretty nasty. "

"Yeah, she smells, " Seth smiled while he rubbed his head.

"And she has an old lady butt, " she added.

For a moment, Seth raised his hopes; only this time he didn't dare act on anything he was feeling. He knew Francesca would enjoy nothing more then to crush him again and again as if she were a machine designed for that very purpose. Francesca saw that he was drifting off to Seth fantasyland and she slapped him on the face, hard enough to knock loose a few more teeth.

"Snap out of it Fucktard, " she whispered, "if we're going to do anything, we do it quick, and by the book. "

In the field where I died.

Chapter 4

John reached the edge of Las Virgenes County roughly four hours after meeting with Major Wall in Ventura. Las Virgenes was the last county before Los Angeles. A week before it served as the point of entry for the quarantined areas that now reached as far south as the Mexican border and as far inland as Baker and the Mohave Desert.

Las Virgenes was deserted as John drove through. The posts further south were believed to be abandoned though there had been little effort to verify this as it was deemed a waste of manpower and dwindling resources. In fact, the only post that was still manned was Baker, which like Ventura had served as an evacuation (and detention) site for Southern California.

John rode down the 101 freeway in a red Vespa that had been appropriated for the sake of not knowing the potential congestion on the roads. No one was really sure what he'd face; there's been no southern-based transport and sparse communication over the last week. The Vespa was the optimal choice, it was fuel efficient and allowed easy maneuverability and John had always wanted a Vespa so it was nearly perfect. Had he not crashed the red Vespa it would have been perfect.

John and his Vespa made it as far as the Las Virgenes Canyon exit of the freeway. Beyond that it was blocked by an eighteen wheeler filled in with metal dumpsters in any open space. Only the freeway off ramp was clear. There was an unmanned guard tower and a sign that read; Mont Blanc military base, and an arrow that pointed left. Las Virgenes Canyon would be the only way into the valley. John was at least familiar with the road from a brief stint delivering

In the field where I died.

pizzas and from there it would be straight
down Ventura. John headed through the exit.
Mont Blanc was once a very exclusive gated
community; John remembered them well for the
poor tips he'd always receive there.

The air was still, quiet, the Santa Ana
winds were not blowing. He had to assume
that Mont Blanc was unmanned. He continued
up the road that would lead him to the
valley. Out of habit he stopped at the
intersection where the Las Virgenes
municipal services building sat. John looked
over. The building had been used as a
makeshift mortuary. A shabby sign was still
draped over the doors. The sign read; all
dead in here.

John put his Vespa in gear and pushed
up the hill into the valley.

In the field where I died.

Chapter 5

"So what are we going to do?" Seth
paced about the kitchen floor. Francesca sat
calmly at the kitchen table sipping a Dr.
Pepper, a red folder in front of her.

"Has Paul seen the emergency
Directives?" She asked.

"He threw them at me once," Seth
stopped his pacing and leaned on the
counter.

"Has he ever read them?"

"Paul hates reading as much as I do."

"So it would be a safe bet to say that
he has not seen Sub-section Seven?"

"What's in there?" Seth asked.

**National Security Agency Emergency
Directives Biohazardous/Viral agents
Sub-section 7
Introduction**

- In the event that you, the field
  agent, have received Section 7, the
  governing body in conjunction with
  the N.S.A. have made the
  determination that eighty to ninety
  percent of the population will be
  considered (or have already become)
  acceptable losses to a Biohazardous
  or Viral agent(s). Subsequently, any
  effort to contain, cure or otherwise
  control said agent(s) will be
  suspended indefinitely. It is now the
  duty of the field agent to employ
  what measures may be deemed necessary
  to ensure a future for the American
  way of life in what ever form that
  might take.
- As discussed in Sub-section 4 any
  available 'sleeper' agents should be

In the field where I died.

activated, as additional help will
most certainly be required.
- Of higher importance at this stage
  should be discretionary population
  control. Selective or restrictive
  breeding should be employed.
  Additionally any and all available
  birth control options must be
  employed for any recreational;
  encounters.

"Is that all?" Seth asked. He hadn't
really been listening, He'd realized by the
time Francesca said the words 'National' and
'Security' that from where he was standing
he could see right down her shirt. He
smiled; it was a Jack-o-Lantern smile thanks
to Francesca. "Ya' know, Paul doesn't use
any of the condoms I bought." It was a
clumsy, unsettling proposition, which
Francesca would ignore. She'd already
ignored so many.
     "Doesn't like condoms?" She said.
     "Nope," Seth leered.
     "And has Serenity been tested?"
     "Paul would have given me the test to
process," Seth answered.
     "Good," Francesca placed her gun on the
table and smiled, "lets take care of this
right now."

In the field where I died.

In the field where I died.

Chapter 6

A post coital cigarette was what Paul wanted right now. It was a ritual that Paul had maintained since his first conquest at the age of fourteen. It was the same conquest that paid for college. Whenever Paul had needed something at that time, he would casually make threats to tell the woman's husband. To call Paul a great lothario would not be quite accurate. A charming sociopath would be much closer to the mark. Paul had discovered, from an age earlier then his first sexual conquest, that he could charm, manipulate of influence nearly any person or situation to his benefit.

From the age of fourteen through to the present (age forty-one) Paul has had seven hundred thirty-three sexual encounters, each one accurately documented, categorized and stored on his laptop. This was done partly to avoid repeat encounters (and family of encounters, unless that was also required). Five hundred were simply for pleasure; the remaining two hundred and thirty-three were performed in the line of duty. Seven hundred and thirty-two woman, one man (Colleen Ferguson's husband).

Serenity was different; Paul would reason to himself, this was about the future.

Paul sat next to her on the bed. Out of habit he had started getting dressed again, though he had managed to stop at his socks and boxer shorts (Hanes stretch cotton, medium). Serenity was naked and curled in a yoga position that was supposed to be conducive to fertilization post coitous. She had an orange glow to her leathery skin from too much unprotected sun bathing. Her hair

In the field where I died.

was in dreads, a coiffure trend most commonly associated with not bathing, which in Serenity's case was the truth. Her breasts weren't sagging, though in a standing position they would be.

"Paul, I'm hungry," she said. Her speech pattern tended to be slow, peppered with awkward pauses and whining. It was beginning to grate on Paul's nerves.

"Well I could run down to Safeway and get us a late lunch," he answered, swallowing most of his contempt.

"SAFEWAY!, I don't eat food from a grocery store," she sprang into a sitting, breast sagging position, "you're so stupid sometime Paul, I don't throw money at a giant corporation like that, I want an organic burrito from the Organic Mexican place on third."

"The one across the river?" Paul scanned his bedside table for bus fare to throw at her; there wasn't any, "how about Subway then?"

"Do they even sell food at Subway?" Serenity was indignant, though she had forgotten to say 'Vegetarian' food.

"Yes dear they sell sandwiches, remember we had some last week."

Serenity wouldn't have a chance to answer. Seth and Francesca burst through the door, pistols in hand. Paul had heard the creaking of the floorboards in front of the door and rolled to where his gun should have been but it was gone.

"Move back to the bed Paul," Francesca ordered, "the Sig Sauer behind your headboard is gone as well as your Colt." Paul got up from the floor; he kept his eyes on Francesca and Seth and moved back to the bed.

"What the fuck?" Serenity had just caught on, "guns are like....worse then

In the field where I died.

cancer," she said in her most frantic tone,
"are you guys Paul's roommates?" Serenity
wouldn't let them answer, "I mean hate and
war were created by men, women are beautiful
and animals don't hate or have wars."

"Shut the fuck up honey pie," Paul
hissed.

"Nooo,....but I mean you know what they
do to chickens, they get pumped full of
hormones so they get fat and then we eat
them, I mean you guys not me, and then we
get all those chemicals in our blood and we
get all fat, ya' know, you guys, not me,
cause I don't eat chicken."

"Is she begging for her life?" Seth
could only ask hopefully.

"No, I think they call that shock,"
Francesca pulled the hammer back on her gun.

"You don't have to do this Fran," Paul
said calmly, "she's just an idiot, she
doesn't matter."

"Breeding with an untested civilian,
yes I do have to do this Paul, you fucked
up."

"Humans are so bad for the environment,
I mean we are all so wasteful, you guys, not
me," Serenity turned to Paul, "hey, don't
call me stupid right in front of me."

"I didn't call you stupid honey pie, I
called you an idiot, because you're my
idiot." Paul caressed her cheek, "Francesca
you know as well as I do that those tests
are unreliable."

"Wait, you tested yourself," Francesca
began, "you tested yourself and you tested
positive."

"It was going to be another three weeks
before I would have shown any symptoms
which, by default, means that my D.N.A.
hasn't been altered yet."

"That's hypothetical bullshit Paul,"
Francesca snapped.

In the field where I died.

"Yeah," Seth snorted, it was all he'd been able to add to the conversation so far.

It had suddenly dawned on Serenity that she was going to die.

"You're not the Quality Control Inspector for the Oregon Home Soda Company are you?" She said.

"No such company honey pie," Paul smiled, "truth is I'm a hired gun, so to speak, like these two here, well more like Seth he and I are at least the same species."

"Shut up Paul," Francesca said.

"You may as well hear it Serenity, our Frannie, whom you have just met today and who is going to kill you by the by, our Fran, not only isn't she human, she's a collection of synthesized proteins and enzymes, programmed D.N.A.," Paul sneered.

"What?" Serenity said after a long pause.

"She's not Organic, she's the product of a big corporation," Paul kissed Serenity on the cheek.

"Oh, I'm so sorry," Serenity cooed, suddenly feeling pity for Francesca.

"Don't be, Frannie and all her brothers and sisters are the reason people are dying."

"Is that true?" Serenity turned to Francesca.

"Most of it," Francesca didn't take her aim off of Paul.

"Can't you just let us disappear Fran, let us live out whatever time we may have left somewhere you can forget about us?" Paul put on his best wounded dog expression.

"No," she said without blinking. She quickly fired four shots at Paul, one in each kneecap and one through each hand. Paul fell to the ground.

In the field where I died.

"Fuck all," he shouted, "doesn't matter how many times you've been shot it always feels like the first time." Serenity froze in shock; she'd never seen anyone shot before.

"So what is it going to be Paul?" Francesca asked.

"What the fuck are you on about now Fran?"

"You compromised our mission, you ignored protocol, you fucked a dirty hippie and you're infected, so do you want your Sig Sauer or your Colt?"

"Oh wait, this is the whole 'shoot me with my own gun if I'm ever infected' thing right?"

"That's the one," Francesca answered.

"Right, well I suppose the Colt would be the most appropriate, but could you do me a semi-big favor?"

"Could you make sure that Seth doesn't have sex with the bodies when you're done?"

"No necrophilia for Seth, got it."

"You can't do this, killing people is so wrong," Serenity had finally snapped out of her shock.

"Seth, take care of Serenity," Francesca said.

"Cool, wait to you mean," Seth did a series of pelvic thrusts with accompanying grunts and 'oh yeah, take it bitch's', "or do you mean," Seth pointed a finger gun at Serenity and made shooting noise with plenty of spray.

"The one that involves your gun, not the one that involves your penis fucktard," she answered. It seemed to make sense enough to Seth. He raised his Glock and leveled Serenity with the entire seventeen rounds. "I didn't want to miss," Seth snorted with a bit of victorious chuckle.

In the field where I died.

"Right, well goodbye Paul," Francesca pulled back the hammer on Paul's Colt.

"Could you do me one last favor Francesca?" Paul propped himself up by his elbows.

"What now?"

"Take care of the Colt for me," he smiled.

"Paul, you know I hate long goodbye," she said and fired a single shot through Paul's left eye.

"Seth call site cleanup."

"There's a crew for that?"

"Always has been, you call them and I'll get us some lunch."

In the field where I died.

Chapter 7

John Parker's Vespa made it all the
way from Ventura only to die on him in front
of Jim Friendly's. He laughed to himself.
The last time he was here George told him
that there was five years left. Now there
was little better then three and a half left
and it looked as though the world had
already come to an end for the San Fernando
Valley. Ventura Blvd. was never this empty.
There wasn't a sign of life anywhere John
looked. Trash and abandoned cars lined the
streets. Hanging on every other street lamp
was what must have been some sort of
criminal of a collapsed society. They all
wore signs around their necks with varying
numbers painted on them. On the lamp in
front of Jim Friendly's was what must have
been Julie from the tattoo parlor. She had a
twenty on her sign.

John was aware of some movement behind
in what was once Jim Friendly's. There had
been an apparent raid on the place, which
was made obvious by the burned car that sat
in the dining room.

"Probably just a rat," John said. The
silence bothered him a little. The movement
got louder and a warmth drew closer. John
snapped open the release of his shoulder
holster.

"Hey, is someone out there?" A voice
called out from inside. "This is private
property GODDAMMIT!" John drew his pistol
and pulled back on the hammer. "I heard
that you Motherfucker," the voice got
closer till it became a hazy silhouette,
"don't think for a moment that I don't know
what a cocking pistol sounds like," the
silhouette stumbled about what remained of
Jim Friendly's, "SON OF A SEA WHORE, I

In the field where I died.

stubbed my toe." John wanted to laugh,
though he kept his aim on the movement.
"I'm unarmed you pig fucking bastard, so
don't shoot me when I come out." The
silhouette emerged as a gangly old man with
a long beard and potbelly. He was very tan,
almost red and he wore a brown corduroy loin
cloth and dirty fuzzy blue bedroom slippers.

"Good day to you young fella', I am
Jim, shogun of the Western Valley," Jim
said trying his hand at sweeping, dramatic
movements. He was failing.

"Okay Jim, do you have a car I might be
able to barrow?" John asked.

"Why would you need a silly bastard
thing like that for?"

"I have an appointment about twenty
blocks north of here," John answered.

"I see," Jim said. He began scratching
the back of his head which he'd already
scratched raw. It was bare and pink, with
many visible scabs. Occasionally he would
stop and examine his fingers, then flick the
pieces of skin off. John could only offer a
raised eyebrow to this.

"Don't look at me like that you smug
son of a whore, you know as well as I do
that the only Grand Shogun approved method
to keep the fever at bay is to wear an
upside-down, open jar of fleas on the back
of your head at least once a week."

"I'm afraid I missed that one," John
said.

"You're one of those 'Americans' aren't
ya'?" Jim said accusingly.

"You know what's really sad about that,
it's that you really care about that," John
holstered his gun, "as it stands I'm not an
American really."

"Good enough, but you did miss the shit
storm that took place here right?"

"Yes I did," John said.

In the field where I died.

"Okay then, that would make you..., "
Jim paused to flip through a maroon colored
textbook. He had to cross reference several
pages till he was somewhat more satisfied.
"So are you Good, Evil, Chaotic, Neutral,
Lawful, Lawful good..., " Jim rambled
through his list before John rolled his eyes
and interrupted him.

"What does this tell you Jim?" John
tossed his N.S.A. id onto Jim's book.

"Sweet juggling Christ," he tossed it
back, "that makes you Neutral Evil," Jim's
expression changed from excitement to
melancholy in a near instant, "You know
something Agent Parker, can I call you Agent
Parker?"

"John, you can call me John."

"John for this new society of ours I was
supposed to pick a deity from the book to
worship and curse and so on," he started to
scratch his beard and his scalp with a
renewed vigor, "before the shit storm hit
us, long time ago, I was suppose to be a
nice Jewish boy from Patterson but GODDAMMIT
I love bacon, pepperoni pizza and crazy
Mormon broads."

"What's the matter with pepperoni
pizza?" John asked.

"Same thing that's wrong with a cheese
burger, you're not supposed to mix dairy
which represents life, with meat which
represents death, certainly not kosher,"
Jim focused his scratching to the patch of
beard underneath his chin.

"I guess that makes sense," John said.

"A bit off the mark, but what religion
did you abandon?"

"My family was Catholic."

"Oh you poor bastard," Jim replied.

"Oh I survived, it was all just muscle
memory and singing anyway."

In the field where I died.

"Well sure and you had good crackers and awesome wine," Jim huffed, "all we ever got was Moses, Abraham, matzo and Manichewitz."

"That shit sucks."

"Hell yes it does John," Jim beat his own chest like Tarzan he felt so strong about it.

"So what does this have to do with religion from that book of yours?"

"Oh sorry, right, anyway I had to choose a religion, a fake god to believe in when I couldn't believe in the 'God' that my family worshipped. Jim shook his head and looked down at the book.

The title of the book was "Grand Shogun Cory's Dungeon Masters guide to the new order and society." Jim showed the cover to John.

"Shogun Cory?" John asked not really wanting the answer.

"Yeah, of Van Nuys, he rules over the entire Eastern Valley," Jim kicked at the ground, "he has his own army and almost any survivor is his slave."

"Except you," John said.

"That's a damn right, I declared myself Shogun of the Western Valley but with no army I had no way to protect my people so now it's just a big scrap yard."

"So where's the border?"

"Reseda Blvd, a big wall of garbage extends from the Ronald Regan freeway to the foothills of the mountains near Shogun Cory's complex."

"So if I were here to 'rescue' someone...," John began.

"Then you'd have to go see Shogun Cory, if they were left in the valley they're probably his slaves by now."

In the field where I died.

In the field where I died.

Chapter 8

     Las Vegas had become home to many of the displaced residents of San Diego and Los Angeles County. The city itself hasn't changed much since the virus hit the coast. There were immediate threats of Marshall law, wage and price freezes, though these remained only threats as the new Las Vegas population reached nearly four million in three weeks. So the civilian population had a near eighty-five to one advantage over the available military personnel.

     Las Vegas had become the west coast safe city. Numerous N.S.A. teams were scattered about the Northwest and several of the plains states. Their purpose was to eliminate potential problems for when the cities were to be evacuated to Nevada. This was part of the screening process to keep Nevada clear. There were three established points of entry for the state. One was Baker, CA (which was closed but still minimally staffed), St. George, Utah and Taos, New Mexico. These were the only test sights in North America for the virus. A positive testing resulted in detainment, under the guise of treatment, and a subsequent termination. It was determined that killing the host was the only effective means of containing the virus. This method was keeping Nevada ninety-eight percent clear of new infection. The remaining two percent had already resided in the state before the emergency[51].

---

[51] The National Security Agency hit teams located in the other states were all utilizing localized lists containing any registered sex offenders, convicted felons (robbery, assault, manslaughter, spousal battery). Additionally, political dissidents were included among the undesirables, including but not limited all media formats offering a dissenting voice (i.e. internet blogs, public access cable, street protesters). This was not to stack the deck, so to speak. The government has always (and will always be) an a-political form; a vile body taking whatever shape was needed or required. This systematic elimination process was

Jason Parker didn't care about any of this, even if he knew he probably wouldn't care unless he was told to. What did matter was that he was almost out of scotch. He had plenty in his wet bar, but his glass was nearly empty. The scotch might have been a bigger problem but Jason was getting a foot massage. It was a damn good one too. Jason had only recently added an elaborate to his nightly variety show. The dance sequences were reaching the absurd running time of two hours. It was the worst combination of awkward dancing, large breast (Jason's manboobs and the all girl dance squad) late nineteen fifties musical staging and uninspired Bossanova cover tunes that lacked soul in equal parts from the original version and the Bossanova sound that they had failed to capture. It didn't seem to matter; it was the most popular addition to the show since 'White bikini chocolate pudding fight'. Jason felt like the king of a new realm, though he was more of a lucky jester at best. He could do no wrong. Then again neither could his massage therapist. Shirley was fantastic and she was actually certified to touch people. She'd had to explain this to Jason, that she was not a masseuse who tended to work in "Jack Shacks" in bad neighborhoods. No Shirley was a massage therapist. Shirley, like much of Jason's personal staff was female, under thirty and single. Jason, in what was practically ritual, made routine, poor attempts to flirt with them all. He never seriously pursued any of them, however, there was his work to consider. For Jason, his staff was his Family and he was very protective of his ladies. The staff

---

not political, it was more to insure public safety, foster unity and to a greater extent control the populace at large by removing threats both external and internal.

In the field where I died.

included; Shirley, the massage therapist from Spokane, WA, Collette, the wardrobe mistress from San Diego, CA, Annabeth, the valet from Brea, CA and Shannon, the staff coordinator from Studio City, CA. Jason was a shoulder to cry on, a confidant much like a trusted girlfriend.

Jason slurped the last watery ounce of scotch from his glass and again swirled the ice around as if to signal to an unseen force that it was time for a refill. Jason was fully capable of getting up and pouring another glass for himself, but that might interrupt Shirley who at the moment was working both her thumbs up and down the arch of Jason's left foot.

"Hey Shirl, where's Annabeth?" Jason asked.

"I think she has gas," Shirley replied. She usually spoke in a kind of nasal monotone that made her sound like she had a cold. She usually assumed that people were just assholes and usually she was right because they'd be staring at her butt. She suffered from what she only referred to as W.G.G.B. (White Girl Ghetto Booty) disorder.

Annabeth didn't have gas that was just the assumption Shirley made whenever Annabeth disappeared from a room. Annabeth was a petite young woman easily passing for fourteen despite being twenty-five. She usually excused herself to smoke a cigarette. Smoking was something that Jason would never tolerate. Before John got shot Jason would only go so far putting up with smoking as to cough loudly and claim to be dying. The police detective (baring a striking resemblance to George) who came to the door the night John was shot explained to Jason that it was in an argument with a homeless person over cigarettes. It was a highly improbable tale, though Jason

In the field where I died.

believed it. He would step up his campaign
against smoking; this would include carrying
a pair of scissors for slicing cigarettes
and an air horn to blast in smoker's ears
after he cut the cigarette. Jason would have
to resort to scowling when they took away
his air horn and scissors. There was only so
much anyone was willing to take from Jason.

Annabeth was midway through her third
cigarette as she paced the length of the
hallway in front of the elevators. She
wanted to quit this job; she didn't like
Jason or most of the other girls. She had a
degree in Physics from San Diego State and
she wasn't even a glorified personal
assistant she was a fucking valet. But the
show was the best paying job around. It was
federally funded and had great health care.

"Fuck!" She screamed. She would have
had more but the elevator chimed. "Who the
fuck is this," she said. It couldn't be
room service that would have gone through
her; anything else would have gone through
Shannon. Now, each of the girls were
supposed to carry their walkie-talkie cell
phones. Shannon and Annabeth were the only
ones who really bothered with it. Annabeth
retrieved hers; she hated it and had named
it Carlos[52].

"Shannon, are you available?" She
called into Carlos.

"Go ahead Annabeth," Shannon replied.

"Who's on their way up here?"

"Need to know basis," Shannon replied.

"Well I fucking need to know asshole
'Need to know' is getting off the
elevator."

---

[52] Carlos McDermott was a boy she dated in College. He was
gay but dated girls to please his mother. He was an
intrusive nuisance much like the phone.

In the field where I died.

"So this is a smoking floor?" A voice called from behind Annabeth. This caused her to leap forward with a yelp.

"You fucking scared the shit out of me," Annabeth turned to the voice, "and who the fuck are you?"

"I'm not the issue here Annabeth," the man said with a cloud of smoke. Annabeth straightened out her clothing.

"Who you are is the fucking issue buddy," Annabeth said in her best saccharine voice, "so unless you show me something that...." Before she could finish the man produced his credentials.

"Agent Dekalb," Annabeth began, "National Security Agency?"

"So you're familiar with us?"

"Only enough to know that you're not a cryptologist."

"Cryptology is only a fraction of what we do, it's what we want people to know, there isn't really the time to cover everything that the N.S.A. encompasses."

"Then what can I do for you Agent Dekalb?"

"Well for starters you can call me George."

"Okay, George what else do you need?" George smiled, back in the day he would have shot her when he got off the elevator. Not really a personal issue but more of one of time management. This compromise would have bothered George more so had Annabeth not been a healthy American woman and he of all people knew how rare that was going to be.

"Now you can give me a light," George took a cigarette out of his pack, "then you can take me to see your boss." Annabeth leaned forward to light the cigarette.

"Pardon me George," she began as she stepped back, "but what could National Security want with Jason Parker?"

In the field where I died.

"Well believe it or not it has to do with a matter of National Security," George smiled.

"Bullshit, he's a moron George how could he be trusted with a matter of National Security?"

"Well," George began.

"Have you missed the ukulele hour?" Annabeth interrupted. "I mean come on, the song "Fatties", "Bumblebee please let me be" you most have heard "A Song for Johnnie" that's the most atrocious[53]." Annabeth seemed more then slightly out of sorts over the quality of these songs.

"I'm well aware of Mr. Parkers 'talents' Annabeth," George said.

"You're going to use Jason for something aren't you?"

"Hmm, if you figure out anymore I may have to kill you," George broke into an unsettling laugh which caused Annabeth to laugh albeit nervously until George's laughing stopped abruptly.

"You're not kidding are you George?" Annabeth said. George smiled weakly. In the past he'd never hesitate to eliminate any potential or actualized problem. He took a pull on his cigarette and sighed.

"Motherfucker."

"It's part of my job," he replied.

"Right, lets go see the moron," Annabeth said.

---

[53] These three songs were among the worst of offenders in Jason Parkers ukulele repertoire. Highlights of these include; from "Fatties" *Fatties/eat all my ice cream, Fatties/break all my wicker chairs* the song closes with *Fatties/need love too* followed up by a fifteen-minute ukulele solo. "A song for Johnnie" was Jason's most personal composition since "Who ate my Ding-Dongs?" "A Song for Johnnie" was a forty-five minute mini opera featuring a coral tit for tat argument about smoking, a progressive jazz backbeat, and the screechy falsetto of Jason himself.

In the field where I died.

Chapter 9

"I like tacos," Jim sang at the top of his lungs, "I like tacos, lots of lettuce, lots of hot sauce." Jim then leapt into the taco dance. Which, like all of Jim's dances was a combination of the 'Chicken Dance' and 'The Electric Slide'. This had been the first such dance that John had witnessed. The 'Taco Dance' relied heavily on the chicken dance.

"True story John, funny too, first taco I ever had was at this taco shack in one of the flyovers, it was a Taco John's taco shack."

"Really?" John was trying to find the funny part.

"Yes sir, true story," Jim's dance had mutated into a shuffle as he and John walked along.

"So Jim there wasn't another funny part to that story was there?"

"Well of course, ya see there was this young gal behind the counter, probably seventeen, pretty easy on the eyes, smallish boobage, great heart shaped hiney." Jim paused to spin with his shuffle. John stopped to tie his shoe and shake his head.

"Well, ya' see, she was a fan, like a big fan saving up for a tattoo of me that she was going to put on her inner...anyway I always said and I quote myself 'If there's grass on the infield, LETS PLAY BALL."

"If that means what it sounds like that's pretty appalling Jim."

"Hey don't be jealous just cause you never got any rock star quality ass."

"You were a rock star?"

"I was better then that," Jim paused his shuffle and thrust himself into the pose

In the field where I died.

that adorned the cover of his first album,
The Defiant Desperado[54],
"ring any bells?"

"Afraid not Jim," John shrugged,
"though it's kind of familiar."

"Um, okay, what about this, *I was
walking down the street/with the country at
my feet/when Jesus came along/said 'son you
got it wrong'/ain't no way to play my song*,
anything?"

"Nothing, sorry," John said.
Jim shrugged and began dancing a modified
electric slide. "You really don't know?"
Jim said with a nudge.

"Yeah, no I still don't Jim sorry," He
said.

"GODDAMMIT," Jim cried, "what, have
you been in a coma or something?"

"Fairly recently actually."

"Honest injun[55]? Shit, is your long term
memory affected?"

"Not that I've been able to tell Jim,"
John replied, "only been up and about for
around five months or so."

"Well, that's forgivable John," Jim
said as he slide into a more thoughtful
shuffle, "you're not pulling my leg right,
you were really in a coma?"

"Yes sir, got shot in the back of the
head," John turned to show his scar covered
by short hair, "you see that?"

---

[54] The pose was used on four out of five Jim Friendly
albums, it was better known as "the Sassy Pirate". The
pose required feet at double shoulder width, hands on hips,
chest thrust out, head cocked defiantly toward the sun.
Only the wildly unpopular double Christmas Album featured a
different pose. It was Jim lying naked on his stomach on a
bear rug. "A Christmas Postcard/Chanukah in a Disco
beat/Happy Holidays from James included the songs "Lox on
the dance floor", "Jesus the mad cat space Jew from beyond
the stars" and the entire twelve song set from the last
Jim Friendly concert in the Clover lounge at Fitzgerald's
Casino in Reno. Heckling included.
[55] Feather, not dot.

In the field where I died.

"Damn, that's a good one," Jim was amazed, it wasn't terribly visible but it was pretty ugly, "who shot ya'?"

"A friend of mine," John laughed.

"What's funny about that?"

"Honestly I don't know everything is almost like he said it would be, and I guess I should really be scared but I don't really feel anything."

"Don't think I can't help you with that John," Jim sounded disappointed.

"Wouldn't be fair of me to ask Jim, though there really isn't anything that would help."

"Well, okay then, you'll let me know if there is though right?"

"Of course I will."

"Right, I should properly introduce myself, before the shitstorm and all the bullshit that's followed I was known as Jim Friendly the country singer."

"Oh my brother Jason was a big fan of yours."

"Jason, as in Jason Parker, he's your brother?" Jim was excited.

"You know him?" John raised an eyebrow.

"Hell John he has the only show on the air right now, live from Vegas."

"I heard about it, I guess people really are starved for entertainment these days."

"Oh hell yes they are, they don't know an entertainment giant like me is still around," Jim snorted and thrust his chest out.

"That is really a terrible shame Jim," John added dryly.

"Say you don't think you could hook a crazy old Jew up do ya'?"

"Considering that I haven't seen Jason in nearly two years, when I finish up, sure why not."

In the field where I died.

"Fantastic," Jim broke into a faster shuffle and hopped back and forth.

In the field where I died.

Chapter 10

      Philip Carl Streckler had reached the
bottom. It did take fifty-seven years but
every aspect of his life had bottomed out.
And now he was drinking well bourbon. It's
not that Phil was a booze snob, he was a
Jack Daniel loyalist though even that seemed
too expensive right about now. Kentucky
Cellar was his drink of choice now. It was
an undistinguished Kentucky style whiskey
bourbon that was fifty-four percent alcohol
by volume and has a very distinct after
taste of dirt. It was bottled in Detroit and
fortunately for most was only available on
the North Eastern most states (it wasn't
even for sale in Michigan).

      Phil was in Burlington, Vermont, which
sat four hours (if you drove like Phil) from
the border. Many Americans were trying to
flea to Canada figuring that since there had
been few reports of virus related outbreaks
it would be safe up there. This was not a
virus that was exclusive to America. So many
Canadians were running further north (an
actual recommendation from the Royal
Military research laboratory which had
reasoned with little data and no hard
evidence that the virus could not survive
the colder it got). Safe harbor seeking
Americans would find abandoned cities,
scavengers and pockets of militia and piles
of bodies. The border had been sealed the
week Phil got to Burlington. He was never
going to make it to the border anyway, his
eighty-eight Corsica died in front of his
current residence, the South Burlington
Holiday Inn. The Corsica dieing was nothing
unexpected to Phil or to anyone who'd ever
driven the model. Phil bought the car for
two hundred dollars (which had not been easy
to scrap together) from an old co-worker

In the field where I died.

who'd lost an eye in a fight during a job interview.

Phil finished his glass with a painful gulp. His eyes watered from the vileness of the liquor.

"Ho there barkeep," he bellowed, "one more please," he shook hi empty glass.

"You sure about that?" The bartender wasn't so concerned about Phil being drunk as she was serving anyone Kentucky Cellar.

"Never been more sure of anything in my life before Caroline," he declared.

"That's really kind of sad James," Caroline answered as she poured another.

"Yeah it is, isn't it," he added. Phil's real troubles began fifteen years earlier. He was the assistant manager of a Montgomery Wards auto shop in Brea, CA and unbeknownst to Phil he was neither a good husband nor father. Phil had worked hard his whole life, but he was really nothing beyond tired and brake pads. He hadn't even purchased a new suit since a spring of seventy-eight trip to Sears. His wife Meredith and their son Phil Jr. left about a week before Montgomery Wards closed their Brea location. Phil had to scramble to get what he could, there wasn't much call for unimaginative middle management Sears hired him on part time, but it was back to sales. A couple of years in Sears closed up a better majority of their auto shops and Phil was left to rely on what was left in the retirement nest egg (half having already gone to Meredith and Phil Jr.)

So there he was, fifteen years gone, sitting in the Patriot lounge with three hundred dollars left to his name and a buffalo wing sauce stain on the lapel of his burnt orange three piece suit. He had to tell people about the stain, it was his conversation starter; the stain was the same

In the field where I died.

color as the suit. Phil choked back another sip of Kentucky Cellar. He was beginning to feel warm all over.

"Say isn't it about time for the Jason Parker show?" Phil said trying not to sound drunk.

"Yeah it is, lucky son of a bitch," Caroline replied.

"Tell me about it," Phil sighed.

In the field where I died.

Chapter 11

The curtain was closed the theatre was full. It was a sea of whispers; talk of a special announcement for tonight's broadcast. The stage crew raced about making final changes to pieces going with the assumption that tonight's announcement didn't cause a riot. Jason was a wreck. So much had come to light the previous evening, so much horrible truth. He was so wrapped up in his new opening monologue he didn't even scold Annabeth for smoking like a chimney next to him.

"Jason honey, calm down GODDAMMIT," Shannon barked as she approached, "Collette come here and check Jason's tux."

"You don't know how big an announcement this is Shan'," Jason said, "how do I look Col'?"

"Bow tie undone, shoe look good, but Jason the show hasn't even started yet and you're sweating like a whore in church."

"Is it that noticeable?" Jason sounded worried.

"Well you're already soaked through your shirt," Collette answered.

"Should I change?" Jason said.

"No we go straight into the wild west number after your monologue."

"Right, you're right," Jason answered.

"What the fuck Jay'?" Shannon slapped him on the arm.

"This is bigger then anything we've ever done...," Jason began.

"You said that," Collette interrupted, "so tell us what it is."

"It's about his brother," Shirley spoke up.

"Shut it Shir'," Jason snapped.

"Which brother?" Collette asked ignoring Jason.

In the field where I died.

"Yeah, the jerk or the dead one?" Annabeth added.

"Which ones which?" Shirley asked.

"Ladies please," Jason pleaded.

"I think Johnnie was the jerk and Jeremy's the dead one," Collette offered.

"No that's not it," Shannon growled.

"Yeah it's the other way around," Annabeth corrected.

"Really?" Collette said.

"Yeah, I mean the ukulele thing is called "A Song for Johnnie not for Jeremy," Annabeth said with a heavy amount of disgust.

"Okay so we've established that John's the dead one and Jeremy's the jerk," Collette said to Shirley.

"Good, now Shirley what's the big secret?" Shannon said.

"John, the dead one, isn't really dead," Shirley began.

"Shut your mouth Shirley please," Jason finally interrupted.

"Jay this isn't really about you hun," Shannon said with her arm placed firmly on his shoulder.

"But John's my brother," Jason whined.

"No really, this isn't about you," Annabeth said.

"You were saying, Shirley," Collette prodded.

"Okay so the dead one, who's not really dead he's like some rogue assassin or something."

"Or something?" Collette said.

"Yeah I really wasn't listening," Shirley held up her hands in a defensive, hamster like pose.

"Jesus motherfucking Christ Shirley what were you doing?" Annabeth screamed as she lit another cigarette.

In the field where I died.

"I was painting my finger nails with liquid paper, see," Shirley held her fingers out, but maintained her defensive posture.

"What the fuck did you do that for?" Collette shrieked.

"Because it's fun to scratch off," Shirley muttered.

"What's your problem?" Annabeth punched Shirley on the arm.

"Don't hit me," Shirley said.

"What did you say?" Annabeth snorted.

"Ehhh, I said don't hit me," Shirley said.

"No, before that," Shannon said.

"That it's fun tom scratch off," Shirley offered like a question.

While this was going on Jason had slipped off to the stage. The Luther Cole Four was warming up the audience, which was starting to take on the energy of a full prison cafeteria that was about to be denied food.

"Hey buddy," Jason said as he approached the bandstand.

"You look like shit tonight Jay," Luther said.

"Yeah, really?"

"Damn straight buddy," Luther set his guitar down and stretched, "me and the boys can play longer if you need more time."

"I appreciate that Luther, but this is something I gotta do, kind of like ripping the band aid off your sisters hairy leg, ya gotta move quick and hope you don't get smacked."

Luther chuckled. He was one of the few people on staff who really enjoyed Jason's brand of humor. Luther even helped Jason compose most of his original pieces.

In the field where I died.

"So what can I help you with?" Luther
asked.

"Could you play something on the somber
side?"

"You got it big Jay," Luther said.
Jason gave a quick smile and walked over to
the center of the stage. He raised his hand
to signal for a spotlight, which hit dead
center on the stage. When Jason was lit up
the audience exploded in wild applause.
Annabeth ran out from the shadows to bring
Jason his show scotch, which was ginger ale
on the rocks. Jason looked at the glass;
tonight he almost wished it was real scotch.
He looked out at the audience and set the
glass on a black bar stool next to him.

"Ladies and gentlemen, my friends, last
night I met a man who told me about the
past. Gave me a history lesson on some
pretty strange, science fiction sounding
stuff." The audience grumbled a bit, but
they were mostly silent. A man at a table in
the back coughed, but it was only because he
swallowed his vodka tonic wrong.

"He's dying out there," Collette said.
"I've seen him do worse," Annabeth
lamented.

"Okay, my baby brother John, who we all
thought was dead, he ain't dead, in fact
he's healthier then a lot of us," Jason
paused again. There was a confused muttering
going through the theatre. "And you'd think
I'd be happy, overjoyed to get my brother
back, well I was and then I wasn't. As it
turns out, he never really was my brother
and this is sort of where it gets
complicated," Jason paused tom sip on his
ginger ale.

In the field where I died.

"Shirley GODDAMMIT tell me you know
more about this?" Shannon demanded.

"Only that it has to do with the
plague," Shirley whined and held her liquid
paper finger nails up in defense.

"You see, my brother was never really
my brother at all. John Parker or whatever
he calls himself was part of a cold war
program, a Soviet fail-safe to infiltrate
manufactured sleeper agents on our shores.
And there are thousands of them. Sure my
folks thought they were saving a child from
communist clutches. They were misled; so
many patriotic parents were lied to. Well
our boys took some action and knocked out a
couple of hundred of them Russian
bastards," Jason paused again while a few
idiots in the back tries to start a
"U.S.A." chant. "Fella's wait a second,
there's more," Jason called out to them.
"They may have lost hundreds, but we're
losing thousands and those Russian bastards
are the ones responsible for the plague
spreading like it has. So we have to do our
part, we have to be vigilant if we're to
save this country of ours. I know what
you're thinking and no it won't be easy and
no there is no easy way to spot the
distinguishing features of the Russian
bastard children cause they don't really
have any. However, they are all between
twenty-five and thirty-five, they heal
quickly, they have fast reflexes and they
have no remorse for the things that they've
done." The spotlight disappeared for a
moment as a large screen lowered behind
Jason. A picture of John appeared on the
screen. "Very often in life we don't know
the face of our villains. This is no longer
true for my former brother John Parker. He
is the face of our enemy, the grandest of

In the field where I died.

our villains, he is our monster, this man I
called brother." Jason paused for his
trademark hand on heart, look to the
heavens. "No more is he my brother," Jason
shouted. All the stage lights went dark with
that statement echoing through the theatre.
"With your permission," Jason began from
the darkness, "we will now present you our
show.

In the field where I died.

Chapter 12

"Hey John," Jim whispered, "did you
ever see the first Dracula?"

"Probably a few times, when I was a
kid, why do you ask?"

"Do you remember that guy who was all
crazy and he ate flies?"

"Oh yeah, Reinfield right?" John said.

"That was pretty cool huh," Jim said as
he changed his shuffle to a Tai Chi/break
dance/karate chop walk.

"Yeah, wait what are you talking
about?"

It was near midnight on what used to be
Monday evening in a quiet neighborhood in
the valley. John Parker and Jim Friendly had
almost walked the entire length of Tampa
Avenue to bring themselves up to the back
end of Shogun Cory's compound. The entrance
was on Reseda and Jim thought it'd be to
heavily guarded for them to simply just walk
up and ask to see the slaves.

"Hold on a minute Jim," John threw his
bag on the ground and began digging through
it.

"What is it?" Jim asked

John glanced up for a moment and then back
to his bag from which he produced a slim
silver tube, though Jim couldn't see it too
clearly.

"What the hell is that?" Jim sounded
worried. John said nothing but he placed his
index finger to his lips to try to tell Jim
to be quite. "Was that a shushing?" Jim was
suddenly very animated, as if someone had
thrown a jar of bees into his loincloth,
"that was a silent shushing too GODDAMMIT
nobody shushes Jim friendly silent or

In the field where I died.

otherwise," Jim shouted and danced about. A motion in the surrounding brush became apparent to Jim. He turned to say something to John about it but froze when he saw John connecting the silver tube to a silver pistol. John locked eyes with Jim as he stood up and chambered a round.

"I was hoping that you would understand the need for quite," John paused to fire two shots to his immediate left without looking away from Jim, "I probably could have said something," John extended his arm to the right and fired twice more, "we've been followed for the last four blocks and I was trying to figure out if they numbered five or six." John finished by raising his gun at Jim.

"Wait a minute John was it five or six?" Jim was swept panic. He didn't like having weapons pointed at him in any threatening manner whatsoever. The last person, with any apparent intent of harm, had been Jim's third wife Sylvia and it had been a butchers knife not a gun and it had been pointed at his crotch not his head. Jim braced for the shot. He wasn't ready to die but he at least figured out that John would politely listen to him plead for his life and shoot him anyway, so why waste the time pleading. John was a nice guy right, Jim reasoned to himself, and he's got plenty to do and doesn't need a time burglar. John pulled back on the hammer and fired.

Jim was still braced for the end, though he certainly didn't feel dead.

"Did you shoot me John?"

"No."

"Did you miss?"

"No Jim I didn't miss," John answered.

"So you weren't trying to kill me?"

"No present reason to buddy," John smiled, "and I wasn't trying to kill you

In the field where I died.

either pal, " John walked up to Jim patting
on the shoulder as he passed. John was
approaching the black clad figure hat was
wailing behind Jim. Jim had been so
engrossed in his own demise that he'd been
oblivious to the fact that the first four
shots killed four figures that were
preparing to strike. These shots were not as
Jim had assumed which was to make sure that
the gun worked. The fifth shot, which Jim
was certain was his doom was intended to
maim but not kill the supposed leader of the
group.

"Stop your bawling or I'll make it
worse, " John said as he approached.

"What? " The leader cried out. John
kicked the leaders hand away from his
shoulder wound and pressed the heal of his
shoe into it.

"See what you made me do, " John said as
he grinded his heal in.

"He won't tell you anything John, " Jim
tried intervening, "he's a member of the
elite Black shirt guard of Shogun Cory. "

"I see that Jim, " John looked over the
leader. The leader was dressed in head to
toe black, black knee-high boots, black gun
belt with an ornamental black shoulder
strap. The leader had four black pips on his
collar which John could only assume was his
rank.

"So what's your name Sarge? " John
asked.

"It's Captain, " the leader whined,
"and that's none of your Goddamn business
ya piece of shit. "

"Really, piece of shit, uh huh, " John
fired two rounds off to the side, "open, "
he jammed the barrel of the gun in the
leaders mouth, the heat and the force
cracking several teeth in the process, "do
you feel that burn, taste fresh gunpowder? "

In the field where I died.

the leader nodded his head. "Good, now consider this the last threat you will ever get from me, do we have an understanding now?" John pulled back on the hammer of his of gun, "if you don't give me the assistance that I request, that will be the last taste you will ever know." John smiled, pushed the hammer back in place and took the gun out of the leaders mouth.

"Yates, Ian, Captain of the Black shirt guard," Ian shouted.

"Okay Captain Yates give your gun belt to Jim."

"What?" Ian had an unnatural love for his gun seldom had anyone else ever touched it.

"I don't like repeating myself Captain," John said.

"I get a gun!" Jim sounded excited, "give it here Cap'n." Jim leapt on Ian and began grabbing at the gun belt.

"Leggo ya old bastard," Ian cried and struggled.

"Captain I though we had an understanding here."

"Yes sir we do, it's just.." Ian stuttered.

"I don't want excuses here Captain, are we clear?"

"Yes sir," Ian replied.

"Jim, give the Captain some room," John looked him over for a moment, "while you're at it Jim go to the bushes and grab yourself a uniform, I've got an idea."

In the field where I died.

In the field where I died.

Chapter 13

Shogun Cory's compound was surprisingly well organized and more surprisingly well guarded. However, this utopia was on the verge of collapse. It had all started simply enough, with a mutual love for porno comics and Advanced Dungeons and Dragons that Cory and the only regular customer to his book store, Ian Yates shared. Promises of a new order and life regulated by dice came to bare in the Battle for Los Angeles. Cory and his rag tag, rowdy army of skinheads were given the larger chunk of the eastern valley. Originally the valley had been divided in to four pieces. Cory declared himself Shogun of the kingdom of Gondor (Northridge and Reseda); the North Hollywood Boyz had control of North Hollywood and the city of San Fernando. The Vietnamese Thug Cult had Chatsworth and surrounding neighborhoods, while a group of Russian mobsters took Woodland Hills and Canoga Park. Time, the virus and a few strategic strikes and (food supply tampering) took care of Russians and the Thugz. Jim Friendly as installed as the Shogun of the Western Valley after Cory and the North Hollywood Boyz took everything they wanted.

At the present moment grand Shogun Cory was posing for his official state portrait. By posing this meant sitting in front of his television covered in orange cheese puff dust. He was dressed only in a pair of blue paisley boxer shorts, which did little to hide anything at his current weight. Prior to the Battle for Los Angeles (which took place in Studio City, on the edge of the San Fernando Valley, so it was L.A. county, not the city) Cory was at the slightly more functional weight of two

In the field where I died.

hundred eighty pounds, still not quite
running shape, but still mobile[56]. Several
months of post victory both private and with
his skin head army had pushed Cory's weight
into the mid four hundreds thusly ending
both his mobility (with the exception of his
personal mobility scooter which was now a
modified A.T.V.) and his ability to wear
clothing not in muumuu form. This didn't
bother Cory too much, though he did miss his
uniform, which made him the highest
decorated officer in the history of the
armed forces. These were by no means
arbitrary awards for valor; they were
however based on his many Advanced Dungeons
and Dragons campaigns. Given his gaming
prowess and having been an eleventh level
wizard it seemed only natural to make
himself an eleven star general.

His uniform consisted of a crushed blue
velour tunic covered shoulder to shoulder
with all manner of medals and each was
adorned with comically large gold epaulets.
The pants were a horse-riding cut from the
same blue material as the tunic. The only
piece of his uniform that wasn't custom fit
to Cory (the slimmer Cory) was his gun belt.
It was an old western style fitted for a
pair of nickel-plated six shooters with
mother of pearl handles. The pistols were
the 'payment' Cory 'received' from Jim
friendly for the Western Valley. It was also
the only part of his uniform that Cory had
handy at the present. Normally the pistols
rested on the handlebars of Cory's scooter.
But with Captain Yates out on patrol the
threat of assassination was higher then
usual. This wasn't simple paranoia, which

---

[56] Notable exceptions to Cory's pre-war mobility were as
follows; uphill, downhill, stairs numbering greater than
twelve, large parking lots, large shopping malls, medium
sized convenience stores, and a multitude of other walking
related activities.

In the field where I died.

with Cory was true of anything he might
face; there were plots against Cory and his
rule, several in fact.

The court painter, a former associate
of arts professor at the local community
college Philippe St. Croix (St. Croix was
his mothers name from her second marriage,
legally he was still Philip Carl Streckler
Jr.) was counted among the conspirators. He
had plotted for many weeks; however, lacking
his father's conviction had not acted on any
plot thus far. What Phil Jr. did do was
absorb Cory's abuse, drink cheap wine and
cry himself to sleep. The picture that James
was painting was of a glorious, svelte but
noticeably muscular Cory in an orange (to
help highlight his eyes) version of his blue
uniform. The vanquished foe at Cory's feet
was beginning to resemble John Parker.

In the field where I died.

Chapter 14

"You'll never pass for one of us stupid old man," Captain Yates hissed at Jim.

Jim was dressed in a black uniform taken from one of the guards shot by John. The uniform didn't fit him well at all. Jim further weakened the ruse by clumsily chopping off his beard with a throwing knife he'd taken from the same guard he took the uniform from. All that had succeeded in doing was making Jim look older then his fifty-six years[57].

"Did you hear me old bastard you and the marksman are going to die," Yates growled.

"Wait a minute Captain," John said.

"What?" Yates responded. He didn't really have a chance to turn as John belted him across the back of the head. "What was that for?" He cried.

"Well, first off, you told Jim that he'd never pass for one of your guard which is pretty obvious if you see him up close anyway." Jim shrugged while both Yates and John looked him over. "And apparently that was some sort of death threat or maybe a death mark, you weren't really clear with it," John raised an eyebrow to the Captain.

---

[57] One of the key rules for Cory's new society was to deny citizenship to women over the age of forty-two. Forty-two, Cory reasoned was the official end of "hot chickness", which would make repopulation more of a chore then it should be. Truthfully, forty-two was a number Cory arrived at in the same manner her made all his decisions, which was by the roll of a die twenty (a twenty sided die employed by gamers like Cory). For the greater majority of his life Cory has been a slave to the roll of the dice. All new citizens to Cory's society were issued a bag of dice (die twenty, twelve, ten, percentile, six and four) to be used to conduct business, settle disputes and so forth. As for the male age for acceptable citizenship, that was a floating number. It was felt that it would better serve the community to determine a man's abilities and potential contributions then to restrict his potential admittance his standing against to an arbitrarily conceived number. Again, truthfully, this was due to Cory rolling a combined twenty-nine when attempting to define the male age. Cory was thirty-two at the time.

In the field where I died.

Yates was busy wiggling his dentures,
looking really annoyed.

"John I think it was more of an
implied or understood 'you're going to die'
sort of thing," Jim interrupted.

"Really, did you feel threatened when
Captain Yates spoke to you just then?" John
asked.

"To be honest John I didn't really
hear all of it the first time," Jim reached
under his pants and began vigorously
scratching his ass, "these pants are
chafing like a son of a bitch."

"Right, so, the first chance we have
we'll get you some boxers."

"Sounds like a plan," Jim continued
his scratching assault adding a second hand
as he went.

"All right good, moving on," John
turned to Yates, "okay Captain let's clear
the air between us."

"Just don't fucking touch me again,"
Yates said. John blinked his expression
remained blank. Palming his gun he cracked
Captain Yates in the mouth, sending Yates to
his knees, clutching his mouth.

"You see a marksman is usually a
distance shooter or perhaps even a big game
hunter."

"Now you've done it asshole, you broke
my fucking dentures," Yates snorted. John
slapped him across the face, "don't be
rude, let me finish," John buzzed, "you
see, I'm an engineered killer, a
manufactured monster..."

"What does that have to do with not
being a marksman?" Jim interrupted
maintaining his ass assault.

"Ya know Jim, you're right, that is a
little off topic," John laughed.

In the field where I died.

"Some pretty weird shit buddy," Jim answered, "the man-made killer thing I mean, that ain't the truth now is it?"

"It is yeah, synthetic from the ground up, so to speak," John answered.

"Are there more like you?" Jim asked.

"Something like three hundred left in America I've been told," John said.

"Are they all like you?" Captain Yates asked as he pulled his denture pieces out.

"Well, as I understand it of the twelve hundred of us that were designed only the first two generations shared similar D.N.A. sequences so technically speaking no there are no more like me specifically, but we were all designed for the same purpose and share many of the similar attributes."

"What?" Captain Yates said.

"So you're like a clone or something?" Jim pondered.

"Or something would be closer, there were only fifteen variations of my sequence."

"What, you're a clone!" Yates said.

"No a variation is more accurate," John corrected, "it was difficult enough creating one complete sequence that was wholly independent of organic proteins, so much so, that it was decidedly easier to copy and modify a successful sequence then to make every one from scratch." Jim looked bored. He'd even stopped scratching his ass he was so bored. Captain Yates looked horrified. He was still stuck on the idea that there was twelve hundred more like John.

"I know what you're thinking and yes not all the generations were trouble free, the earlier groups were far more susceptible to cancers, degenerative skeletal diseases and any manner of neurological and

In the field where I died.

psychological disorders you could think
of. "

"What the fuck! " Captain Yates sprayed.

"Well the nervous system is extremely
complex on it's own so try to imagine
designing and then making a working
synthetic model, correcting for your
mistakes each time, once you have the
solutions applying them is rather simple
apparently, " John lit a cigarette as he
finished.

"I'm not much of a Mr. science guy
John, but I don't think that that was what
he was asking, " Jim yawned.

"Yeah asshole, what the fuck are you
telling me all of that shit for? " Yates
brushed himself off with his uninjured arm.

"I guess I needed to share that with
someone, even a skinhead fucktard such as
yourself, I mean there's only so much I can
absorb without feeling a need to share it
with someone, " John exhaled, "but please
don't misunderstand me, you haven't suddenly
become more important to my mission, you're
the one who is going to die when we reach
your compound whether by my hand or by your
compatriots. "

"They respect me asshole, " Yates
defended.

"No they needed you, and that need
ceases when they see that you've brought me
into their home, " John said.

"John, what are you talking about? " Jim
asked.

"It's about eleven o'clock right, " John
said.

"Something like that pal, " Jim glanced
at his watch.

"So the Jason Parker Variety Show is
more then half over right? " john asked.

"Yeah, but what's so important about
that? "

In the field where I died.

"Let's go find out," John threw his
cigarette to the ground and grabbed Captain
Yates by the wounded arm, "come on Yates."

In the field where I died.

Chapter 15

"Gun Boy, where's my gun boy?" Cory squealed. He'd been screaming this at the top of his lungs for then last twenty minutes. The gun boy, who ranked only above the towel boy and the sponge bath boy but below the court painter as far as seniority went, was busy ignoring Cory. His name was Leonard Murray Franklin. His older brother was murdered the in the summer time but that didn't bother Lenny much (he preferred Len of Lenny to Leo which is what Cory always called him when he dignified people by using their names instead of their titles). Lenny's brother was an asshole and many people who knew him thought he got off easy bleeding to death after having his testicles ripped off like he did. Lenny thought this too; he even had a lot of trouble containing his laughter at Russell's funeral.

As Cory hollered Lenny was playing Ms. Pacman on one of the old tabletop machines while Philippe St. Croix watched. Lenny knew that Philippe was really just a Phil. They had decided to break into Cory's private liquor cabinet. Most of the private stock had been chosen for the look of the bottle of even the color it contained. In some cases it was the name that gained an elixir entry into Cory's cabinet. This led to there being several yellows, pinks and blues as well as many liquors named after Norse gods. Cory never drank; he had never been very good with drinking. He had once gotten the spins from drinking a lite beer, a story he no longer told when it became clear that usually blood donors and anemic children got the spins from lite beer not over weight men in their thirties. Cory made the decision that the manliest thing he could do would be

In the field where I died.

to have the manliest liquor cabinet around.
It was not.

Lenny and James were halfway through a
bottle of 'Loki's Potion', which was
Mango/Raspberry flavored schnapps. This was
the second bottle they'd opened which was
only evident by the fact that James was in
his underpants (white Jockey's, small also
known as 'tighty whities') having decided
that he didn't want to vomit all over his
uniform. Lenny thought that was a fine idea
and had gotten as far as one boot and his
gray uniform shirt before giving up to play
Ms. Pacman.

"Is that fat piece of shit still
yelling for me Phil?"

"I do believe he is," Phil answered
before taking another swig of schnapps,
"you know what I don't like about our
situation Lenny?"

"No, what would that be Phil?"

"Well, here we all are, waiting on the
undelivered promise of women and steak an
what did we end up with?" Phil's European
accent always slipped back to Orange County
when he drank. Lenny shrugged his shoulders,
he thought he knew the answer but he was
also too buzzed for any test taking. "What
we got Lenny, in exchange for our loyalties,
bologna, Wonder bread and a near total
sausage fest."

"Fucking sausages man," Lenny truly
didn't like sausages in any variety, "ah
man, my guy died, your turn Phil."

"Now don't get me wrong Lenny, I dig
hot babes just like the next man, but they
really aren't my thing ya' know?"

"Phil, you're like a brother only I
wouldn't laugh at your funeral so far be it
for me to judge where any dude would want to
stick his baby maker but mine is strictly

In the field where I died.

for chicks, hot or otherwise passable,
understand? "

     "Fair enough brother Lenny, " Phil sat
down, "you said it was my turn then? "
     "Indeed. "

In the field where I died.

Chapter 16

At the opening gates of the once exclusive community Mulholland Heights Jim Friendly staggered in, doing his best to act like an army guy which was somewhere between a swagger and a mosey. He was followed by Captain Yates who was being followed very closely by John Parker. John glanced to his right, then to his left. He counted at least eight more black shirts and he had to assume that they were armed.

"Jim, are you any good with a side arm?"

"John I am from New Jersey," Jim answered confidently.

"What do you mean?" John asked.

"He means he's a retarded old man who's going to get you both killed in here," Yates interrupted.

"Shut up Yates," John snapped.

"No he's pretty close to the mark, I fried more of my brain in the seventies," Jim paused for a moment and began kicking dirt around with his slipper.

"Was there more to that Jim?"

"Oh sorry, yeah no not really, I am a fair shot shooting that is."

"All the same lets try to avoid a fire fight at any cost," John said.

"You got it buddy," Jim gave a thumbs up and continued to kick at the dirt. At this point the inconsistencies of the trio had been spotted by one of the more and vigilant Black shirt guard. He pressed the button for the silent alarm, not to avoid alerting the trio but to ensure he received credit for corralling them. The alarm consisted of a single red flashing light

that had only flashed once before and
shortly after it was installed[58].

Cory saw the light flashing and was
swept with panic. Images of an evil and
sneering John Parker dancing on the ashes of
Cory's kingdom ran through his head. His
voice was horse from thirty minutes of
screaming for the gun boy who never did
arrive. Cory began to cry. It was an
uncontrollable sobbing that only another
paranoid, bloated ruler with a society on
the verge of a collapse could understand.

"I can't believe this is happening," he
sobbed. This surprised Cory. He had
convinced himself that he'd lost his voice.
This had been based on an article he'd read
in The Cyclops, which described the last
hours of a plague victim who screamed till
her vocals cords bleed out. The estimated
time for this was twenty-five minutes. Cory
took this to heart; he didn't read the rest
of the article that mentioned the actual
cause of death. No, Cory was far more
concerned with what he felt was an important
break through in screaming. Cory had
employed screaming for most of his life as
his last ditch effort to get his way and up
until now it had rarely failed him.

"Oh gun boy," Cory called out, his
voice still shaking, "Leo gosh darn you,
get yourself armed and get your monster
father self in here." Lenny staggered in
the room with a goofy smile on his face.
He'd thrown on a gun belt and was dragging
his rifle and an ammo belt behind him.
Philippe had decided to join in the game

---

[58] The perpetrator had been Lenny and it was his first and
last shift as perimeter watch leader for the Black shirt
guard. A pack of dogs had gotten into the compound on his
watch and Lenny was terrified of dogs. His older brother,
the deceased Russell Franklin, had trained the family pit
bull (Snuggles) to attack Lenny on a whistle command.
Lenny panicked and hit the alarm. He was demoted to a
position determined by a roll of Cory's die twenty. Lenny's
most egregious offense had been interrupting Porno Night.

In the field where I died.

play fun, equipping himself with every
weapon and belt he could hold. Somewhere in
the process he put his shoes back on and
took off his under wear.

"So what up fats?" Lenny tried to
steady himself by leaning on Cory's
shoulder, he was so very warm and foggy
headed.

"Leo, why are you touching me?" Cory
heaved his indignities at Lenny. Lenny was
irritated but as focused as he could be
considering the circumstances. He was trying
to remember all the clever things that Phil
told him to say to Cory. He smiled over at
Phil and waved, but he couldn't remember a
damn thing.

"Leo you are red in the face and you
are sweating, just what have you been
doing?"

"Jesus fucking Christ dude, I'm trying
to think here shut up for a minute," Lenny
swayed.

"No I will not, as you put it, 'shut
up'," Cory glared, "'dude' we have a red
alert, you are out of uniform and Philippe
is naked." Cory wheezed until he was out of
breath. Phil was still waiting for Lenny to
slam Cory and he shook his rifle anxiously
in anticipation. Lenny was still fighting
his liquor-fogged memory, his eyes twitched
as he tried to remember what it was he was
going to say. . Cory was beyond impatient
now, Lenny just stood there laughing or was
it arguing with himself, what was going in
Leo's head, Cory wondered. Philippe on the
other hand, hopped nervously around on the
balls of his feet. He was surprisingly
hairless. "He must shave his entire body,"
Cory muttered in amazement. He tried not to
stare; he was already covered in sweat that
had combined with cheese puff dust to make

In the field where I died.

him orange and sticky as well as out of
breath. He stared breathlessly at Philippe.

"Sir," a voice called from the intercom
on the wall, "Captain Yates is brining two
civilian prisoners to see you," the voice
paused for a moment, "are you there sir?"
Lenny jumped over to the intercom and
pressed the button.

"We've come to fit you for a man-bra
fattie fuckstick." this was the verbal slam
that Lenny had been trying to remember. Cory
shook with rage though he couldn't take his
eyes off of Philippe.

"Leo," he began through his teeth,
"tell them to bring the prisoners to me."

"Hey Grippo, fuckstick says to bring
them in," Lenny shouted into the intercom.

"Leo come here and bring me my dice,"
Cory was still talking through his teeth,
still staring at Philippe.

"Ah not that bullshit again," Lenny
whined thought he was already stomping over
to the dice cabinet.

"It is not bullshit Leo, gosh darn it,
it happens to be the rules of our
enlightened society."

Lenny set his rifle against the filing
cabinet that held Cory's massive collection
of dice.

"James, make yourself useful and fetch
me a drunk critical chart[59]."

"Fuckstick gonna' roll for critical,"
Phil said as he bounced over to the charts

---

[59] A critical chart was a playing device for the dice based
gamers. A critical chart covered both hits and misses based
on attack (failed or successful) and then a percentile roll
to determine effect and or consequence. For Cory's needs
this process was made slightly more complicated. Various
charts were drafted covering a number of grievances and
crimes. The system was allegedly fair, however, the charts
tended to favor the accuser unless the defendant was Cory
who always employed his own personal charts. The desired
effect seemed to be public humiliation at the hands of the
accuser, though if the dice favored the defendant the
circumstances would reverse.

In the field where I died.

and maps filing cabinet. Cory's eyes never
left Phil's form, he was mesmerized.

   "Stop staring at Phil asshole," Lenny
said as he threw a tray of dice at Cory.
Cory wouldn't be able to retaliate short of
huffing and scowling which were the current
limits on his mobility inhibited girth.
During this Lt. Gary Gerard Grippo entered
with Captain Yates, John Parker and Jim
Friendly in tow.

   I should be noted that aside from the
odd surname there were very few oddities to
Gary's life. They should, however, be
mentioned. Most summers since he was sixteen
and too old to play, Gary officiated as an
umpire for Woodland Hills Little League. The
only notable oddity here was Gary's
insistence on wearing his custom fit, near
indecent, short navy blue umpire shorts. The
shorts did little to hide his 'thunder'.

   Despite living a full decade more than
Donald "Donnie" Martin Grippo who was a
paraplegic, Gary counted nineteen (with an
asterisk) less sexual encounters then
Donnie. The asterisk referred to Donnie's
much-disputed (by Gary and Donnie's
headstone) twentieth encounter, which killed
Donnie[60] so Gary considered it as an
incomplete. Gary, himself, has never had a
steady girlfriend despite twenty-three years
of eligible studness (counted from the age
of sixteen). The only noticeable quirk to
Lt. Grippo was his ambition. He had been
perfectly happy as the senior league umpire
and the daytime cashier at Whytes Hardware
in Canoga Park. He lived in a converted
garage at his mom's house in Reseda and
drove a faded blue Dodge Shadow.

---

[60] Number twenty was a jumper. She jumped up and down on
Donnie hard enough to break his ribs and collapse his
lungs.

In the field where I died.

The world around him changed, Gary changed very little. He was a little more ambitious. Though it was very simple. Gary didn't like sentry duty so his plan consisted of doing something amazing, then getting promoted to something other then sentry. He'd been stuck on the doing something amazing part for a couple of months now. He'd become comfortable enough to have his uniform modified to his umpire standards (quarter sleeves and short shorts).

The short shorts were holding him back now; Gary would have been off sentry duty if it weren't for those. Gary thought by helping Captain Yates bring in the dangerous criminal civilians that he would get his shot, maybe a cushy desk job somewhere with air conditioning, maybe inventory, porno librarian, or maybe even mess hall captain.

The job Gary really had his eye on was over at the slave quarters[61].

Gary bounded into the throne room. He was drenched with sweat having run the full two hundred yards from the entry gate to Cory's house. The scene he ran into had a naked and armed Philippe dancing to a tune in his head while he tore through a filing cabinet. Lenny, who looked very drunk and punchy, lurched over a very orange and sticky looking Cory. This was not at all a surprise to Gary; this was not a shocking scene for the throne room. Gary brought himself to attention, straightening up and bringing his feet together on the black

---

[61] Slavedom was determined by age, criminal history and ability, or lack there of. Woman were designated as slaves automatically since as determined by, in his only dice free decision, that women served only two needs for the new world; pleasure and reproduction. Astoundingly, there were no women in camp, subsequently there was no Harem for Cory, nor was there the much promised 'Breedin' Barn' for the Black shirt guard. Furthermore, this lack of action was serving to foster a volatile and somewhat hostile movement against Cory and any open loyalist.

In the field where I died.

marble floor[62]. The noise brought everything but Philippe's dancing to a halt. He continued to throw charts and papers onto a floor already littered with dice, weapons and cheese puffs. Gary directed his eyes to the ceiling. He didn't want to get caught staring at Philippe's buttocks again. This was not impossible to accomplish, however, Philippe was frequently naked and his buttocks were surprisingly hairless and pimple free.

"What do you want Gar-bear?" Cory's wheeze was indignant. He could feel that he was losing control of the situation and that really bothered him.

"Captain Yates has been injured, but he is brining the prisoners, they asked to see you," Gary shouted to the ceiling[63].

Cory snapped himself out of self-pity. It was his only skill beyond rolling dice, which was to channel his cowardice into rage.

"Bring the prisoners to me." He screeched, "Philippe, put something on gosh darn it." Phil danced away to the next room. Gary breathed a sigh of relief; he could finally take his eyes off the ceiling. "Leo pull

---

[62] Black marble was the theme to Cory's palace. It was not what Cory installed, but it was the home he commandeered. The previous resident had been a philandering, motorcycle riding, wife beating mediocre actor with a greasy mullet and a proclivity for stripperesq wives. The house had remained much as Cory had found it, save for the actor's sixth wife's underwear and the actors German pornography collection. Cory appreciated both as much as he could. The main drawback to the extensive black marble motif was Cory's more recent inability to wear shoes. Cory could hardly tolerate cold on his feet, though given his size he rarely had to. To combat the few times his feet would touch marble he had sandals made from thick, yet comfortable doormats and a spare pair from carper remnants.

[63] Gary was employing the best-known method for not staring at Phillipe's glistening buttocks. The punishment for that (or any other variety of naked man ogling) would be an hour in the 'fairy shed'. The 'fairy shed' was formally a port-o-pottie that had been secured by concrete poured into the waste receptacle and a series of silver dollar sized holes, not enough to compromise the structural integrity but enough to allow proper administering of the punishment. The punishment consisted of a die-determined volley of broomstick pokings.

In the field where I died.

yourself together and try to look like a
soldier, okay? " Lenny looked down at Cory
with hate, he wanted to say something but he
felt really warm and vomity, he wanted to
take a nap next to the toilet. "Oh and Leo
load my six shooters would you? " Gary
remained at attention, waiting for his next
order. "Oh, Gar-bear, you're still here,
please go fetch Captain Yates. "

"Right away sir, " Gary turned sharply
to leave the throne room. Immediately he
bumped into Captain Yates.

"Out of my way asshole, " Yates growled.
John Parker and Jim Friendly were right
behind him. "Cory, these pricks wanted to
see you, " Yates said. Cory's eyes widened.
His greatest and most recent (as recent as
an hour ago) fear was coming to life right
before him.

"Jim, shogun of the western valley, we
have no quarrel with you, you may go, " Cory
said trying to sound kingly. Lenny walked up
to him with his six shooters in his hands.
They were chrome and nickel-plated colts
with mother of pearl handles. Each handle
had 'J.F.' laid out in turquoise.

"No, I'm with John, we just came for my
guns before we left town," Jim said.

"So be it, however, you seem to have
forgotten that I won these fairly in a game
of Jujubees[64], " Cory felt he had the upper
hand; it was the only contest he'd ever won
out right.

---

[64] The game Jujubees had little to do with the candy,
unless that was the disputed or desired item. The game
consisted of catching your victim off guard, punching him
in the dick, shouting "Jujubees" in the victim's ear and
then claiming your prize. The game works on a similar
principle to that of "Roshambo", (settling basic ownership
disputes with dick punching), however, "Roshambo" requires
that the aggressor propose the game before the dick
punching can commence (I'll Roshambo you for your lunch).
This leaves the aggressor in the possible position of
getting punched first and then not getting what they
desired in the first place. Neither game works well or can
even be recommended with a female target.

In the field where I died.

"Ain't nothing fair about Jujubee's ya' dick punching, cheating cur," Jim was doing his best to sound like a wise old cowboy which was never really all that easy.

"Jim, we will deal with the pistol matter as soon as we dispatch Mr. parker."

"Agent Parker," Jim corrected.

"What?" Cory squealed, panic stricken once more.

"Hey what do you mean we Fuckstick?" Lenny finally interrupted. Before Cory could answer, Phil burst back into the throne room wearing blue hot pants and a green and pink tube top. Cory looked at Phil in an awkward mixture gape mouthed horror, annoyance and jealousy. Cory had never been able to fit in any of the tube tops, not even over his arm.

"Quite an army you have here Cory," John said.

"We'll deal with you soon enough Agent Parker," Cory sneered, "Leo shoot the Captain."

"Ah, fuckstick he's not going to like that," Lenny whined.

"Yeah fuckstick, I ain't going to like that," Yates added.

"Ian, you brought a great villain into our city and he is here to kill me."

"Well, actually, Fuckstick, if I may, I'm here for Angela and Richard Parker both of whom should be in your slave quarters," John said.

"We have no women in camp," Cory's voice was shaky.

"Really?" John removed his Baretta from its holster.

"Yes sir, total sausage fest sir," Gary shouted to the ceiling.

"No women, so what good is Cory then?" John asked.

In the field where I died.

"Very little sir," Phil shouted. He was
running in place trying to do the dance
"The Running man".

"Right then, it would seem that you're
expendable old pal," John smiled and raised
his gun at Cory.

"Your not my friend John Parker," Cory
shouted as he pawed at Lenny for the six
shooters that were held in their holsters.
They were held in by small leather hoops
resting over each hammer. Without warning
Jim ran up to Cory and punched him in the
dick. He shouted "Jujubees" and grabbed his
guns from Lenny.

"That wasn't very nice Jim," John said.

"Paybacks a bitch ain't it," Jim paused
to giggle, "fuckstick."

"I can't take you anywhere can I Jim?"
John chided.

"Well hell John you're just going to
shoot him."

"You're right, I was and am," John
answered pulling the hammer back on his
Baretta.

"Wait, don't you want to hear what I
have to say?" Cory tried to plead. John
thought for a moment. He wasn't considering
Cory's potential information; he was just
trying to be cruel.

"Frankly speaking, no," John said as he
fired twice. Each shot slammed into Cory's
forehead. Phil took his queue and unloaded
his rifle into Captain Yates's stomach.
Lenny stood frozen, he wasn't moving save
for his trembling. Phil leapt on the fallen,
dieing Captain and began to beat him with
his rifle.

"Asshole, motherfucking asshole," Phil
shouted.

Lenny looked pale; he'd never seen
anyone die before, especially two so
quickly. John turned his attention to Phil.

In the field where I died.

"Are you finished?" John asked.

"He was such an asshole," Phil said, "are you going to kill us now?"

"Of course not," John smiled briefly, "I do, however, need some names."

"Sorry, yeah I'm Phil, that's Lenny over there and that's Gary, he's a lieutenant," Phil said.

"Okay, good, Phil and Lenny I'm going to need you fella's to gather weapons, ammo, supplies and a sturdy vehicle and meet me at the front gate in thirty minutes," John paused as Jim nudged him to remind John about something, "right, almost forgot could you help Jim find some clothes that fit him better."

"Agent Parker can Phil and me go with you?" Lenny asked.

"Phil and I," John corrected.

"Huh," was Lenny's only decipherable response.

"Sure, so long as Phil puts on some big boy clothes, but hurry okay we have a lot of ground to cover."

"Right away sir," Lenny snapped to attention.

"Don't call me sir, John will be fine," John said.

"We won't let you down John," Phil straightened up, "Lenny, Mr. Friendly, lets get moving."

Gary was still at attention with his eyes fixed on the ceiling. Tears filled his eyes and he was biting his lower lip to suppress his sobbing. He figured that since he was the ranking officer he was the next to go. He wasn't ready for death; he'd never even really had his life threatened.

"You're going to kill me aren't you?" Gary finally said.

"That would be off mission Gary, if I can call you Gary?" John smiled.

In the field where I died.

"Was Cory part of your mission?" Gary asked.

"No, but that seemed to be a necessary deviation."

"So it wouldn't be necessary to kill me?"

"No Gary, in fact think of this as a promotion, call yourself whatever you like, you know Admiral, Generalissimo, Emperor, king of the mountain and so forth," John said. Gary beamed with pride; a promotion like this was beyond belief.

"I like the sound of Captain Grippo," Gary said hopefully.

"Thinking a little small there," John said as he holstered his Baretta.

"Do you think General would be too much?" Gary asked.

"That's up to you buddy, but if you want my opinion you'd be foolish to call yourself anything less."

In the field where I died.

Chapter 17

The slave quarters were at the back
of the compound. They consisted of eight
corrugated fiberglass sheds sitting on the
last two undeveloped lots. Across the way
(on what was called Aspen Way) was what was
supposed to be the camp bordello. The only
resident the bordello would ever have was a
woman by the name of Frederica Ann Elliot.
Freddie, as she insisted on being called,
was in every conceivable aspect a woman.
However, for the sake of survival she'd
claimed to be a pre-op transsexual. She even
gone as far as to show her "member" to a
few of the other men of the camp to give her
story some credibility. Freddie was once a
florist and part time dominatrix from North
Hollywood. She was a mother twice and a wife
three times. She was an attractive thirty-
seven, though she highlighted her harsher
features to give herself a more mannish
appearance.

Freddie's experience as both a
dominatrix and a wife taught her that most
straight men lived in fear of being
dominated by another man (there were also
those who would pay extra for that, but that
was a separate matter). This worked to her
advantage. The skinhead army was always too
confused and too unorganized to commit any
hate crimes and Cory, however vaguely
curious he might be he was too afraid of
breaking his own laws to try anything.
Freddie watched from her porch as John and
Gary approached.

"So, who are you here for again Agent
Parker?" Gary asked.

"Well I suppose only Richard Parker,"
John shrugged and lit a cigarette, "he's
about six foot, white hair, black moustache,
pain in the ass."

In the field where I died.

"That's sounds familiar," Gary said.

"And you're sure you don't have any women in camp?"

"No sir, Freddie at the bordello's the closest we got," Gary smiled.

"We have, the closest we..never mind," John began, "so this Freddie's not a woman?"

"Chick with a dick my friend," Gary patted John on the shoulder, "come on he has the slave manifest."

"How does Freddie usually present himself?" John asked.

"Well, usually as a hot chick John, why does that matter?" Gary said.

"Well etiquette would dictate that you refer tom him as a she when he dresses as a woman," John said.

"Oh, makes sense, okay," Gary scratched his nose, "she still has the slave manifest."

In the field where I died.

Chapter 18

In the third shed of the front row Richard Parker was winning at his favorite game. It was something he'd come up with during his first week as a slave. It hadn't been a particularly good week. Angela had died that week, her brain leaked out through her nose after she tried to attack Richard. He wasn't terribly upset by this but it was still unsettling. He'd always been certain that he would meet his end first, probably at John's hand. He never had any contingency plan beyond Angela. He wasn't prepared to be single again. She was supposed to be his wailing widow, too distraught to marry again (in many scenarios she committed suicide at Richards wake). This had been most inconvenient.

Richard and Angela had married in the spring of nineteen sixty-eight. They were both eighteen and had just graduated from high school. Richard shipped out a week later for boot camp and officers school. Richard had gathered honors serving in his schools R.O.T.C. program. It was really just an excuse for authoritative cruelty which Richard would exploit to it's fullest extent. Officers school would do very little to improve Richards treatment of his subordinates in fact it only served to confirm what many had felt Richard was capable of. Which was of course a brilliant, callous, mechanical and yet artistic approach to violence. Richard was a functional sociopath, not visible to the naked eye; however, given the correct circumstances he was like a master craftsman. Moral boundaries were never an issue. It wasn't a matter of passing judgment, feeling righteous or even deriving pleasure in the act. Richard saw nothing

In the field where I died.

extraordinary in what he did, he equated it
to picking up the paper in the morning, of
getting out of bed to have a sensible
breakfast.

Lieutenant Parker shipped out to Asia
expecting to serve a tour or two in Vietnam.
Instead he was sent to Southern Japan. On
paper he would serve three tours with
distinction and modest decorations and
commendations for valor. All his letters
home would be post marked from various
military installations throughout south East
Asia where he was supposedly stationed.
Between tours, Jeremy and Jason Parker were
born though then Captain Parker would be
little better then a picture on the
mantelpiece.

The reality was that Richard Parker
arrived in Okinawa in early nineteen sixty-
nine to find himself assigned to a special
project. Officially he was still a Marine,
still fighting a lost cause for freedom and
democracy. Unofficially he was an active
field agent for the National Security
Agency. Upon arriving in Okinawa he was
thrown, almost immediately, into an
aptitude/proficiency test. It was well
documented that Richard was well armed,
especially when traveling. He arrived in
uniform showing only his holstered Colt 45.
He also had a thirty-two caliber snub nose
revolver strapped to his ankle and a Sig
Sauer nine millimeter tucked into his belt.
He also carried a pair of stockless pump
action twelve gauge shot guns loaded with
short-range scatter shells. These rested in
his duffle bag.

The test was a bank robbery turned
hostage situation in a down town hotel
orchestrated by the N.S.A.. Local police
picked Richard up at the airport and
explained the situation. Richard then met up

In the field where I died.

with the swat team in front of the hotel.
They explained the situation again,
stressing that there was one way into the
room. Richard thought about this for a
moment and then retrieved a shotgun from his
duffle bag. He took another moment to
chamber a round in his shotgun and each of
his sidearms. "Hold this," he handed his
duffle bag to one of the swat members and
moved inside the hotel. There was a full two
minutes of silence. Richard had wandered
through the lobby to the elevators he was in
no hurry. From outside the policemen heard a
quick blast from a shotgun followed by the
report from several small arms. This was
followed by another minute of silence broken
by two more shots. Richard emerged a minute
later; he hadn't taken off his trench coat
or even broken a sweat. He had, however,
shot both the robbers and the hostages. From
his debut he rose quickly through the rank
and file of the N.S.A.. His main purpose was
eliminating rival genetic development, which
included both developers and their product.
After twenty years of loyal service, active
service Richard was allowed to go into semi-
retirement. He didn't know the full extent
of the damage the project had caused or was
going to cause. He did know that time was
short, maybe twenty years (if calculations
were correct) and he wanted to spend time
with his family. The project director had
been understanding, especially since Richard
and Angela had adopted a product of the
project, it was felt it would be best for
all concerned that Richard be there to
protect the boy till he was old enough.

In the field where I died.

In the field where I died.

Chapter 19

The game that Richard was winning at was "Ball Buster Blackjack". Richard and his older brother Daniel would play a hand of blackjack and whoever lost a hand would get punched in the testicles. Richard had won fourteen consecutive hands and the game was starting to lose its thrill.

"Ready for another hand Danielle?" Richard smirked. Mocking Daniels wounded masculinity was a commonly employed weapon for Richard. Daniel, however, was beyond having his feelings hurt, he was close to blacking out from the pain and the numbness.

"Richard are you there?" the intercom suddenly buzzed with Freddie's voice.

"We'll continue this later princess," Richard said patting Daniel on the leg, "yeah Freddie we're both here, what do you want?" Richard rolled his eyes. "You're lucky my punching hand is getting tired," he said to Daniel. Daniel could only look up with a pained expression and tears welling in his eyes. He couldn't cry Richard would pound on him for it.

"There's somebody here to see you and Dan," Freddie answered back.

"It isn't that twisted monster father Cory is it?"

"No, fuckstick is dead," Freddie replied.

"You said a swear." Richard was astonished. Cory's laws of language had always been very strict. Daniel stared at the speaker box in amazement, for a moment he didn't even think about how much his balls hurt.

"Fuckstick must be dead," Daniel muttered.

"Indeed," Richard snorted, "they must be here to appoint a real man as king," he

In the field where I died.

looked at Daniel, "and they don't mean you
Cinderella Princess."

"Still there Richard?" Freddie called.

"Of course, yes, so where do you want
us?"

"The appell yard will do nicely,"
Freddie chirped.

Moments later Freddie was standing next
to John and Gary. They stood on the edge of
the appell yard which was a dirt octagon
closed in by chain link and barbed wire.
Once a week the slaves were counted and
inspected for signs of the virus, which no
one really knew till it was too late.

Once a month the yard was used for
ultimate fighting, which was the sorriest
exhibition of pasty, middle, aged slap
fighting.

"Hey Gary old pal could you check to
see how Jim and the boys are coming along?"

"Sure thing John," Gary said
cheerfully. He had never been that
comfortable with the slaves, they never
showed him any respect and they usually made
fun of his shorts.

"If you don't mind me asking Freddie,"
John began once he was sure that Gary was
out of ear shot, "how long did you think
you could fool them?"

"What are you talking about?" Freddie
tried to sound more masculine.

"That you're a real woman," John said.

"Oh that's sweet of you to say,"
Freddie tried to play this off, "but
flattery will get a spanking."

"No really, you may want to get out of
here real soon," John drew his Baretta and
chambered a round, "this camp has a week,
maybe two tops left and if I were you I
wouldn't want to be here for the end."

In the field where I died.

"What makes you so sure that I'm a woman?" Freddie was still trying to maintain her mystery.

"The details wouldn't be polite, suffice to say there's about a fifteen degree difference in your body temperature."

"What does that have to do with anything?"

"Well you're warmer where you shouldn't be," John said.

"Maybe I have a rash or something," Freddie tried to take offense at this, "and just who the hell are you?"

"Oh, sorry, I can be terrible with introductions," John retrieved his id with his free hand, "John Parker, N.S.A.."

"Is that supposed to scare me or something?"

"Not really part of my mission to scare you Freddie," John smiled.

"Okay Freddie," Richard bellowed as he approached, "I'm ready to be the leader, a daring combination of Spartacus, Moses and Mussolini."

"What are you on about Richard?" Freddie asked.

"Well with Cory dead I assumed I would be the logical replacement," Richard slowed his speech as he got a clear look at whom Freddie had been talking to, "so this is how it's going to be eh."

"What is how it's going to be, John what is he talking about?"

"Freddie he was my father," John answered.

"You're no son of mine you motherless bastard," Richard shouted.

"Listen, we're headed to Vegas as soon as I'm done so if you like..."

"Will you explain some of this along the way?"

In the field where I died.

"Sure," John answered, "meet us at the front gates."

"Don't be long," Freddie said as she ran back to the bordello.

"So you're a full agent then?" Richard said.

"Yes," John said holding his id up for Richard to see.

"That's quite a clearance, good for you, how's the old man doing?"

"George is, well, cagy, up to something, nefarious, ya know."

"Still calling himself George?" Richard lamented.

"Has he always?" John asked.

"As long as I knew the man," Richard sighed.

"It's an easy enough name to forget I suppose," John added.

"Slightly off topic John, but I really didn't expect that you would be the one sent to deal with me," Richard pondered.

"To the best of my knowledge there's a bit of an agency schism," John answered.

"Really? So there are two camps?"

"Possibly more, communications been pretty spotty."

"So from a technical standpoint you don't have to kill me."

"You know, somehow that doesn't work for me," John said as he lit another cigarette.

"At the very least you don't have to kill Dan, he's harmless," Richard argued.

"Harmless? how many times did he try to kill me when I was growing up, six or seven."

"Seven, but you were a monster, he knew that."

"I was and am what I was designed to be."

In the field where I died.

"That's a horseshit copout and you know it!"

"You really think so don't you?" John said.

"Damn straight, in fact I'd go so far as to say that you and your kind should be hunted down and cleansed from the face of the earth."

"I'm only going to disappoint you there old man," John shook his head.

"That was never really an issue between us John you could never fail to meet my expectations nor could I fail you as a father since you were never really my son," Richard said in a matter of fact tone of voice.

"That's really fascinating," John wasn't really paying attention to Richard, he was however, watching a figure that appeared to be working it's way around the back carrying a large tool of some kind.

"If you're still holding on to some sort of childhood resentment because I never said 'good job son' or posted some crappy picture on the refrigerator or ever showed up to one of your little league games you'll need to put that gun away and think about what you're really trying to do."

"Are you trying to buy Dan enough time to ran around the back of me and hit me in the head with a shovel?"

"What?, no it's supposed to be a backhoe, Daniel if you're running around with my shovel I'm going to kick your ass," Richard shouted. John raised an eyebrow to his father. "What, I claimed the shovel," Richard defended, "that pig fucker knows perfectly well that he has the backhoe."

"You'd better tell him to come into the light, dad, Richard, whatever," John stopped himself as Daniel trudged by, "I

In the field where I died.

guess that really doesn't matter now does
it. "

Shots rang out and then silence.

In the field where I died.

In the field where I died.

Part V
And I don't believe in God so I can't be saved.
Chapter 1

"'Chesca, you're like a hermit grab that everyone wants to catch and cook in garlic and butter," Seth smiled. It was the best line he'd ever heard and he's even seen it work the night before. Francesca hadn't quite been paying attention. She had been busy watching their last Portland target. What she did hear was something about garlic, catching her and 'Chesca?

"Are you fucking retarded?" She asked.

"What?" Seth sounded hurt. It shouldn't have surprised him that the line had failed, but it still hurt. He'd mutilated family members in their sleep for more or less similar comments[65].

"Where in God's name did you get a stupid line like that?"

"I over heard it at a party I was invited to,"
Seth answered meekly.

"Seth you jackass you were on assignment, no one invited you," Francesca turned toward him, "and so that we are painfully clear and that there are no uncertain terms, I would sooner practice self mutilation with a pair of pliers and a butane torch then ever see your rot and fungus covered penis."

Seth looked down toward the ground. Francesca had never been that particularly

---

[65] When Seth was twenty-four and had completed his N.S.A. training he returned to the town he grew up in. It was spring in Palo Alto just before Seth disappeared for good. The home he grew up in belonged to his maternal grandmother. Seth had been the product of his mother's liaison with her slow-witted cousin. Seth's mother was sent off to live in a convent after his birth. He would never meet his mother, which Grandma Oliver said was all right, cause his mother didn't love Seth as much as Grandma Oliver did. On that spring morning Seth crept into Grandma Oliver's home and slit her throat with a jagged can lid while she slept.

And I don't believe in God so I can't be saved.

vague in her past rejections; however, she
had never been that specific. The only love
Seth ever had freely he destroyed and the
love he wanted would never be his.

And I don't believe in God so I can't be saved.

Chapter 2

Francisco Ricardo had dismissed his crew for the afternoon. The only members of the crew that remained were the brothers, Juan and Pedro Swartz. The Swartz brothers were having an argument; they were always having an argument. Francisco Ricardo, also known as Derek Wall the fugitive baby killing skinhead/Satanist, did what he always does which was ignore the argument until it became a fight. When it became a fight it was never very hard to break up given that both men were out of shape and in their sixties.

"You have no idea what you're talking about," Juan, also known as Earl Myers shouted and shoved Pedro also known as Walter Myers.

"Oh really tubbo!" Walter said.

"Sweet Jesus Walt you spent forty years as a journalist and 'Oh really tubbo' is the best you got," Earl answered.

"Shut up Earl," Walter retorted.

"Hell if I didn't know that Roman Franco was some kind of giant moron I'd be really worried and maybe somewhat afraid."

And I don't believe in God so I can't be saved.

And I don't believe in God so I can't be saved.

Chapter 3

On the afternoon that lead to Portland, landscaping and hiding out an angry Derek, a shirtless Earl and a mostly indecent Roman Franco arrived in Needles, CA. From outward appearances Needled was empty except for an oddly well-staffed Diamond Cafe. Needles had been evacuated by the National Guard and most of the residents were taken to a camp near Victorville. Needles was then commandeered by the California Church of Satan. The Diamond Cafe was their guardhouse.

What made the staff unique is that they were a collection of aged bodybuilders, all but one were once protégés of Roman Franco. They were the security force of Needles as a satanic commune. The head of security was Abe Herschfelder, the fifty-five year old kid of the group.

When trio arrived Roman would accept only a mesh muscle shirt for himself and Earl.

"Gentlemen," Roman began, "this young man is our future, our champion," Roman slapped Derek on the back, "and I do believe you all know 'Blobbo' Myers here, who has returned to our church." The name 'Blobbo' caused fits of laughter amongst the old muscle men. To this group Roman was the great leader, teacher and of all things comedian. Though never to be mocked himself, Roman felt it was his duty as the leader to keep things a bit loose. Since the better majority of his people were California Satanists they were familiar with Earl Myers, consequently Earl was the source of many, many jokes by Roman.

"Come on Derek let me introduce you to the boys," Roman took Derek by the shoulder, "this is my right hand, Abe."

And I don't believe in God so I can't be saved.

"Pleased to meet ya kid," Abe grabbed
Derek's hand and shook it aggressively.
There was a kind of resentment in his
presence and in the way he gripped Derek's
hand. Abe didn't like what Derek was
supposed to be.

"The here is Kurt Wheeler my hammer,"
Roman said. Kurt heaved his hand on to
Derek's and gave him an awkward, limp and
sweaty handshake. For being known as 'the
hammer' Kurt was, in appearances at least, a
misnomer. Though Kurt was six foot seven (a
full foot taller then Derek) he was easily
four hundred pounds with no discernable
musculature. Kurt Wheeler had many things
that begged explaining. The most would be
his missing fingertips. All eight of his
fingers were missing a good inch giving his
thumbs a freakish quality. The fingertips
Kurt lost were the 'trophies' of an
industrial fan that very nearly bested him
in a fight. Another, though no longer
visible due to a beard and an extra chin was
a scar that ran like a half circle around
his neck. It was Kurt's souvenir from when
he was last normal. Kurt was once a married,
church going man who worked as a Ventura
county Sheriffs Deputy. Sheriff Deputy's
worked as prison guards half the time and
one unlucky Sunday Kurt got caught up in a
prison riot in which he was brutalized,
tortured and received the neck scar for his
troubles. He stopped going to church, quit
being a Deputy and left his wife. Kurt had
always been slightly worse then average for
intelligence and it was something he
compromised after leaving his wife. It was
hard to notice, you had to watch Kurt for a
few minutes to catch it. It was the way he
blinked, one eye at a time. His eyes were
out of sync, though one eye was practically
useless and white. This stemmed from time

And I don't believe in God so I can't be saved.

spent on an underground boxing circuit (where he mostly fought other transients). The boxing circuit is where he met up with a younger Abe Herschfelder (forty-three at the time). From there Kurt was brought into the service of roman Franco, who if nothing else, gave Kurt Wheeler a focus to his violence.

The two remaining muscle men were Alberto Alejandro Aramendez or 'Triple A' as Roman had dubbed him, and Heliodoro Pasqual Benitez, 'Big Bad Eli'. Alberto, who sported a thin moustache, was the closest to normal the room had to offer. Though unusually lean for a muscle man, he had made up for his lack of bulk by being limber and flexible beyond most conceivable human limits (to which he credited the Prince of lies ad a rigorous training regimen). Heliodoro more resembled a forties muscle man. Very little discernable muscle definition, he looked very much like a trapezoid with feet (he wore high wasted pants and appeared to be constantly sucking his gut in). He considered himself Castilian, which was only partly true. He spoke a rich, royal Spanish and only through Alberto. It was not that he didn't understand English, he was simply that he sounded foolish and uneducated when he spoke it. Roman bounded over with Derek in tow to introduce the pair.

"These boys are special Derek," Roman said, "much like you these brothers came from a hateful group to join us in our impending triumph."

Alberto and Heliodoro were not brothers. Roman knew this and it made little difference if they offered protest to this, which they no longer bothered to do.

"So where did they come from?" Derek asked.

And I don't believe in God so I can't be saved.

"These poor bastards were with the Catholics, if you can believe that," Roman bellowed smugly. He was proud of any time he could 'stick it' to the Catholics, whom he saw as one of the chief enemies of his church.

"It's a bit of a stretch," Derek began in a deadpan sort of voice, "but I think I could go that far with you."

"Good," Roman slapped his hands together, Derek's sarcasm was lost on him, "I thought you'd be able to handle this my boy," Roman sneered, "I know in past times you would have committed some manner of hate crime on these boys because they're Mexicans," Roman nudged Derek knowingly, "but these boys are your brothers now Derek, not literally of course, but they will fight for you like brothers would."

With that said there was a full two minutes of silence. Derek exchanged nods with Alberto and Heliodoro. He only knew enough Spanish to be insulting so he didn't bother.

Abe knew what was coming, so he was busy using similar anger management techniques as Derek did. This involved deep breathing and joint cracking.

Kurt maintained the clearest mind in the cafe. He had the same two thoughts running through his head in sequence. They were; breathe in, breathe out. Largely due to brain damage, there was a very good chance of Kurt forgetting to breathe. Thankfully though, his breathing sounded like thick mucous and rocks being forced through a small cylinder (Kurt had a severely deviated septum).

Roman had often fantasized, and during the silence did, about giving Kurt a 'Mcmurphy', but given that there was never a standing agreement between the two men that

And I don't believe in God so I can't be saved.

should Kurt ever become brain damaged that
he would wish that Roman would smother him
with a pillow and then proceed to smash a
window with a water fountain so that he
could run off to live in the wilderness.
This was the fantasy, sadly for Roman never
the reality (plus Kurt had been brain
damaged since before Roman knew him so it
probably wouldn't count anyway).

Earl stood trying to hide his hairy
nipples revealed all too easily by his black
mesh muscle shirt. He was trying to figure
out just what sort of hideous surprise Roman
had in store for him. Normally it would be
some sort of illustrated pamphlet or a slide
show that depicted the whole world having
carnal relations with Earls Francine. Roman
had always considered himself Earls chief
rival for any potential love (or truly
anything for that matter) and since Roman
could never effectively woo what's her name,
the whole world would have there with her by
way of Romans illustrations[66]. This would
have bothered Earl more had things not
already been so strange.

"Gentlemen, Derek," Roman broke the
silence
and raised an eyebrow, "Earl," he lamented,
"we are about to enter the end of days, not
just for the Judeo-Christian world or even
the secular world, this is for all of us."

"Have we been wrong all this time?" Abe
wondered aloud.

"No Abe my friend, this is no rapture,
no day of judgment forth coming," Romans
smile widened for a moment, "that pompous
bastard God has nothing to do with this."

---

[66] Roman Franco never really wanted Francine Myers. Roman
Franco was a bully who had spotted the easiest target he
would ever know in Earl Myers.

And I don't believe in God so I can't be saved.

"Does this have something to do with Derek and the bus?" Earl asked.

"I believe so," Roman said, "though there is a man who will better explain this to you all."

And I don't believe in God so I can't be saved.

Chapter 4

Seth was lying on the grass on the hill above Francisco Ricardo and the Swartz brothers. He was lost in a daydream watching the movement of the clouds above. His daydream wasn't anything more specific then a genderless naked person dancing just for Seth. He tried, but couldn't put a face to the figure. Regardless this was enough for Seth to have drool collecting in both corners of his mouth and for him to rub his gun on his cheeks. Francesca was aware of the movement and perhaps even mild writhing, but she didn't care to look.

"Hey numbnuts, that's not our guy," she said.

"What?" Seth snapped out of his daydream.

"Listen, according to the file, Francisco Ricardo, the one we're supposed to kill, is some tubby guy around five foot seven."

"An your point?" Seth chuckled. He wasn't paying attention to their target; he was twirling his fingers around on the grass underneath his hand.

"Well Seth," Francesca began through clenched teeth, "that guy down there is about six foot six and probably only has three percent body fat."

"FINE, why don't you MARRY him," Seth rolled away from Francesca.

"Don't make me break something," Francesca growled, "now gather your stuff we're going to have to follow them home."

"Why? why can't we just move on to the next target," Seth whined.

"Francisco Ricardo is our last Portland target and after we deal with this situation then we can move on to the next target."

"So what's our next assignment?"

And I don't believe in God so I can't be saved.

"We don't have one yet," she answered.

"So we could have a little holiday after this," Seth said as he scrambled to his feet, "we could go up to Vancouver," he chambered a round in his Glock with a look of determination on his face, "we can get stoned and have sex and authentic Chinese food."

"Are you high?"

"No, but all we have to do is finish this assignment and all these things are possible."

"Have I not made myself clear?" Francesca stood up.

"Hell yeah, we kill the fatties and the hulk
and then we can go sexing up Canada." Seth broke into a run toward Derek, Earl and Walter.

"You're a big idiot sometimes Walt," Earl sighed.

"Well at least I'm not pussy whipped," Walter said, Derek chuckled offering this insult a level of credibility, "am I right Derek?"

"Somewhat, but Earls right too, you're a douche bag," Derek leaned back on the truck. Walter was preparing a slamming and potentially volatile comeback for the both of them, something involving fornicating their own mothers, the underlying problem being that it would be suggesting that Earl have sex with their dead mother, so Walter held it in. thankfully their was what appeared to be a lunatic running down the hill toward them shouting something like "I am loved!" Seth was in fact shouting that as he ran. Francesca was a good ten paces behind, partly due to her roadrunner running in place start that dated all the away back to high school track.

And I don't believe in God so I can't be saved.

"You see Earl, that's what I've been trying to tell you about," Walter finally said.

"What? idiots with guns, running down hill?" Earl answered.

"The idiots are just a symptom, the worlds coming to an end Earl and a lot of people are going to die, a lot of people have already died."

"You can't seriously expect me to buy that Satan Children bullshit you've been pushing in the Cyclops."

"No brother, that's just the crap I feed my public, I still don't have the full story."

"That's not what Roman believes," Earl said.

"Romans a pasty beef jerky moron," Walter smiled.

"Something we can finally agree on," Earl smiled.

"Boys, I don't wanna' break up happy shiny time or nothing but we still have a moron with a gun running at us and I think he's a retard," Derek interrupted.

"Don't they like to be called mentally challenged?" Walter wondered.

"No I think it's Person or Persons with special needs, though I do suppose we will have to agree to disagree on the matter," Earl said.

"But we can agree it's not 'retard' yes?" Walter asked.

"Well yes, certainly it isn't 'retard'," Earl rolled his eyes at the word.

"Well hoo-fuckin-ray for the retards," Derek said, "I'm gonna have to deal with this one ain't I?" Both Walter and Earl looked at Derek and then at the ground. Earl started to say something. "Oh shit save it

And I don't believe in God so I can't be saved.

Earl," Derek said as he got up and moved to the back of the truck.

"So where was I?" Walter said, "right, Roman well you know he kidnapped me when he heard about you and the skinhead, he was going to kill me when you both arrived, but I had enough time to convince him of how important I was, more important then the funny joke he had planned."

"Which was?" Earl asked, not really wanting to know.

"He was going to shove C-4 up my ass and have me 'explode with excitement' when you arrived," Walter answered.

"That sounds like Roman, I don't have to tell you he's a sick bastard right?"

"No sir, he spends all day in a thong, yeah that's not a mental picture I need ya' know."

By this time Seth had reached them. He was out of breathe and drenched with sweat.

"What can we do for you young fella'?" Earl chimed.

"Just gimme, phooo, a sec," Seth replied, "I really gotta get more exercise."

"We can see that my boy," Walter said.

"We're not really a pair to talk Walt," Earl chided as he patted his own belly.

"You are so right, hell we almost have our own orbits," Walter chuckled and elbowed Seth.

"Jesus, you're both fat, I have a gun see," Seth held his Glock out, "so you both shut up so I can kill you."

"Is he threatening us Walt?"

"I do believe so Earl," Walter answered.

"Well that's not very nice son," Earl began, "say, what is your name?"

And I don't believe in God so I can't be saved.

"You fatties just need to know that I'm the guy that's gonna kill you both to death," Seth snorted.

"That seems a bit redundant, 'the guy who is going to kill us both to death," Walter laughed, "son, as an American, a tax paying, Satan worshipping American, I have a constitutional right, handed down from the all mighty, to face my killer or killers with full knowledge of who he she or what they might be," Walter bellowed trying to sound official.

"That sounds like complete bullshit," Seth shouted hoarsely. It was a method that more often succeeded where it should have failed. It was the old I'm shouting louder then you so I'm more right then you are.

"No need to shout young man," Earl began, "my brother may be an oaf but he does have you there."

"Really?" Seth sounded shaky.

"I'm afraid so," Earl replied.

"Oh," Seth patted himself down for his id, "here it is," he said as he flipped it open, "read it and uh...read it."

"Agent Seth R. Oliver eh," Walter said.

"Pleasure to make your acquaintance Seth," Earl rolled back on his heels, "may I ask what the 'R' stands for?"

"Rodgers," Seth offered.

"A bit odd, Rodgers I mean," Walter said.

"It's a family tradition," Seth defended.

"What Rodgers?" Earl asked.

"No the 's'," Seth said.

"Pluralized middle names is a family tradition?" Walter balked.

"I suppose," Seth shrugged.

"So what was your fathers name?" Walter asked.

And I don't believe in God so I can't be saved.

"Jeremiah Roberts Oliver," Seth said automatically, "he was also my uncle."

"And his father?" Earl asked.

"Allain Fontaines Oliver I think," Seth replied.

"Sounds like a family a idiots to me," Derek said from behind Seth.

"What?" Seth swung around to fire and got met by swinging shovel.

"Fucker, you broke my nose," Seth cried into his hands.

"Ain't the first time is it princess," Derek wasn't waiting for an answer. He raised the shovel for another strike when a gunshot rang out against the shovel, knocking it back but not out of Derek's hands.

"It's been my experience that a gunshot typically knocks things out of a persons hands," Francesca said. She threw her burning cigarette filter to the ground (she always smoked down to the filter).

"Where were you?" Seth whined.

"I took a fifteen," Francesca began, "I had a feeling that these two would distract you while the big one attacked you."

"Why didn't you step in, he broke my nose," Seth stood up and held his shirttails up to his nose. Francesca didn't answer she just shook her head. "Okay, fine, we can kill them now right?" Seth hadn't been looking past his shirt.

"No," Francesca answered calmly, "we didn't come here to kill the wrong man."

"But if they don't die I don't get sex."

"Seth, I am going to say this the last time and be as lucid as I can be, we are never going to fuck, never be friends, never be anything."

"But what about...," Seth began.

And I don't believe in God so I can't be saved.

"Any pleasant memory you might hold is either a lie or a fantasy, which up until now was a endurable problem," she interrupted.

"But Miss Fran you belong to me," Seth pleaded and demanded at the same time.

"It doesn't have to come down to this does it Seth?"

"Come down to what, you belong to me, Paul said," Seth shouted. Francesca kept her gun on Derek who tightened his grip on the shovel. Francesca drew Paul's Colt from the back of her belt and fired. The bullet exploded though Seth's left knee, dropping him to the ground.

"Pardon me for a moment won't you?" She said to Derek.

"What? yeah sure," he answered.

"I'm going to fucking fuck you up," Seth screamed from the ground. Francesca raised an eyebrow and then emptied the Colt into Seth. He laid still for a second then started to twitch and gargle on his own blood until he was silent, his own blood pooling around him. Francesca tossed the Colt on top of him and turned her attention back to Derek, Earl and Walter.

"Please tell me you have a Portland exit strategy?" she asked them.

"And who might you be young lady?" Earl asked.

"Special Agent Morrison, National Security Agency," she replied.

"Given your unflinching dispatching of what must have been an associate of yours are we to assume that you are not a cryptologist?"

"That would be fairly accurate," she smiled, "I do not like wasting words so here is, at some point, fairly soon, someone other then myself is going to figure out

And I don't believe in God so I can't be saved.

that Francisco is really Derek Wall as
accused baby killer an Nazi piece of shit."

"Ex-Nazi piece of shit," Earl
interrupted.

"And you would be Earl Myers?" she
said.

"In the flesh," he smiled.

"Delicatessen owner and excommunicated member of the California Church
of Satan."

"Actually just 'C.C. of S.' maam, it's
what most of us call it," Earl offered.

"I'll make a note of that Mr. Myers,"
she said.

"Earl would be fine," Earl said.

"I'm sure it would be Mr. Myers,"
Francesca coolly replied, "and you would be
Walter Myers, the missing tabloid
journalist?"

"You bet your sweet sexy ass I am,
damn I'd like to," Walters sentence was
interrupted by Francesca pulling back on the
hammer of her pistol, "okay then, what if I
were to give your cheeks a squeeze?" Walter
salivated. Francesca thought about this for
moment.

"Walter, are you right or left handed?"

"Like many great Americans I am right
handed."

"Then would you please hold your left
hand up and away from your body." Walter
raised his hand without a thought. "Spread
your fingers out please?" She asked. Walter
started to wiggle his fingers.

"I can do this with both hands ya
know," he leered. Francesca smiled and
fired a pair of shots at his hand. The first
took off his thumb and the second removed
the tip of his middle finger.

"Were you flirting with me Mister
Myers, Derek bandage his hand up and throw
him in the truck, Earl make sure you have

And I don't believe in God so I can't be saved.

all that you need, we're going to see my
Supervisor. "

And I don't believe in God so I can't be saved.

Chapter 5

Jason's suite was dark save for the light emanating form an upstairs bathroom. The bathroom is where Jason had spent the last three hours. He was on the white marble floor in his tuxedo shirt that he wears at the end of every show and a pair of powder blue boxers (Merona small). He hugged the toilet like it was his only friend praying to it for his nausea to end. Jason wanted the angry, bubbling mix of scotch, seafood and sake to erupt in a liquid fire from his throat, but it wasn't coming.

Three hours and forty-five minutes prior Shirley had helped him back to his room, even helped undress him to a point before Jason dismissed her. On her way out the door she scolded him for even thinking about more drinking.

"What?" Jason had swayed, "I have neither the desire," he paused for a horrific sake burp, "no the means for such."

"Good," Shirley smiled before leaving the room. The suite was one of several, palatial and somewhat extravagant suites that had been appropriated for the Jason Parker Show crew and production staff. Jason's own suite outstripped his previous living accommodations by twenty-eight hundred square feet[67]. It had two upstairs master bedrooms each with their own jet tub. On the main floor there was a piano room with the grand piano where Jason did the majority of his song writing. On top of the piano sat four bottles of port which Jason considered composers fuel and normally had

---

[67] Jason's previous apartment was a junior studio in an older building just off of Melrose and La Brea in Hollywood. For seven hundred fifty dollars a month Jason had luxury amenities such as walk-in kitchenette/bathroom and great alley views.

And I don't believe in God so I can't be saved.

no taste for the stuff. On the opposite side
of the main floor was the home theatre with
a sextant of leather recliners arranged in
an amphitheatre configuration. Neither of
these served as the centerpiece to the main
floor of the suite. The honor went to the
twelve person Jacuzzi that sat in the middle
of the room and over looked the strip. The
Jacuzzi was empty except for the bottles of
scotch that Jason hid in there. He never
really made an effort to hide them; no one
had ever accepted a hot tubbing invitation
(secretly, much to Jason's relief). Jason
stumbled over to the Jacuzzi and swiftly,
and to his own amazement retrieved a bottle.
The first pull was swished around loosening
grains of rice and odd flecks of seaweed.
Jason continued this swishing for the second
pull and had developed some rhythm and a
hip-swaying dance. This swishing scotch
dance had Jason thinking about a new routine
for the show, that was until he looked at
the bottle he was drinking from. It was his
one and only bottle of Glenfiddich Ancient
Reserve Single Malt, aged eighteen years.
"Jesus Christ," he slurred, "it's a
Goddamn single malt." Swishing and swaying
was no way to treat single malt. Eighteen-
year-old scotch wasn't quite the royalty of
scotch, but at the very least it was a
respected ambassador. Jason tried to do his
best sober walk over to the wet bar by the
piano (trying to show his friend the
eighteen year old scotch the reverence he
thought it deserved). He grabbed a highball
glass and nearly forgot his purpose. From
his position behind the wet bar he could
survey almost the entire layout of the main
floor. In the several months that he'd
occupied this space there was never a wild
bash, a sexy party or even a poker game.
He'd have felt miserable and unloved if the

And I don't believe in God so I can't be saved.

sake hadn't already made him feel that way.
He filled his glass and held it up to look
at the room the icy scotch. The last person
to really spend any time hanging out with
Jason in his "Swankienda" and all they'd
ever done was eat popcorn and watch Jason's
favorite musicals (The Jazz Singer, South
Pacific and Westside Story to name a few).
Tears filled his eyes. He was ready to throw
his glass and run upstairs. Instead, he
sniffed the glass, he could never come to
terms with the fact that scotch always
reminded him of a strong, acidic organ
preservative. He drank it down anyway which
caused him instantly to gag and wretch on
his own poison. He started to sweat as the
contents of his stomach began to churn and
bubble.

And I don't believe in God so I can't be saved.

Chapter 6

Jason had managed to fall asleep. A couple of minutes of heaving, some false starts on vomiting and overwhelming nausea and he was out. It would not be a restful sleep, drunk sleep, especially while hugging a toilet. All this sort of sleep ever was lost time. Jason snapped awake. It was nearly six-forty and he'd lost about three hours. He wanted his bed. He felt weak and unsteady. His eyes were heavy and even stung just a little. Real sleep, a pillow, didn't matter if the vomit never came. That's what Jason wanted.

"So what if Shirley has a boyfriend now," Jason muttered to himself, "she deserves to be happy." Jason pushed himself up from the toilet, "but who wouldn't want some of this sexy beast," he said as he caught himself in the mirror, "don't I deserve some happy, don't I deserve some ass?"

"What's her name this time?" John asked from the doorway.

"Her name is Shirley," Jason said. He was still transfixed by his own by his own reflection and he hadn't realized whom he was talking to, "wholly shit John do you realize what kind of mob is looking for you right now?"

"That's not the issue right now Jason," John said as he set a bag down and lit a cigarette.

"You're right John, you're always right John I'm sorry," Jason made eye contact with John's reflection and felt a sudden return of nausea.

"Don't be sorry brother," John exhaled a cloud of smoke, "what makes Shirley so special?"

And I don't believe in God so I can't be saved.

"Oh so many things," Jason began to run some water, "she's got this large and perfectly pear shaped bottom, she always smells like rosewater and spring rain and she laughs at all my jokes."

"I wouldn't take that last one as a good sign brother," John said.

"What are you talking about?" Jason swayed.

"Well you were never very funny Jay," John shrugged.

"Well you were never really my brother John," Jason snapped, "oh my God I'm sorry John."

"Be that as it may I never thought you were particularly funny."

"The world might disagree with you former brother," Jason said as smug as anyone who'd just been sleeping on a toilet could sound.

"Jay, I'm not here to debate your lack of funny," John paused to pop open the cap on a small white bottle, pour two orange pills out into his hands and then throw them in his mouth and swallow, "I've got something for you, a few things actually and then I was going to be on my way."

"So are you going to kill me?" Jason asked nervously.

"That's not part of the agenda old pal," smiled and lit a fresh cigarette.

"Well I kind of figured you'd want revenge," Jason turned to face John and nearly fell over before catching himself on the sink.

"I'm not here for revenge or to kill you brother, I knew my part in the plan, I knew that the people needed a monster to fear," John slide the bag at his feet toward Jason, "there's one less for you to fear."

And I don't believe in God so I can't be saved.

And I don't believe in God so I can't be saved.

Chapter 7

"So you're one of them aren't you?" Earl asked. Earl was behind the wheel of a fifteen-passenger van that had been appropriated from a Mormon youth group earlier the previous evening. It was nearly seven in the morning and they were headed down Mount Shasta.

"Pull into the rest stop up ahead we're going to over heat soon," Francesca said, "and to answer your question, yes I am one of 'them', Satan's children or whatever garbage Walter spewed out to his readers."

"I never met one of you before, you know a synthetic person," Earl said.

"You have you just didn't know it," Francesca said.

"What are you talking about?" Earl asked.

"Alex Combs."

"Ah hell, Al was a little fire cracker, he drank too much for his size and he had a vicious temper, but I never had a better employee," Earl paused to reflect, "I didn't cry at my own mothers funeral like I cried for Al, he died so young and so pointlessly."

"Alex Combs was a product of Generation three which still employed an accelerated growth protocol, fortunately it was realized that the accelerated growth, among everything else, caused cancerous developments, limited physical growth and chemical imbalances that could neither be regulated of corrected, but rather managed after each synaptic episode."

"You mean like an angry shouting match over a bagel?"

"Yes," Francesca said.

"Short and angry, that was Al all right," Earl chuckled.

And I don't believe in God so I can't be saved.

"It also made him a liability which is why he was processed," Francesca added.

"You mean shot right?"

"Yes."

"So it was an agent then?" Earl asked.

"Following established protocols, yes," Francesca answered.

"You don't have to defend it Agent Morrison, Al was a troubled kid with a lot of anger and a lot of hate, it was probably better that way, he didn't ever get a chance to hurt anyone," Earl lamented.

"I would imagine that you're right about that," she said.

"Slightly off subject, but how did you know we were over heating? I mean you didn't even look at the dash, is that one of your powers? ya know like a motor psychic or something?"

"Okay, we've been driving up hill for about four hours yes?"

"Four and a half tops," Earl smiled.

"And this is a Ford, am I correct?"

"Yes maam it is, they don't make them like they used too."

"Right," Francesca said with a raised eyebrow.

"What's the make have to with anything?" Earl asked.

"It's the most common problem with a Ford, prolonged up hill climb and the radiator can not cool off."

"One other question if I may?" Earl said.

"Sure," she answered.

"What do you think of my boy Derek?" Earl smiled.

"Excuse me?"

"He's single, bit of an anger problem, but otherwise he's all right," Earl tapped the steering wheel. There was no rhythm to his tapping as there was very little music

And I don't believe in God so I can't be saved.

on the radio. The van they had appropriated had only an AM/FM radio. Further limiting the radio was their present location of Mount Shasta, which limited their reception to broadcasts from Modesto and Redding. This left them with a choice of the Tejano music station, talk radio (which lately had been over run with conspiracy theorists convinced they knew what was killing everyone) and the very best of thirties and forties radio comedies. At the moment it was a comedy.

"Mister Myers," Francesca began.

"Earl, really, please call me Earl," he interrupted. Francesca waited she did not like interruptions.

"Are you finished Earl?" She said with raised eyebrows. "Is it all right for me to speak now?" She had already holstered her pistol, several hours before, and yet she remained just as threatening if not more so.

"Please, by all means," Earl said not taking his eyes off the road.

"As much as I might appreciate what your intentions are, I have neither the time, the interest nor the desire for such an encounter and before you ask the fact that he was a skinhead had very little baring on my feelings, to be perfectly honest I don't find him very attractive," Francesca finished by lighting a cigarette.

"So that would be a no then?"

"Yes, in fact I would consider the matter closed as of this instant."

Earl simply nodded his head as they pulled into the Mount Shasta rest area. The rest area, by all appearances was deserted.

"Stay alert Earl," Francesca said.

"No problem," he turned back, "Derek, Walt wake up its time for a pee break."

And I don't believe in God so I can't be saved.

Chapter 8

"So what's in the bag?" Jason asked. His body ached and he was sobering up in a way he had not intended for. His eyes still burned with a need for sleep but he was able to fight that for a moment.

"Open it and find out," John said. Jason squinted at John and then at the bag. With two fingers he poked the bag and crinkled his nose.

"It's more squishy then hard," he said.

"That's an appropriate description of it," John said. Jason started to giggle. He worked to maintain it as a giggle for fear that laughter would bring the vomiting he'd so far avoided.

"Open the bag already," John prodded.

"Right, right," Jason leaned in to open the bag. His hands fumbled with the zipper on it. It was a black bowling ball bag that John had picked up on his way out of Los Angeles County.

"Sweet Christ," Jason slapped his hands on his mouth and fell back on the toilet.

"It was a bonus from my last assignment," John said.

"You call a head in a bag a bonus?" Jason looked horrified.

"Well, maybe you could consider it a token of good will," John yawned, "the last one form a brother."

"Goddamit I hated Uncle Dan he was such a bastard," Jason said.

"Yeah, I remember how he used to torture you," John laughed.

"It wasn't funny," Jason whined and weakly slapped the head in the bag.

"Come on, you can do better then that," John said. Jason glared at John. He

And I don't believe in God so I can't be saved.

had tears welling in his eyes. He looked at
the head in the bag; the face stared back at
him as lifeless and dull as when it was
attached to a body. Jason began a slapping
barrage that quickly evolved into a fist
pounding, crying jag.

"Stop calling me Gay Jay," Jason
screamed. John entered the bathroom, tossed
his cigarette into the toilet and put his
hands on Jason's shoulders.

"It's all right now brother, he's dead
now," he said.

"What about dad?" Jason asked.

"Yeah him too," John answered.

"Good, he was a piece of shit," Jason
began, "did you kill mom too?"

"No, she died from the virus, and
besides in regards to mom I was only going
to do what was necessary in respect to her
well being," John answered.

"So you would have killed her?"

"If the situation dictated the need."

"She loved you, you weren't even her
real son and she loved you," Jason growled.

"Yeah, I know," John said.

"Is that all you have to say?"

"Jason, in my present line of work
personal connections, feelings what have
you, are a liability, though by design I am
able to suppress the greater majority of
things of that nature."

"Like I give a shit what you are
Johnnie," Jason turned on his heels and
tried to motion for John to get out of the
way, "if you'll pardon me for a moment?"

"Of course," John stepped aside. Jason
slid to his knees and lodged his head in the
toilet.

"You all right there big guy?" John
asked.

"Hang on brother," Jason tried to push
the contents of his stomach out with no

And I don't believe in God so I can't be saved.

luck, "apparently I will not be vomiting today," he said with a toilet bowl echo.

"Feeling any better?"

"Like hot shit in a blender," Jason stood up.

"I'll take that as a yes I suppose," John began, "so clean yourself up and we'll go get some breakfast."

"Groovitude, I'm just gonna shower 'kay?"

"Don't need more details Jay, but if you could hurry it up, I've got some people down stairs excited to meet you."

"Fans?"

"Something like that," John said as he stepped out of the bathroom.

And I don't believe in God so I can't be saved.

Chapter 9

Maude Kolby was a woman with a large appetite. She was also one of the two single women versus the forty-two single men in the satanic commune that now encompassed Needles, CA. The other woman was the unattainable daughter of Roman Franco, Romana (pronounced Roman-a). She was the promised bride of Satan's champion on Earth, which was Derek Wall who presently wasn't in camp.

Maude was on her second double cheeseburger with extra Thousand Island dressing. She never bothered with fries they were only a distraction. Abe Herschfelder was behind the grill working on double cheeseburger number three. As a rule Abe didn't go for fat chicks or sluts like Maude, but that aside, as one of Roman's 'Diabolical Four'[68] he had to abstain from frolicking with women or men. As Roman put it "It weakens the spirit, mind and knees." Eventually the four were to become the 'Diabolical Five' as lead by Derek. Abe didn't like this anymore then he liked Maude Kolby.

Maude finished the last bite of her burger.
She grabbed hold of her drink (a Diet Pepsi float with strawberry ice cream). She started to suck on the straw like it owed her something. Her dining companion stared at her with a heavy level of disgust. Roman, of course, was having sour dough toast, light butter, cherry jam on the side and a black and white shake.

---

[68] The Diabolical Four were Roman's idea. They were to be superheroes for Satan and the champions of the new world to come. Herschfelder, Triple A, and Big Bad Eli all sported twenty-two carat 'D4' rings. Kurt Wheeler had a gaudy medallion made because his remaining fingers were not long enough for rings.

And I don't believe in God so I can't be saved.

Maude's makeup matched her outfit to ear perfection, purple eyeliner and eye shadow with gold lipstick. These colors didn't work for her at all. The gold or purple alone would have been bad enough. Given her very tan complexion and the combination of the two colors they gave her face a poorly animated corpse appearance. Her choice of wardrobe was another mistake on it's own. She was wearing purple velour with gold trim and a gold embroidered 'M' over the left breast.

Roman made a mental note that her breasts, however voluminous they may be, were still a shapeless blob on her chest that, in particular disgusted him. To his dismay, even further, the active wear that now encased her burnt skin (he desired no mental picture beyond that) had been equipped with all manner of easy access ports. Maternity snaps allowed some unsuspecting fiend to see part or the entire breast blob. More snaps ran up and down the length of each pant leg; no doubt she wasn't wearing underpants to allow quicker admittance to her pink parts. Roman wondered why she even bothered to wear clothes at all, though the sudden image of Maude Kolby naked made Roman shudder.

Maude Kolby was by no means an unattractive woman though not particularly memorable. Her most distinguishing was her massive breasts that while still very large, appeared disproportionate in comparison to her diminutive frame. Additionally, her breasts compensated for the fact that she had an almost concave ass. Maude always looked like she needed a shower, someone to wax her sideburns and then perhaps yet another shower.

And I don't believe in God so I can't be saved.

"I don't like this Derek guy," she began with a belch, "I don't think he deserves your Romana."

"Were that any of your business I might have asked for your opinion on the matter," Roman breathed in, "as it is, as it now stands I will ask for your opinion when I need to know the carnal appetites of the single men of this town and how best to serve them."

"Wait are you...," she twitched and scratched her cheek, "are you calling me a whore?"

"I wouldn't dare dignify you with such a prestigious vulgarity," Roman laughed, "what's more an escort can make quite a healthy living, say what do you pull in my dear?"

"I don't know who has time to count these days," Maude immediately locked her eyes on the melting pink glob in her soda.

"What was that my dear, I didn't quite hear that?"

"I don't really know," she admitted.

"I'll tell you what you make, a place to sleep, the occasional bottle of hootch, all for acting like a harlot for a bunch of men half of whom are in no condition to be cavorting with the like of you."

"The likes of ME!" Maude rolled her eyes and fumed, "YOU KNOW WHAT THIS IS ROMAN, this is fucking bullshit."

"Watch your language my dear," he smiled and took a bite of toast.

"Don't give me that language bullshit, back when I was sucking your wrinkled sac you like my filthy fucking mouth."

"Let's not dwell on the past my dear," he said.

"You motherfuckering asshole it was seven months ago," she screamed.

And I don't believe in God so I can't be saved.

"One year and seven months would be more accurate," Roman corrected.

"You're still an asshole," Maude pouted.

"Must I refer you to my earlier common on the value of your opinion?" Roman bellowed.

"Fuck you wrinkle sac."

"Come come dear Maude you did ask me to meet you for lunch today didn't you?"

"Right," she adjusted her top, "okay what's this I hear about you trying to bring more women to Needles?"

"Wouldn't just be women Maude, it sounds as though one of your paramours is having you on while he's having you.

Maude tightened her fists digging her acrylic nails into the palms of her hands. She drew blood, but succeeded in containing an unholy stream of profanities. "So Roman," she began through clenched teeth, "you're getting everyone boy whores and girl whores?"

"I frankly don't know what their professions might be," Roman answered.

"More bullshit, I know you Roman you need you know every detail down to the freckle on a fly's ass or you don't act," Maude looked down at the table and finished her soda.

"Under normal circumstances you would be right, however, these times we inhabit are quite far from normal."

"Then what the fuck are you doing?"

"Trying to ensure the survival of our church and to a lesser extent humanity."

"So how do you go about that?"

"It's a very simple concept really, breeders, we need them," Roman said.

"We need WHAT?" Maude seemed horrified with the concept.

And I don't believe in God so I can't be saved.

"Of the one hundred eighty that comprise the faithful we have doctors, nurses, policemen but we only have one woman capable of bearing off spring. "

"You mean Romana, I'm a woman too ya know, "
Maude defended.

"Yes, physically this is true, but the child boat set sail for you a long time ago. "

"But I'm only thirty-nine, " Maude said.

"I had you examined when we first met, do you remember? "

"So that was about..., " Maude began.

"Testing your fertility, yes, " Roman interrupted, "and you are no more capable then Abe or Myself. " The caused Abe to burst into laughter as he brought Maude he next double cheeseburger.

"Fuck you Herschfelder, " Maude threw a wad of napkins at him as he moved back to the grill.

"Maude, you have contributed very much to our fledgling society, but we need to consider the next generation and hopefully the generation to follow."

"So you're not brining in whores? "

"No, just people, whatever they might bring to the table so to speak, just people. "

"Church members? "
"That would be ideal and hopefully tomorrow night negotiations will go well enough to where we can open our first recruitment office in Las Vegas. "

And I don't believe in God so I can't be saved.

.

And I don't believe in God so I can't be saved.

Chapter 10

Derek pressed down on the gas pedal. Reno was on the horizon and it was nearing dusk. Francesca was still awake and still in the passenger seat. Earl was asleep in the first bench seat with Walter cuddling up next to him. Derek looked in the rearview window and caught a glimpse of the pair.

"Ya know...," Derek began.

"Are you going to tell me that you hate fags," Francesca interrupted, "or wait, you wish all fags would catch aids and die, is that it?"

"What? no, why do you hate me?"

"Why do you hate gay people and Mexicans?"

"I don't hate gay people of Mexicans," Derek offered.

"Don't tell me, some of your best friends were gay Mexicans."

"You know something, you're right, I hate fags, are you happy, and yeah I probably hate Mexicans too, ya happy now lady?"

"No it doesn't make me happy," Francesca answered, "you're some kind of hate monger."

"No, it's just fags and Mexicans, spent eight years in Chino."

"So your incarceration is supposed to justify your pre-existing hatred?" She asked.

"Well I did go to high school in Santa Ana," Derek offered.

"Must have been rough for the beefy, misunderstood white kid."

"How'd you know I was a fat kid?"

"I didn't, it just makes sense, doesn't justify you, but it helps explain you a little better."

"So what explains you?" Derek asked.

And I don't believe in God so I can't be saved.

"What do you mean? "

"You're cold blooded lady. "

"That's by design, no joy, no
pleasure, no remorse just duty. "

"What about the retard I hit with a
shovel or hell, even Wally's fingers, was
that duty? " Derek asked.

"They both had it coming, and yes,
maybe I did enjoy it, that would mean that
there is a flaw in my design. "

"So you can act without feeling? "

"As much as possible, " Francesca
began, "I turn them off."

"That's fucked up lady, " Derek shook
his head.

"Pretty sure of yourself for a
skinhead, " she smiled.

"What does that have to do with
anything? besides, that's ex-skinhead. "

"You still hate people right? "

"So. "

"So, whether you wear a uniform or not
you're still a skinhead piece of shit, " she
said maintaining her smile.

"At least I'm not some heartless
psycho killer, " he snorted.

"Are you trying to flirt with me? "
Francesca stared him down. "Now listen
close because I will not repeat myself for
anything; my purpose, by design, is to kill
without any question or regard to
sentimentality, a simple addendum is that I
do, very much, enjoy my work, this should
disturb me but it does not, so please don't
think for a minute that I won't crack open
your skull and tear your brains out with my
bare hands that very minute that you cease
to be useful, " she paused momentarily to
lite a cigarette, "are we clear? "

"Yes maam, " Derek looked
straightforward. He tightened his grip on
the steering wheel, burning with a sudden

And I don't believe in God so I can't be saved.

rush of hate and focused on the road ahead.
" So where are we headed maam? "

"Needles, you know where that is right? "

"Yes maam. "

And I don't believe in God so I can't be saved.

Chapter 11

On mornings that he didn't work, the Red Stallion would play video poker on the computer in his mother's living room. Though he no longer lived there he still had a key for when she would be out of town and he was needed to feed her dogs. The dogs (seven in total) didn't like the Red Stallion very much and the Red Stallion didn't like them either.

Alan Aaron Camden was the Red Stallions Christian name and very few people aside from the Red Stallion actually called Alan the 'Red Stallion'. Alan was, at forty-three, one of the night cashiers at Super Mart, which was an all night drugstore on Las Vegas Blvd. It was the stretch between the high-end part of the strip and downtown. Across the street there was the Aztec motel, which had a swimming pool, three slot machines in the lobby and free HBO in every room. Next door to the Aztec was Candies. Candies was also open twenty-four hours a day. It was an adult bookstore with exotic dancing in the back. Alan had gone once, though he didn't like paying six dollars for a can of cola and hadn't returned since.

Alan wasn't the shift leader, he wasn't regarded for his intelligence and on his last review his supervisor told him that he was not promotable. Alan had flirted with the idea of a transfer to the Super Mart further down the strip, where there'd be "more awesome babes" but he never bothered to put in the application.

Alan was an anemic five foot eleven. He slouched, which made him look shorter. He was pasty and wore think glasses. What did make him stand out was his shaggy mane of red hair, hence self declared nickname. Alan was a cheap man, never tipped, wore thrift

And I don't believe in God so I can't be saved.

store sweaters year round and had no luck
with the ladies. His last girlfriend was two
hundred pounds heavier then him. She had
three children she never saw, they lived
with their father in Fresno after the courts
decided that she was an unfit mother. Sasha
Margaret Pierce and the Red Stallion were a
couple for three years. She even went so far
as to have a silhouette of a horse's head
tattooed in red on the back of her neck. And
like his mother, Sasha had a scent of burnt
cotton candy, which was mostly a side affect
o the lithium she took.

Alan lived in an efficiency complex down
by the Greyhound station off of Fremont and
across from The Golden Gate casino. His
dreams of awesome babes and success as an
angry standup comic had been cast aside for
the time being. Last week he'd taken the
mimeograph out of his mother's garage and
started a newsletter. It was nothing more
then the ramblings of a bitter man about the
state of things. Alan did make the mistake
of advocating several kinds of civil
disobedience, including jaywalking and
public urination. But what caught someone's
attention was his paragraph about why no one
had returned from viral treatment.

Alan had called in sick to work,
something he'd rarely done, but he wanted to
get started on next week's newsletter. It
was going to be a full page on why there
should be discount coupons for brothels.

Alan sat in front of a blank page in his
typewriter. He took his glasses off and
wiped sweat out of his eyes. It was hot and
he didn't have air-conditioning. He kept
most of the lights off and the window (there
was only one) open. He sat at his typewriter
in his underwear reveling his unnaturally
pale skin for a native of the desert. He
cracked his knuckles and set to type when

And I don't believe in God so I can't be saved.

there was a knock at the door. He was
suddenly annoyed and put his glasses on.
Maybe if he ignored it they would go away.
There was a minute of silence and then
knocking again. Alan peeled himself out of
his folding chair and stomped, bare foot,
over to the door.

"What do you want?" Alan called to the
door.

"Mr. Camden?" The voice said.

"That's me, what do you want?"

"I need to speak with you, it's a
matter of security," the voice answered.

"Who the hell are you?" Alan adjusted
his underpants. They were sticking to his
body.

"John Parker, National Security," John
held up his id to the eyehole in the door.

"I can't see that clearly," Alan said.
John had quietly drawn his gun, fired two
rounds through the door. Alan fell back and
cried out, he'd never been shot before. John
kicked the door open to find Alan blubbering
on the floor.

"Why are you doing this?" He cried.

"Your newsletter," John answered.

"I know too much don't I," Alan said.

"No, you really don't," John smiled.

"Then why kill me?" He said.

"My supervisor doesn't want the idea
spreading," John pulled back the hammer on
his pistol, "it's nothing personal Mr.
Camden."

"Oh, okay then," Alan began, "so you
shooting me is not a personal thing?"

"Not at all," John fired a round
through Alan's forehead, "not at all."

And I don't believe in God so I can't be saved.

And I don't believe in God so I can't be saved.

Chapter 12

The audience in the Jason Parker
Theater was buzzing with excitement. Extra
seats had been added and sold to the extent
that just before show time it was standing
room only. The audience, theater and
television alike, had been chomping at when
the show announced new editions. These
included a permanent guest star who would
remain a mystery until the first curtain
call, an Irish dance number, performed on
trampolines added to Jason's all girl dance
squad pudding fight and finally the "Death
of a former brother" one hour mini opera
that was to take the place of the ukulele
songs.

The Luther Cole Four had been augmented
to include a seventeen-member horn section
that included trumpet players, several
saxophones trombones and at least three full
time flautists. There was also an electric
piano player, a regular piano player and an
extra percussionist whose chief instruments
was a pair of kettledrums and a large gong.
Despite their enlarged ranks they were still
called the Luther Cole Four and had the
initials LCF cascading down their
bandstands.

Presently they were playing a funk
rendition of Beethoven's "Moonlight Sonata"
which had been chosen by the producers to
try and help lull the audience. The
producers wanted to avoid the result of last
weeks show when Jason announced that not
only was his brother John alive but
responsible for the plague itself. The
audience had stormed out and grabbed anyone
looking remotely like John. Anyone who
hadn't seen the show was given a vague and
slightly misinterpreted description and
began grabbing a hold of any person wearing

And I don't believe in God so I can't be saved.

a tie or named John. It would have been
comical pandemonium had an overzealous Clark
County Sheriff not summarily executed four
of the 'Johns' first shooting them in the
head and then cutting the head off. The
reasoning to this was that a 'John' could
come back to life if you didn't remove the
head. This among everything else lead to
aiding the growing myth of John Parker and
subsequently those like him. Firstly it was
considered a given that, enraged or not, he
would have the strength of fifty men.
Secondly an ability to fly had been
discounted as no one could claim to have
seen it (having nothing to do with how it
would defy physics). In a similar fashion
resurrection was also discounted, but it was
more the method of displacement that had
been called more into question then the
actual act of resurrection itself. One
faction reasoned that you only needed to
destroy the brain while most maintained that
in order to insure death you needed also to
separate the brain from the spinal column.
There were also, not so hushed whispers
about an ability to transform into various
animals. This particular portion of the myth
was feared and debated though never
(officially) made public as it was reasoned
that no one wanted angry mobs hunting down
and killing animals that resembled what John
Parker might look like as a cat or dog. This
would be until transformation could be
proved.

   The extraordinary abilities that John
did posses were mostly unknown. He did have
enhanced night vision, which did allow him
to track movement while seeing body heat.
The trade off to this was that he could only
tolerate about fifty to sixty percent of the
sunlight a normal pair of eyes could.
Further was a heightened, hypersensitive

And I don't believe in God so I can't be saved.

olfactory nerve. This allowed John to
accurately pinpoint pheromonal secretions
relating to fear, anger, love, lust and so
on. He could also pick up the scent of blood
(fresh or dried) and used or unfired
gunpowder among other things. The most
practical of his unknown abilities was the
ability to change the color and length of
his hair and the color of his eyes. This was
achieved through very particular
combinations of vitamins, proteins and
enzymes. It took up to six hours and only
allowed him to change to the next logical
color and never anything radical or
unnatural.

Currently John was backstage watching
the Luther Cole Four warming up the
audience. His hair had gone from short, dark
brown to shoulder length dark red. His eyes
had gone from green to dark blue. Jason
paced back and forth near by. Shirley,
Annabeth, Collette and Shannon stood in a
semi circle behind Jason's pacing. The four
of them were trying to size John up. Shirley
maintained her defensive hamster pose.
Annabeth was chain smoking with a pile of
butts at her feet. Collette glared holding
Jason's first costume in her hand. It was a
pastel cowboy outfit with a rhinestone 'JP'
on each sleeve. Shannon had the straightest
glare; she cracked a single knuckle at a
time and cracked her neck without taking her
eyes off of John. Behind John, Lenny and
Phil stood in front of Jim Friendly's
dressing room door. They were dressed in
identical crimson sharkskin suits with white
shirts, black ties and pointed black boots.
The suits had been Jim's insistence. He
reasoned that security should have more
class then just some fat dude in a black tee

And I don't believe in God so I can't be saved.

shirt that had a yellow 'Security' on it[69].
The fat dude was walking the perimeter of
the audience. He was in the same as Lenny
and Phil were wearing with the exception of
his shoes. He wore black loafers because
they didn't make the pointed boots in triple
e size. The security trio did also differ in
their choice of armament. Lenny had decided
to be like his new hero, John, and carry a
Baretta. He also packed a Walther P-88 as
his backup and he had a straight razor
tucked into his left boot. Phil chose style
over practicality and had a chrome .357
magnum as his first weapon. Phil felt that a
revolver made things more sporting. He did,
however, copy Lenny and carry a P-88 and a
straight razor. Peter Saturday, the fat
dude, professed to liking to add some
"fuckin' boom" to a firefight[70]. Peter
carried a pair of modified sawed off double
barrel shotguns. He wore a blazer two sizes
larger then he needed to help conceal them.
On a lesser man this wouldn't have done the
trick, but for Peter it worked quite nicely.
Realizing that he would have to compensate
for the poor reloading time and seriously
compromised accuracy (of an already weak
principle) of the shotgun Peter also carried
a pair of Chinese ten-millimeter pistols in
his belt. Further there were six weapon
lockers located throughout the theater each
containing three sub machine guns and

---

[69] In fairness to the pre-existing security detail, neither
the Casino nor the show provided him a wardrobe budget.
Peter Saturday Jr. had always been a faded Levi's, black
tee-shirt guy to begin with and despite his best efforts he
was always far from menacing. Peter had a baby face so no
matter how mean he tried to look, how vicious his scowl it
would still come across as cute. Peter was also lead vocals
and rhythm guitar for the local Vegas speed metal band
"Sauramon's Heir's". He was also a regular fixture at
every Nevada Renaissance Fair and was Shirley's current
boyfriend.
[70] Peter Allen Saturday Jr. had yet to be in an actual live
round firefight. Further, outside paint ball, Ren Faire
combat simulation and Dungeons and Dragons in the park
(full costume and props) he was something of a pacifist.

And I don't believe in God so I can't be saved.

reserve ammunition for the weapons that the trio carried.

"God I want to throw up," Jason said whipping sweat from his brow.

"Come on Jason, you've done this hundreds of times already," Shirley said.

"Come on honey you're an old pro at this," Collette added.

"You fucking rock Jay," Annabeth sounded the most unenthusiastic between cigarette hits.

"He's like this before every show isn't he?" John asked.

"Pretty much yeah," Collette answered.

"He's such a fucking pussy," Annabeth answered.

"You haven't changed at all Jason," John said.

"Shut your fucking mouth pretty boy," Shannon shouted at John. Lenny ands Phil responded by each drawing a pistol and raising it toward Shannon.

"That's not necessary guys," John said without turning around.

"But John, she's a goddamn gorilla," Phil said.

"She fucking scares the shit out of me John," Lenny added.

"All the same fella's, don't draw your guns unless you intend to use them," John said.

"But she's mean John," Phil said.

"Yeah, hell yeah, she's a fucking monster bitch," Lenny added.

"Do either of you intend to kill the monster bitch gorilla?" John asked.

"Not as such...," Phil began.

"We only wanted to scare her," Lenny finished.

"Don't you think she knows that?"

And I don't believe in God so I can't be saved.

"Maybe," Phil answered. Lenny shrugged his shoulders.

"And what if she called your bluff?" John said.

"We'd kick her ass, right brother Lenny," Phil said.

"Damn right brother Phil," Lenny answered.

"No you'd have to shoot her," John corrected.

"What?" Phil and Lenny cried.

"Physically she has the advantage," John began, "you could pistol whip her but that means that you would both have to get close enough to do so and additionally be running the risk of just pissing her off," John smiled briefly at Shannon.

"But what if we really just wanted to scare her a little?" Phil asked.

"No point to that really, you see from a technological standpoint you have the advantage, albeit one with a finite conclusion so you have to assess the situation as quickly as you can determine what, if any, action you take."

"So what would you do in our situation?" Lenny asked.

"Well, let's see, Shannon is basically the team leader and somewhat of a legendary bully from what I understand, now given the existing evidence and behavior her likely response to being threatened would be to take the offensive and aggressive stance, further simply injuring her would most likely only exacerbate the situation even more given her lingering presence. The only course of action would be to shoot her dead, keeping in mind that this wouldn't be an issue of crowd control but more to the point about time and resource management," John said.

And I don't believe in God so I can't be saved.

"I think we're a little confused by
that John," Phil scratched his head. Lenny
put his gun away and lit a cigarette.

"Okay, real simple then, evaluate the
situation, resolve it and then move on."

"Yeah, E.R.M. got it," Lenny exhaled

"You understand that brother Lenny?"
Phil sounded astonished.

"Indeed I do brother Phil," Lenny said
with a measure of pride.

"Well that's good enough for me," Phil
put his pistol away.

"Hey, three FAGATEERS you wanna start
something?" Shannon postured and rolled on
the balls of he feet like a cat ready to
pounce. It was just then that Shirley and
Annabeth realized that they were between
Shannon, bullets and the wall.

"Jesus," Annabeth exhaled, "better
move your fat ass Shirl."

"I feel like I'm going to pee myself
if I try," Shirley whined, "don't call me a
fat ass."

"Chicken shit Motherfucker move your
fat ass," Annabeth screamed in her squeaky
voice, "if I get shot because of you or
Shannon I will kick both of your giant
ass's."

"Say kids what the rub?" Jim Friendly
said bursting through his dressing room
door. He could see that Jason was drenched,
Shannon was on the verge of a meltdown,
which she completed by throwing down her
clipboard and storming off, and John was
just smiling. Jim was dressed; head to toe,
in a maroon colored leather suit. It was a
combination bolero jacket, with red, whit
and blue rhinestones spelling out 'Jim
Friendly' on the back and high wasted pants
that flared out a good eight inches at each
led. He had a red cape draped over his left

And I don't believe in God so I can't be saved.

shoulder and a red flamingo hat rested
cockeyed on his head.

"What? too much," Jim said.

"Jim it's beautiful," Jason couldn't
have been more sincere.

"Okay, then what's up everyone ass?"
Jim said.

"I think it's my fault Jim," John
said.

"What'd ya do buddy?" Jim asked.

"I think it was as simple as just
being here," John answered.

"Na, she probably just needs to get
some, if Freddie and I didn't have a thing
I'd be more then happy to give her the ole
high hard seven and a half, know what I mean
buddy?" Jim nudged John.

"I do and that would be pretty
appalling if I didn't already know you
Jim," John laughed.

"Jim, apologize to your friend for
being a filthy liar," Freddie interrupted
from the doorway of Jim's dressing room.

"Excuse me?" Jim was caught off guard.

"There is no excuse for you Jim, you
know at best it's a hard six," Freddie
said.

"Right, sorry dear and sorry John a
more accurate estimate of my penis would be
six and not the seven and a half that I
previously boasted of," Jim offered meekly.

"You know Jim, you naked is not what I
would want to think about if I were to go to
sleep tonight," John shook his head.

"Good thing you don't sleep buddy,"
Jim chuckled.

"I kind of miss it sometimes, I mean I
don't feel like I miss it but sometimes my
mind does," John lamented.

"Don't know how you manage, can't
manage myself without at least five hours of

And I don't believe in God so I can't be saved.

sleep," Jim absentmindedly started scratching his ass.

"Jim stop that you're only going to give yourself an infection," Freddie snapped

"Yes'm," Jim thrust both his hands to his sides.

"So Freddie, if I may, what was the thing Jim mentioned?" John said.

"Oh, well the skinny bitch and I are getting married," she answered.

"Congratulations I suppose," John shrugged.

"Number five," Jim beamed.

"And till death do us part is going to count this time right Jim dear?" Freddie said with a hint of menace.

"You bet your sweet sweet," Jim began till he was met with a sharp glare from Freddie, "uh yeah last time for me honey," Jim sputtered.

"So when's the happy day?" John asked

"Tomorrow night," Freddie answered.

"We were kind of hoping that you'd be there," Jim said.

"Wish I could buddy, I have an engagement south of here tomorrow night and I don't know how long it will take," John said.

"You mean like," Jim made a quick finger gun and fired, "pow bang, you got me I'm dead," Jim stuck his tongue out and closed his eyes.

"That's the most likely scenario," John lit a cigarette. This caused Jason to cease his pacing and angrily at John.

"You have some nerve former brother, smoking backstage when there are clearly posted signs," Jason ranted and heaved. His arms flailed about sending drops of sweat flying about the area.

And I don't believe in God so I can't be saved.

"Jay, come here a sec," John waved him over to which Jason reluctantly responded. "Now look brother, I know it bothers you, you know what I do," John put his arm around Jason's shoulder, "brother, it's okay to hate me, I kill people and feel nothing, then again you entertain people and you try to destroy yourself the minute you feel unloved." Jason stared at the ground, he knew that this was true and there was no sense in denying it.

"But you're going to continue killing people and I'm going to continue drinking,' Jason paused to look over at his staff, Shannon was gone, probably min the parking lot taking her rage out on a dumpster, Collette just looked annoyed, still holding Jason's first costume change, Annabeth had her usual semi-pissed off expression on her face as she churned out an industrial quality of smoke.

Then of course there was Shirley who was Jason's most recent excuse for self-destructive drinking. She had the most sympathetic look on her face, though instinctively she wouldn't make eye contact with anyone.

"But you're a monster and no one loves me," Jason sobbed.

"Jay, buddy, I am what I was designed to be and I accept that, that and that the woman, well, serious feelings for, before I knew what I was is dead, these are things that I cannot change, but this isn't about me, it's you."

"What are you Talking about?" Jason sniveled.

"People love you, you sell out every show shoot Jay they even named the flipping theater after you," John said.

"You can swear in here John, this ain't church," Lenny whispered.

And I don't believe in God so I can't be saved.

"Very true Lenny," John whispered back, "but it's not polite to use coarse language in front of mixed company is it."

"Yeah, you're right...what?" Lenny said.

"Don't swear in front of ladies," John said in less then a whisper.

"Even if they do?" Lenny asked.

"Even if they do," John answered.

"You know, you're right John," Jason said finally.

"Awesome buddy, now go give the people what they paid for," John patted Jason on the shoulder as he ran off. The audience exploded with excitement as Jason ran out and began his monologue.

"So that's it then eh buddy," Jim said as he approached John, "you really gotta go?"

"Afraid so pal, gotta go where I'm needed," John said.

"But we're going to see you again after your done right?" Jim said.

"No, I'm a little to well known around these parts buddy," John lit another cigarette and looked at Jim. He could see the disappointment pour over Jim's face. John shrugged his shoulders and turned and nodded to Lenny and Phil who both shared Jim's expression to a certain extent. John moved past them and stopped at Freddie.

"Good luck with Jim and everything," John smiled.

"Yeah, you too," Freddie sounded distant, "don't be a stranger now." John slipped out through the fire door, strolled past where Shannon was beating on a metal dumpster and then he was gone.

And I don't believe in God so I can't be saved.

And I don't believe in God so I can't be saved.

Chapter 13

Roman Franco paced the dirt road at the edge of Needles. He was dressed in his normal desert uniform, which consisted of a black mesh tee shirt and a snakeskin, blue man thong. He was also wearing a pair of orange flip flops which were exceptionally out of character and would have been more of a concern had it not been hot enough to where even roman couldn't wear socks and his regular orthopedic oxfords. It was a hundred and ten even with the sun fading over the edge of the horizon.

The compound behind Roman was silent but active. Those who had the means were preparing whatever form of weaponry that they had available. A good seventy yards behind Roman and his pacing was the Diamond Cafe. The cafe provided the only visible lights from the commune. Inside Maude Kolby was drinking her second strawberry float and annoyed as all hell that she had to prepare them herself. She stared out intently at Roman and trying her best to ignore the activities behind her. The Diabolical Four were behind her preparing for their first potential adventure. If it was to be the worst case scenario, then they were to spring into action, smite the enemies of the only free city left in America and show the world it's new band of heroes. If a representative of Las Vegas arrived with intent to grant Roman his wish of recruitment, fair trade and supplies then the Diabolical Four were to remain hidden. Roman didn't want to seem crazy.

Alberto (Triple A) was feeling a bit over exposed as he flexed and stretched in his unitard. It was red and black with a gold "Triple A" across the left breast. It was also a size too small, which is where

And I don't believe in God so I can't be saved.

Alberto was left feeling over exposed. He
looked over to Heliodoro with envy burning
in his heart. Heliodoro's uniform consisted
of gold, knee high boots, red baggy
knickerbockers and a loose fitting black
tunic. "Big Bad Eli" was written across the
back in bold letters of gold outlines in the
same color red as his pants. These were
meaningless to Alberto. What he did envy was
the red satin cape that Heliodoro wore over
his right shoulder. With that cape, Alberto
reasoned, he could at least mask how ill
fitting his own uniform was. Heliodoro was
quietly enjoying how much more flattering
his uniform was then poor Alberto's. Kurt
"The Hammer" Wheeler on the other hand was
in heaven. "Breathe in," a pretty lady was
close enough, "breathe out," that he could
smell her skin, "breathe in," and she was
touching his beard, "breathe out." Kurt
continued his laborious breathing trying
very hard not to stare at the woman. Kurt
would always have an easier time doing this
then most men. With only one eye that worked
well enough to see and that was under
voluntary control all he had to do was close
his good eye and breathe. The eye that
didn't work, the one with a scar that ran
through it he was never able to close. When
he closed his functional eye he saw nothing.
He would feel the blood rush through his
dead eye, and if he stopped his breathing
long enough he could almost hear it. In
front of Kurt was Roman's daughter and only
living child Romana. It was clear at a
glance that Romana was not the flesh and
blood child of Roman Franco. She was, as
Roman long believed, of Spanish heritage,
somewhere near Madrid. She had an olive tone
to her skin though she never did tan. Roman
almost always had an orange glow the
hallmark of a tanning bed. Romana had

And I don't believe in God so I can't be saved.

piercing whitish blue eyes; Roman's were a
mud brown. Romana spoke a variety of
languages including Romany, German and
Castilian Spanish where Roman new only
enough Lithuanian to procure snuff films.
Romana was gentle and kind, in stark
contrast to Roman who was well known for his
sadism and sheer unwavering cruelty. Romana
exuded a warmth that couldn't be expressed
too much in words; Roman was best described
as clammy and somewhat unsettling.

Romana finished trimming Kurt
Wheeler's beard. His idiot's grin and warm
drool had been unveiled slowly with each
snip of scissors. Romana didn't mind the
smile or the drool she knew Kurt Wheeler was
mostly harmless. The purpose to the trimming
was to allow for a custom tempered steel
neck brace to both cover and support Kurt's
neck. The neckpiece connected to what could
best be described as a chain mail girdle.
This connection was achieved by a series of
steel cables. Another set of cables ran down
each of Kurt's arms connecting to and
oversized steel glove that restored Kurt's
fingers to a full length hand a somewhat
comical size, the gloves also gave Kurt a
grip that could apply upwards of one
hundred-eighty pounds of pressure.

Kurt felt like a whole man in his
metal contraption and contented by the
presence of a beautiful lady, so graceful,
she even dared to approach. His breathing
slowed and for the first time since he could
really remember he was happy.

"Kurt Breathe!" Abe shouted. He was
the first to notice that Kurt had stopped
breathing. Abe threw down his cinder block
hammer and rushed to Kurt's side, "sweet
Jesus breathe Kurt!" Abe cried and beat on
Kurt's chest. Abe tried shaking him which
caused Kurt to fall back on the table he was

And I don't believe in God so I can't be saved.

sitting on and let out a loud belch. "We
gotta start his heart, come on, somebody
help me," Abe pleaded. Alberto, Heliodoro
and Romana remained still. Romana's gaze
fixed on the tiles beneath where Kurt
Wheeler lay. Alberto continued to fidget
with his costume, preferring to primp rather
then face a fallen comrade. Only Heliodoro
approached. His eyes met with Abe's tear
filled eyes.

   "Jesus Eli help him, he's my best
friend," Abe said.

   "Abrahams, let him go to the dead,"
Heliodoro spoke slowly as he placed his hand
on Abe's shoulder, "so many summer I have
known Kurt Wheeler, Kurt Wheeler was the
best and we must let him go."

   Roman continued his pacing. He grew
angrier and sweatier with each passing
minute. Behind him was the cell phone he
tossed in the dirt. It started to buzz and
chirp. "Damnation," he called out. Roman
stomped over to the noisy source of his
irritation. "Yes, what?"

   "Father Kurt Wheeler just passed
away," Romana said calmly.

   "Well sweet shit pie doesn't that just
tare it," Roman shouted, "what happened
daughter?"

   "Well, he just stopped breathing," she
answered.

   "I don't suppose any of those fuckless
wonders TRIED MOUTH TO MOUTH RESUSCITATION
DID THEY?"

   "Father, please watch your language,"
she admonished.

   "SORRY DARLING DAUGHTER, "Roman caught
himself before he shouted anymore, "you
understand the kind of pressure that father
is, roughly speaking, under right now?"

And I don't believe in God so I can't be saved.

"That's a poor excuse for such language," she answered. Roman had no good retort after all she was right. He was, however, tremendously disappointed that not only had he missed Kurt Wheeler's death but that it hadn't been at Roman's hands. He choked back a tear; he'd wanted so much to have been a part of Kurt's death. "Are the men still getting ready?" He said after some silence.

"They're awaiting your orders father," Romana answered.

"Tell the men," Roman paused to choke back how much he really hated Kurt Wheeler and how it pained him to say this, "we will have a service for our great fallen hammer as soon as this Las Vegas business is settled."

"Yes father," she said.

Breaking the horizon but nearly hidden by the setting sun some manner of vehicle approached. It wasn't entirely clear to Roman but he knew what it meant. "Finally," he hissed.

As it drew closer, Roman could see it was some sort of armored truck. Roman smiled and wiped sweat from his brow. Roman was slightly puzzled by the truck. Usually they were just used for transporting money. His smile broadened when he surmised that some very important members of the Las Vegas community were coming to welcome Roman. He thrust his chest out, adjusted his thong and stood beaming with pride.

"Daughter dear," he bellowed into the phone, "you and the men come and see the important people who have come to meet father."

"What about Miss Kolby?" Romana asked.

And I don't believe in God so I can't be saved.

"Oh no, she has to be kept away, can't she clean or suck something?" Roman snorted with disgust. Before Romana could answer the armored car stopped ten feet away from where Roman stood. It bore no markings, the plates were Government blue and white that gave no hint of a point of origin. The two-panel windshield was mirrored so that no one could see inside. This annoyed Roman until the engine stopped. Roman half expected showgirls and fireworks or something spectacular like that. Instead, George climbed out from the driver's side and walked toward Roman.

"No, you're not the Las Vegas representative," Roman protested, "I know you and I don't like you."

"Come now Roman, I would have thought it would have been long enough since we last met," George smiled, "at least twenty-seven years." Roman did not answer, he glared at George and squeezed the cell phone in his hand, "daughter, hurry the men up," Roman spotted another pair of vehicles speeding toward him from two different points, "and gather up some of the more able citizens."

"What's wrong father?" Romana said.

"We may have a villain or two to squash," he answered.

"Does that mean no Las Vegas father?"

"Not the way we planned it daughter dear," Roman said. He hadn't taken his eyes off of George and the most menacing thing he'd done is light a cigarette. George hadn't even taken off his blazer despite the sweltering heat.

"You're responsible for all of this you filthy son of a bitch," Roman snarled.

"Name calling aside," George exhaled, "I've long since accepted my share of the responsibility in the end of the world."

And I don't believe in God so I can't be saved.

The new vehicles drew closer. From one direction was the van that carried Walter and Earl Myers, Derek Wall and Francesca. From the direction of Las Vegas a Cadillac convertible driven by John Parker. The Diabolical Four, minus one, Romana and a sorry collection of pudgy old men armed with rifles were marching up to where Roman and George were standing.

"You cost me both of my sons and now you will face the retribution you rightly deserve, Roman sneered. This was a mighty show of force for the community.

"I think you're forgetting that we already made our efforts at restitution for your sons," George smiled.

"What are you talking about," Roman raised an eyebrow, "I don't remember receiving a check or a parcel of land," he stepped forward, in part out of indignation and in an effort to intimidate George.

"You daughter, I believe you named her Romana," George paused as Roman's eyes widened in horror, "I trust the pronunciation is correct."

"You're trying to tell me that my dearest daughter is synthetic?"

"Did you honestly think that there was anyone desperate, reasonable or otherwise who would ever trust you with a child?" George said it was the closest anyone would ever hear his voice raised to shouting.

"I am a tremendous father," Roman snorted.

"You never had any business parenting in any fashion," George snapped, "you are deranged, delusional and a lunatic, the real reason you were given Romana was to hide her away, you would never be able to cause her any harm, as you did your sons." Roman couldn't speak, his eyes twitched, no one

And I don't believe in God so I can't be saved.

ever contradicted him like that, he bit his lip hard enough to cause it to bleed.

Maude Kolby broke the tension by running up ahead of the pack of old men. She was shouting obscenities at Roman. "Suck something," she screamed, "fuck you ball dry Motherfucker Goddamit..." George cut her stride and profanity short with three shots. Roman pursed his lips and stared George down.

"I should thank you for that save for two problems," Roman began as John's Cadillac pulled up next to the armored car. John sat behind the wheel finishing as he watched the Diabolical Four, minus one, Romana and several somewhat well armed join the belligerent half naked old man, "my first problem," Roman continued watching nervously as John got out of the Cadillac popped a couple of pills in his mouth and walked over to George, "is that you just killed this towns whore which leads me to the next and very much related problem which is that now my men will have no sex." George smiled weakly at John and offered him a cigarette. They both lit up as the van pulled to a stop on the opposite side of the armored car.

"We seem to have started early, or was I late?" John said.

"A little of both, though you did take care of that last minute assignment I trust?"

"It was a bit out of the way, but easily handled."

"And I see you're headaches haven't gone away," George said.

"They're manageable," John smiled.

"Well," Roman snorted and folded his arms, "now you cannot ignore us, I see that our champion has returned to us." Roman was

And I don't believe in God so I can't be saved.

referring to Derek as he climbed out of the
van.

"What's going on sir?" Derek stretched
and yawned.

"My boy, it is time for you to take as
my right hand, it is time to grasp your
destiny and squeeze fates tits," Roman
shouted and waved his hands towards George
and John. George gave an amused smile.

John made eye contact with Francesca as
she climbed out of the van. He wasn't quite
sure what to do and neither was she? In the
past they'd only ever really shared a kiss
on her doorstep.

"Your eyes are different," she began
as she stepped towards him, and so is you
hair."

"I know, I had to," John said.

"He told me that you'd killed
yourself," she said pointing to George, "I
wanted to hate you for being a coward, but I
missed you."

"What do you mean?" Derek said as he
walked over to Roman. Earl kept right along
side Derek,
Walter staggered behind them.

"Walter, you look like warmed over
monkey poop," Roman laughed.

"Walter Myers?" George perked up.

"Present and mostly accounted for,"
Walter replied briefly waving his bandaged
hand.

"Wonderful," George began, "I've
followed your career for a long time now."

"Ah, my public," Walter chuckled,
"Roman who's the nut job?"

"He is one of the villains in our
midst, he as well as two of his bastard have
arrived to bring about the end of our way of
life."

And I don't believe in God so I can't be saved.

"Makes sense enough to me," Walter nodded.

"I couldn't agree with you more brother oh mine," Earl added.

"Would you two please shut your fat faces," Roman stomped and demanded, "and you," he turned to Derek, "it is time for you to smite our enemies with the flaming sword of Lucifer and lead our people to the promised land of Las Vegas."

"This is supposed to get done with the help of twenty or so old, out of shape riflemen and your Diabolical Four?" Derek wondered.

"Precisely, well except that now it's the Diabolical three," Roman giggled.

"You finally kill Kurt?" Derek asked with no surprise.

"Kurt passed on without my assistance," Roman answered disappointingly.

"Okay so if the guy talking to Francesca over there is anything like her we might be able to do a little damage if we had a battalion of Marine snipers and about a thousand yards between us, otherwise..."

"Otherwise Horsefeathers, Otherwise Balderdash," Roman interrupted with a shouting fit.

"Otherwise," Derek began with a raised eyebrow, "we'd be better packing it in lest we risk what kind of future this town could have, cause these two alone could wipe us out just as easily as breathe and you wouldn't even get out a 'Hail Satan' before you hit the ground."

"They're monsters, we can destroy them, are you afraid?" Roman said accusingly.

"Fella's come on, let's have some pie and talk this through," Earl tried to intercede.

And I don't believe in God so I can't be saved.

"Ain't no talking it through Earl,"
Derek said.

"Yes finally we see eye to eye my
boy," Roman sneered, "and shut your
blubbery, briny face Earl, we fight and we
will win and then we will take what we need
from Las Vegas."

"No, we lay down arms and we do what
the man says," Derek answered.

"Your champion makes a good point,"
George interrupted.

"He's no champion, he's a coward,"
Roman snorted, "and you're a monster maker
and you destroy families but your not going
to stop us."

"Maybe we should help," John said to
Francesca.

"You're right," she answered.

"Yeah you can't stop us," Walter
stepped up brandishing his good hand.

"Stay out of this Walter," Roman
barked.

"Hey, we have as much right to
reproduce as anyone else," Walter said.

"Walter," George began, "while you
have entertained many of us over the years,
your usefulness is at an end," George
raised his gun at Walter.

"Sir, allow me," Francesca stepped up
with her gun leveled at Walter.

"Christ on a cracker would you people
stop pointing guns at my brother," Earl
pleaded.

"Earl shut up and stand down," Derek
grabbed Earl and pulled him away from
Walter.

Francesca smiled briefly at George and
fired a single shot without looking. The
bullet tore through Walters head and
imbedded itself in Alberto's (who was a good

And I don't believe in God so I can't be saved.

ten feet behind Walter) leg. Alberto cried out, clutching his leg he fell to the ground.

"So that's it is it, that's your master plan, you're going to shoot us all one by one," Roman began and paced like a caged animal that's figured out that the lock is open, "well I tell you now for free, it won't work, no matter how powerful your monsters are our superior numbers will win out in the end."

"No, they won't, not tonight," George sighed, "you and you're people are going to lay down their weapons and return to town."

"The hell we will," Roman snorted, "we will fight and we will win, our way of life and our victory today will be taught to future generations so that they know that when it mattered we fought our greatest villains and we were triumphant." George and John exchanged a look, John shrugged his shoulders and Francesca looked menacing at the crowd of old men.

"This is taking too long if you ask me," John lit another cigarette.

"Have patience John," George smiled and turned to Roman, "your way of life ends tonight with this moment, this space in time," George threw his cigarette to the ground. Roman watched intently as it hit the ground. "You want to live on and spread your idiocy and share that disgusting proteins collection that you call life," George paused to his words sink in on Roman, "you will not carry on, there are to be no future generations and you will have no legacy." George leveled his gun at Roman. Roman turned and ran back toward the crowd as George fired twice hitting Roman in each calve. Roman fell to his knees in front of his daughter. Behind them most of the armed

And I don't believe in God so I can't be saved.

and pudgy men dropped their rifles and made
a break for the town.

"So more of the 'no future for you'
speech?" John asked.

"A test," George smiled. Francesca
continued to say nothing but looked ready to
attack all the same.

Abe tossed his hammer from hand to hand
to make himself appear as a threat.
Heliodoro flexed and sneered as menacingly
as he could.

"You idiots, attack!" Roman called
out.

"Abraham give me your hammer," Romana
snatched it away from him as she asked, "I
love you father, she kissed Roman on the top
of his forehead and stepped back.

"I love you daughter," he smiled.
Romana swung the hammer up above herself and
then swung it crashing done on Roman's head.

"What the fuck have you done?" Abe
screamed

"I did what was needed," she answered.

"He was your father GODDAMMIT," Abe
berated her.

"Watch your language please," she
said.

John stepped forward and shot Abe
through the throat. Abe fell and gargled on
his own blood. Heliodoro took his queue and
ran for town.

"Now kill me," Romana said.

"What? no," George was surprised for
the first time in decades.

"I just ended the life of the man who
raised me, who loved me without compromise
or pretense, he knew I wasn't really his and
probably that I am not even really human and
still he loved me," she paused to lean down
and brush some dust off of Roman's dead
face, "he was not a good man and he was not
a good father but he was my father and I

And I don't believe in God so I can't be saved.

killed him. " Romana set the hammer down and approached George, John and Francesca. "Whatever I am I don't want and don't deserve to have so please, " she reached out to George and touched his arm, "please kill me. "

"I'll do it, " Francesca finally spoke. She unloaded her gun into Romana. She dropped the empty cartridge out of her pistol and slapped another in and chambered a round. She raised her gun to George.

"Do you have any idea what you have done? " George said as he turned to face her gun.

"John, you and I, she should never have been, " she said.

"I suppose saying I love you would be a little awkward here? " John said.

"Yes and besides it's a little late for that John, " Francesca smiled and pulled back the hammer on her gun.

"I can't let you shoot him, " John stepped in front of George.

"You're leaving me very little choice John, " Francesca fired four rounds into John's stomach. He fell back on George.

"I'm sorry it had to come to this John, I really was fond of you but we are monsters and we don't deserve life. "

John felt the world slipping away again. The world around him was becoming echoes and fading light.

"Cross John out of your notebook old man and then toss it to me, " Francesca said.

"Here, " George threw a pen to her along with the book, "but you will never find all of them, your brothers and sisters are well scattered. " John slumped down and closed his eyes.

And I don't believe in God so I can't be saved.

Epilogue
Fade out....

    This was the end. The culmination of all they had worked for and it was coming to an end. The project on a whole was a failure. It only cost eighty-seven percent of the world's population their lives, not at all the predicted 'ninety- seven'. "Total success was too much to hope for," George grumbled aloud. He was kicking the dirt around the edge of a mass grave that had been dug to account for the former residents of Palmdale, most from Lancaster and the good majority of those from Victorville. Tortured faces looked up toward George from the pit below. Whole families lay in there; even a few of the soldiers who dug the pit were there. The bodies that remained with faces, however deteriorated seemed to be asking George why; he had no answers for them.

    Nearly four years ago this was covered up as a terrorist attack, Sarin gas or Anthrax, George couldn't remember. He planned for it and he couldn't remember. In Shanghai they called it a vicious strain of small pox, or was it Sars. In Paris they blamed it on an abnormally hot summer.

    London had it the closest, they determined it to be a highly communicable form of Syphilis. It wasn't Syphilis but it behaved most like it. Whatever it was called the disease had reached a point where it killed within hours instead of weeks. Violent mobs of the infected still roamed pockets of cities scattered throughout the Americas. From Mexico City to Seattle there was maybe a thousand people left alive on the West Coast. George had taken to living out of a modified Armored car, which at

Fade Out...

Five Years Epilogue

present he was climbing back into. The modifications included; a hand print verification required starting the engine, this system recognized only two handprints those belonging to George and John Parker. Most of the rest of the modifications catered to creature comforts, like a first class airplane seat that served as Georges bed (George hadn't slept in a real bed six he was nineteen), a computer with a satellite uplink, a small bar refrigerator, reading material and a small cache of weapons. The only true innovation was the hydrogen fuel cells that powered the vehicle; they had a half-life of thirty-five years.

George was headed back to Los Angeles, which save for a few scavengers was now truly empty. He barreled down the dirt road leading to Pear Blossom Highway. John would be waiting, he thought to himself, he should be fully recovered by now and there was business to settle. George smiled when he reached the highway; end of the world or not Pear Blossom was never a busy highway. He pushed down on the gas and roared off toward the I-5 for Los Angeles.

Fade Out…

Five Years Epilogue

Fade Out…

Five Years Epilogue

Patrick Fisher lives in the Los Angeles area with his wife Heather and their cats. In his spare time he cleans the pool and mows the lawn and looks for work. He can be reached through Bloodpoolbooks@gmail.com

Fade Out...